The Mad, Mad Murders
of Marigold Way

The Mad, Mad Murders of Marigold Way

a novel

RAYMOND BENSON

BEAUFORT
BOOKS

Hardcover: 9780825309915
Ebook: 9780825308703

For inquiries about volume orders, please contact:
Beaufort Books
27 West 20th Street, Suite 1103
New York, NY 10011
sales@beaufortbooks.com

Published in the United States by Beaufort Books www.beaufortbooks.com
Distributed by Midpoint Trade Books, a division of Independent Book Publishers
www.midpointtrade.com
www.ipgbook.com

Interior design by Mimi Bark
Cover design by Mimi Bark
Neighborhood map by Michael Short

Printed in The United States

Also by the Author

Novels

Evil Hours

Face Blind

Tom Clancy's Splinter Cell (as "David Michaels")

Tom Clancy's Splinter Cell: Operation Barracuda
(as "David Michaels")

Sweetie's Diamonds

A Hard Day's Death

Metal Gear Solid (based on the video game)

Dark Side of the Morgue

Metal Gear Solid 2: Sons of Liberty (based on the video game)

Hunt Through Napoleon's Web (as "Gabriel Hunt")

Homefront: The Voice of Freedom (cowritten with John Milius)

Artifact of Evil

Torment: A Love Story

Hitman: Damnation (based on the video game series)

Dying Light: Nightmare Row (based on the video game series)

The Secrets on Chicory Lane

In the Hush of the Night

Blues in the Dark

Hotel Destiny: A Ghost Noir

The Black Stiletto Saga

The Black Stiletto

The Black Stiletto: Black & White

The Black Stiletto: Stars & Stripes

The Black Stiletto: Secrets & Lies

The Black Stiletto: Endings & Beginnings

The Black Stiletto: The Complete Saga (anthology)

James Bond Novels

Zero Minus Ten

Tomorrow Never Dies (based on the screenplay)

The Facts of Death

High Time to Kill

The World Is Not Enough (based on the screenplay)

DoubleShot

Never Dream of Dying

The Man with the Red Tattoo

Die Another Day (based on the screenplay)

The Union Trilogy (anthology)

Choice of Weapons (anthology)

Non-Fiction and Miscellany

The James Bond Bedside Companion

Jethro Tull: Pocket Essential

Thrillers: 100 Must-Reads (contributor)

Tied-In: The Business, History, and Craft of Media Tie-In Writing (contributor)

Mystery Writers of America presents Ice Cold:
Tales of Intrigue from the Cold War (coeditor, contributor)

12+1: Twelve Short Thrillers and a Play (anthology)

For Randi—
I am so glad it was you
with whom I spent the lockdown

Acknowledgments

The author wishes to thank the following individuals: police officers Lt. Tara Anderson and Lt. Tony Montiel; Jamie Gould; and Stuart Howard.

Warm gratitude goes to Megan Trank, Olivia Fish, and Eric Kampmann at Beaufort Books for their enthusiasm and help.

Special continuing thanks goes to Cynthia Manson. Finally, my love and appreciation go to my wife, Randi, for her help and support.

Author's Note

This book was written between May and September 2020 while the uncertainty of the coronavirus pandemic—among other stressors—placed every soul on the planet on edge. While it began in March that year with a mandatory lockdown enforced in most places, it became more of a self-regulated quarantine over the summer. Even at the time of this writing, nearly two years later, the end doesn't appear to be anywhere in sight.

Every author has influences for various works. For this one, I seemed to have embraced the Americana of Thornton Wilder, the twisted domestic tales of Tom Perrotta, and the quirky, dark-humor sensibility of the Coen brothers. While this story is assuredly a bit of fever-dream absurdity, its creation was, at the very least, personally therapeutic.

Stay sane, safe, and well.

RB
Spring 2022

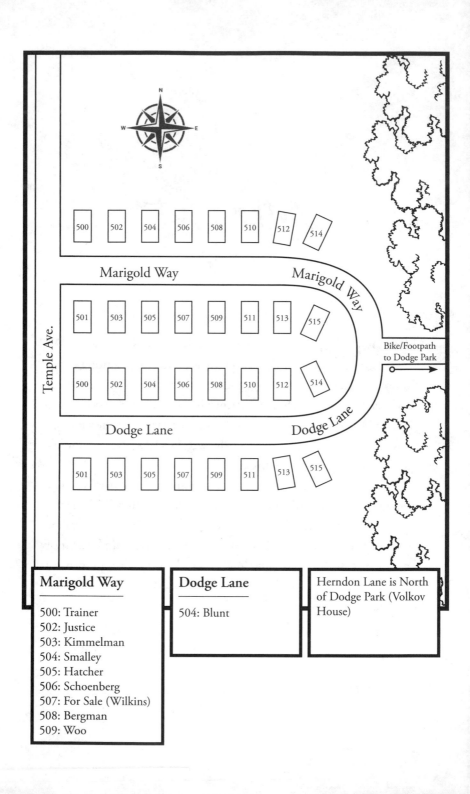

1

Friends, this is a little tale about some murders.

It takes place in a stereotypical American suburb, on a familiar American street, not too far northwest—but far enough—from a major American metropolitan center, Chicago, Illinois. For our purposes, we'll call our suburb Lincoln Grove, although its name, as well as the names of the characters involved, has been changed to protect . . . oh, I don't know. Changing names isn't going to protect anyone.

While no murders make much sense, these are truly wacky. I like to call them the Mad, Mad Murders of Marigold Way.

Our story is set in May 2020. This is significant, for the entire world was under the thumb of this thing called COVID-19. The coronavirus. I'm sure you've heard about it. I imagine every single human being on the planet is well aware of the pandemic that has altered our way of life, no matter if you're rich, poor, smart, or stupid.

Therefore, I ask you to place yourself back to that month. From here on out, we are no longer using past tense to refer to May 2020. It is now.

In most of America, especially in the cities and surrounding suburbs, folks are staying home. Unless you're one of those brave essential workers, you've been working from home using computers, phones, and that newfangled Zoom technology. Or maybe you aren't working at all. Perhaps you are one of the unfortunate ones who got furloughed (a nice way to say "laid off") or even outright fired. If that's the case, then I'm sorry, my friend.

This situation has created a new kind of existence for everyone, right? No more gatherings of clusters of people. No more concerts or movies or live theater. No more shopping malls. Restaurants are starting to reopen, but who really wants to be served a meal by someone wearing a mask? Kind of takes the fun out of "dining out."

The isolation is beginning to take a toll on some. The media says that reports of domestic violence have increased, drug abuse is rampant, and depression and insomnia are common ailments. Whether you're a Democrat or a Republican, the news from Washington, DC, is never pleasant. I don't want to bring politics into our yarn, but it's impossible to allow it to unfold without the background of the coronavirus informing our characters and what they do. If this were a stage play, perhaps the set design would contain subtle representations of those ugly tennis ball-like things with the suction-spikes sticking out of it, the germ as depicted under a microscope. Yuck. I don't know about you, but I don't like the looks of that thing.

Speaking of a stage play, you folks might remember one by a playwright named Thornton Wilder. It was entitled *Our Town*, and it was first produced way back in 1938. It's a hugely popular slice of Americana, a Pulitzer Prize–winning play, and it's been done to death with revivals, movies, TV adaptations, and hundreds of high school and college productions. I was in one myself in my college years—I played Simon Stimson, the town's choir master and resident alcoholic.

And who am I, you ask?

That is a good question, but one I'm not likely to answer during the course of our adventure together. In Wilder's *Our Town*, the main character is really a narrator, a fellow who walks around the stage and comments on the people and the action, addressing the audience directly and becoming their friend. In the program, he is called the "Stage Manager." Well, I'd like you to think of me as something like that. Yes, I am your humble narrator, that omniscient presence hovering over the story, a persona who, I hope, will become your friend and confidant too. I'm male and old enough that central casting would likely consider me to play someone's grandfather—so maybe those tidbits will help you form a picture of me in your head.

Furthermore, in keeping with the conceit of a storyteller, you should be aware that, yes, I do know things about our murders that you don't, and I know things the characters don't. I call those things the Missing Pieces.

Ask any good homicide cop if a closed case is ever fully complete. The answer is liable to be no. A prosecutor might have all the evidence one needs to successfully convict a killer in a courtroom, but there are almost always pieces of the puzzle that are missing. A crime's physical evidence might suggest a timeline of events that go from point A to point E, but what occurred between point F and point P could be unknown to the cops and attorneys. That's a Missing Piece. And there could be more evidence present from point Q to point S, and a bit from V to X, and maybe that's enough to prove the defendant's guilt. The Missing Pieces, however, will always remain cryptic.

Our little murder has Missing Pieces. I'll decide later if I should reveal them to you.

For now, let's concentrate on the arbitrary beginning of the story.

Imagine, if you will, a horseshoe-shaped street in quiet, relatively peaceful, middle-class Lincoln Grove, Illinois. On a map, it's really two streets that sit horizontally, one on top of the other, both open toward the west and connected by a curve on the east ends. The upper leg of the horseshoe is called Marigold Way, and the lower one is named Dodge Lane. The names change at the midpoint of the curve, where there's a small gap the size of a house. A tree-lined foot and bike path begins there and heads east two-tenths of a mile until it hits Dodge Park. Many other lanes and streets kaleidoscope off this large, scenic, pastoral plot that holds a tennis court, playground equipment, and a field large enough for a soccer game. Intersecting the western ends of Marigold and Dodge is north–south road Temple Avenue. "No Outlet" signs stand at the western entrances of Marigold Way and Dodge Lane from Temple, because, well, if you drive east on Marigold, your vehicle will just curve around at the end until you're going west on Dodge and you wind up back at Temple. Eight trilevel houses sit on each side of both lanes, with even numbers on the north sides. The backyards of the odd-numbered houses on Marigold Way butt up against the backyards of the even-numbered houses on Dodge Lane. You get the picture, I hope.

There's nothing but other streets and houses within the radius of a mile around Marigold Way and Dodge Lane. A mile and a quarter to the west leads to a major Lincoln Grove thoroughfare, and one can find a Starbucks, a Walgreens, and a strip mall with a couple of mom-and-pop eateries (now closed, of course) and a dry cleaners. The bigger grocery stores, banks, and other services that are parts of any village lie farther south. Three blocks to the north is an elementary school, and a middle school sits six blocks north of that. One must take a bus or drive to the nearest high school.

It's a fairly diverse neighborhood. Granted, Lincoln Grove is mostly made up of white citizens, but there are pockets of different ethnicities here and there. Maybe a quarter of the population is Jewish. During a single walk through the park, one might hear a variety of spoken languages. Since it's a suburb of Chicago, Lincoln Grove could politically be called "blue," but, like everywhere, that's somewhat of a generalization.

Right now, though, everything is green. It's spring. The sun shines most days. The temperatures are usually in the high seventies Fahrenheit, with occasional forays into the sweltering eighties.

The birds are happy, squirrels are busy, and gardens are blooming. Everything is quite pretty. Residents understandably consider May to be one of the best months of the year.

Since March 2020, though, the occupants in the various houses on the horseshoe have been hunkering down, dealing with the pandemic in their own ways. They're keeping the kids home, working out of their living rooms or bedrooms via their computers, toiling in their yards, taking walks or riding bicycles for exercise, and keeping distance from their neighbors except to speak occasionally while standing at least six feet apart and perhaps wearing masks. No one dons masks when out walking—the paths are never crowded.

There are a few folks who do leave their homes and travel to work. For example, Harriet Schoenberg is one of those heroes who works as a nurse, at NCH Hospital. She is naturally nervous about becoming infected and bringing the virus home to her husband and son. John Bergman, another resident of Marigold Way, runs the warehouse of a medical supply and prescription drug distributor. He had to furlough some employees, but he continues to drive to and from the place daily. John has lately been spending more time at the warehouse due to a recent robbery, and you will learn more about that in a bit.

I suppose the most significant thing about the neighborhood is that no one on the horseshoe has gotten sick. Most everyone has worked to keep safe and practice social distancing. Still, one can almost taste the paranoia and mistrust hanging in the air. Fear of the virus is tangible. Jokes about toilet paper hoarding have long passed. The residents of Lincoln Grove attempt to stay chipper and keep a positive attitude, but there is no question that every person is on edge.

I'm sure you know what I'm talking about.

And this is where our little murder tale commences.

Monday, May 11, 2020

7:33 a.m.

Scott Hatcher reached over to his wife's side of the bed to wrap his arm around her. It was a gesture born out of habit rather than any kind of affectionate impulse.

He didn't feel anything. Marie wasn't there.

Scott half-sighed, half-groaned into his pillow and attempted to shut out the bright sunlight streaming in through the windows of the master bedroom. Even with the blinds closed, daylight was a powerful alarm clock if one didn't have to rise earlier than, say, 7:30. There was also the expected hammering and power tools in the backyard of the house behind his. The noise was likely what woke him up.

Oh man, what time is it? Does he have start so damned early?

It had been a problem since the end of April. Scott's neighbor behind him on Dodge Lane, a Mr. Blunt—Scott didn't know his first name—was building an elaborate addition to his house, and it appeared that he was doing it alone. Scott figured that the guy was probably laid off from his job and had nothing better to do. Scott could appreciate having the handyman abilities to construct something without help—Lord knows that *he* was incapable of doing so—but the early pounding and woodcutting was a nuisance. Blunt never did it during normal work hours, maybe because he enjoyed the cooler temperatures of morning and evening, or he actually enjoyed bothering the neighbors. Come dinnertime, Mr. Fix-It would start up again and ruin what might have been a pleasant meal with the wife. Bang, bang, saw, saw, bang, bang . . . Lovely. For some reason, Marie rarely complained about it. Scott figured that the least his wife could do would be to join him in solidarity against the noise. The family that bitches together, stays together.

But in Scott's case . . . maybe not.

Most mornings, Scott tried to stay in bed as long as possible. His sleep patterns had been messed up for months. He was a light sleeper in times of normalcy, often prone to insomnia. Ever since the lockdown started in March, though, catching forty winks was as elusive as winning the lottery.

"Hon?" he called out hoarsely.

Marie didn't answer. She wasn't in the bathroom or anywhere upstairs.

Scott stretched, felt the familiar urgency, and swung his legs out from under the sheets. After using the bathroom, cleaning his night guard with a toothbrush ("You obviously grind your teeth at night, Mr. Hatcher," the dentist had said), and splashing water in his face, he stepped out of the bedroom in his boxer shorts and called down the stairs.

"Marie?"

Silence. Just the birds chirping outside and the racket from the Blunt yard.

He then checked the guest bedroom where, once in a blue moon, either he or she would sleep if one of them wanted alone time. Last night could have been one of those instances. But the bed was perfectly made and not slept in.

Probably on a walk, he thought. She did that a lot. Marie would get up, not wait for Scott, and head out to the foot and bike paths. There were several to choose from, but the normal route was to head east to Dodge Park and then randomly pick another street from there to traverse. She could be gone for about an hour, sometimes longer.

Scott enjoyed his walks in the neighborhood too. There wasn't anything else to do, that was for sure. The daily routine rarely varied. Get up, have coffee and some eggs, go for a walk, shower, maybe drive to the post office or the grocery store (donned with a mask and medical-grade vinyl gloves), try to write at his computer while sitting in various locations in the house, prepare meals for himself and his wife, perhaps take another walk in the evening after dinner, watch some television or a movie, and go to bed. Rinse and repeat.

Most of that was done solo. Lately, Marie seldom joined him for walks, and sometimes she had no compulsion to eat with him either. The stay-at-home orders were making their already tentative relationship worse. The daily arguments. The sarcasm. The spite.

They had mutually agreed to postpone the talk of divorce when the pandemic hit. Now they were stuck with each other in the same habitat. Scott liked to call it house arrest.

At least neither of them had the kind of tempers that resulted in their throwing things.

Scott spent some time in the kitchen making coffee and toasting a muffin, and then he sat down with his laptop at the table to check email and scan his pathetic social media pages on Facebook and Twitter. His literary agent still hadn't responded to his query about a new novel he was outlining. There was, however, an email from his bank that indicated a direct deposit had been made. It was a damned good thing that he still received residuals from *Blaster Bob*. The television show for kids he had created back in 2003 when he was only twenty-five had run for four seasons and then was syndicated until 2011. It's what had kept him and Marie afloat for over a decade, although those residuals were shrinking with each passing year. Marie now made more money than he did, and Scott had no problem with that. Her job as a freelance realtor had taken a dip when the pandemic began, but she still managed to pull in enough of a salary to cover the mortgage. The stimulus check issued by the government, which they had received a couple of weeks earlier, had helped. Scott was just grateful that they were managing during this time of crisis. Others were not so fortunate.

The only other emails were political begs, spam, and the usual ads from pharmacies and grocery stores. Time to move on and browse the news. He subscribed to the *Chicago Tribune* and the *New York Times*, and that's where he got the latest. These days, it was all bad news.

The *Tribune* site had an update on the recent break-in at Cassette Labs, a company located in Fornham, the next town over to the south. Scott found that item somewhat interesting, because one of his neighbors on Marigold Way, John Bergman, worked there. On the past Friday, May 8, or, rather, early on Saturday, May 9, someone had broken into the medical supply company's warehouse. Whoever had done it had disabled the security system, including video cameras—which would have been no easy feat—and hauled away an impressive amount of PPE—N95 masks, hospital gowns and other protective clothing, gloves, hand sanitizer, antiseptic wipes, and other items that were increasingly difficult for the average consumer to obtain. More concerning to the police was that the thieves had taken a lot of prescription drugs, namely hydroxychloroquine, which was a controversial medicine in the news, but also expensive items like insulin, HIV drugs, narcotic painkillers, and, curiously, erectile dysfunction pills like Viagra and Cialis.

Had Bergman not gone into work on Saturday mid-morning, the robbery might not have been discovered until today, Monday. The *Tribune* article didn't say much about the police investigation except that the thieves had used one of the warehouse forklifts to move pallets and that at least one commercial truck must have carted the goods away. Scott recalled that John Bergman had a significant position at the company—was he the warehouse manager? The guy was likely sweating bullets because of what had happened on his watch. The Bergmans lived across the street and east a couple of houses. Scott didn't know John well. They'd wave hello at each other, but in the few years the family had lived on Marigold Way, Scott could probably count on one hand the number of times he'd spoken to John.

The rest of the *Tribune* and most of the *Times* was all political and Covid news, none of it pleasant, so Scott closed his laptop and prepared to go for a walk on his own. He noted that an hour had passed since he'd risen from bed, and Marie still hadn't returned.

Probably still cooling off from the fight we had yesterday afternoon . . .

It hadn't been the best Mother's Day. Marie tended to sink to rock bottom every year on that Hallmark holiday. It never failed, and Scott could hardly blame her. But if he should attempt to cheer her up or distract her, he was met with derision and curses.

Scott put on jeans, a T-shirt, and tennis shoes. He opened the front door and stepped outside.

He wasn't going to wait around for Marie. Scott shut the door, made sure it was locked, and set out east on his morning walk. A woman was being pulled by an enthusiastic dog on a leash across the street. A teenager rode by on a bicycle.

People were out in the fresh air and pretending that life was normal, but Scott knew that it was anything but.

2

Okay, friends, you've met our hero of the story . . . or is he? We don't rightly know yet, do we? One thing is for sure—he's a minor celebrity on the block. Most of his neighbors know who he is. "Honey, there's that writer walking down the street," someone might say. They smile and nod and wave. Not that they've ever read any of his books. Maybe they had kids who watched *Blaster Bob* on television back in the day. Perhaps there's a *Blaster Bob* action figure lying in the bottom of a clothes closet among other discarded toys that belonged to a boy who is now grown and not living at home anymore.

If you look up the Wikipedia page of Lincoln Grove, Illinois, you'd find Scott Hatcher's name on the list of "notable residents." That said, he's not a big enough celebrity that he is recognized outside of Marigold Way. If Scott goes to the post office or the grocery store, no one stops him and asks for an autograph. Nobody really knows who he is. I suppose that's probably a good thing. Everyone values privacy.

Now let's meet some of the other denizens of the block as Scott leaves Number 505, the third unit down from the corner of Marigold and Temple on the south side of the street.

Monday, May 11, 2020
8:45 a.m.

It was already a warm day, and the air smelled fresh and clean. Scott considered this to be one of the nicer things about living in the burbs. No pollution of the kind one found in Chicago.

One of Waste Management's big garbage trucks was moving slowly toward his house. Scott silently cursed to himself—he had forgotten to take the bins out the night before and place them on the curb. Did he have time to run back inside, go through the house to the lower level, open the garage door, and roll out the bins?

The truck was already in front of the Kimmelmans' home, and they lived next door to the west. Nope, no time. Oh well. The trash would just have to sit in the bins until the next pickup. It wasn't as if he and Marie were producing tons of garbage. They'd survive.

Scott waved at the man driving the garbage truck as it went by. The guy wasn't wearing a mask. Scott frowned. He didn't know if someone could get Covid by handling other people's garbage, but he personally wouldn't want to take that chance. Granted, Scott himself wasn't wearing a mask. It wasn't necessary to wear one just to go for a walk in his community. He wouldn't be within six feet of anyone, and the number of people he'd pass on his trek could be counted on two hands.

"Hello, Scott!"

Ah. Mrs. Kimmelman. Lois. The busybody next-door neighbor stood fifteen feet away from him in her yard.

Lois and her husband, Al, were in their late sixties and were retired. Their kids were grown and gone. Scott hardly ever saw Al Kimmelman. He was known to have health problems, so it was probably just as well that the man stayed inside and didn't socialize with anyone right now. Lois, on the other hand, came over to the Hatcher home every few days with an offer to provide Scott and Marie with a mysterious casserole she had made. The food was always in a plastic container; it seemed she had an endless supply of the things. "There is simply way too much for Al and me to eat, so I'm happy to give you some," she'd say. Scott wondered why the woman made so damned much of the concoctions if there were just two of them at home. Nevertheless, either he or Marie would smile, nod, say, "Thank you," and take the plastic container. "Don't worry about getting that back to me, I've got plenty of them," Lois would remind them.

Yes, we know.

"Enjoy!"

We won't!

Usually after they took one look or sniff of whatever it was, the food went straight down the garbage disposal.

Luckily, it was early Monday morning, so Lois Kimmelman had no casserole in a plastic container in hand. Instead, she stood in her front yard wearing a frumpy housedress and grasping a watering can in her paw, obviously tending to her admittedly well-cared-for garden. The flowers were blooming beautifully—tulips, daffodils, blue hydrangeas, and others that Scott couldn't identify. This was a sore point in the Hatcher home. No one—neither Scott nor Marie—had a green thumb. Scott hated yard work. Mowing lawns for pocket money as a kid had ruined him for life. Now he was perfectly happy to pay another kid to do the work at 505 Marigold Way.

"Good morning, Lois, how are you?" Scott said with exaggerated friendliness.

"Oh, we're doing all right. Al's complaining about his knees again, but that's nothing new. Are you and Marie safe and well?"

"Safe and well as can be, thank you."

"Out for your walk, are you?"

"That's right. You didn't happen to see Marie earlier, did you?"

"No, I haven't seen your lovely bride today."

"Ah, well, she got out of the house earlier than I did. I may run into her. See you later, Lois. Give my best to Al."

"I will. Oh!"

Scott stopped and turned.

"I almost forgot. I'm making the *best* rhubarb casserole today, and you and Marie are going to have to taste some of it. I'll bring over a container this afternoon."

Scott wanted to nip that in the bud. "Thank you so much, Lois, but Marie and I, well, with the pandemic and all, we've really been making it a point to just eat our own home-cooked food. It's a precaution, you know? We haven't even ordered takeout since all this started. Just don't trust it. But I appreciate your offer."

Lois frowned but nodded. "I understand. But if you change your mind, just give us a call. I'll bring it right over."

"Thanks." He turned to go.

"Oh!"

He stopped and turned again. "Yes, Lois?"

"Did you hear about the fire in the park last night?"

"No."

"One of those teenage vandals exploded something in one of the trash cans again. The fire spilled out a little onto the grass. The fire truck came and everything."

"Well, I should hope the fire truck *would* come. Did the police catch who did it?"

"No. They think it's a teenager who's bored and has nothing to do."

"Could be."

"It's been happening a lot in Lincoln Grove. Not only in Dodge Park, but in other parks too. We have a pyromaniac on our hands."

Scott shrugged. "Well, I hope they catch him soon. See you later, Lois."

This time she let him go.

As he left his yard and reached the sidewalk, Scott pulled out his phone to make sure Marie hadn't texted him. He had already sent one message, but he quickly typed another one to her: Going for a walk. See you soon.

He headed east and passed Number 507, the eyesore of the neighborhood. Not that it wasn't pretty—it was ugly *inside*. The house immediately next to the Hatcher home had been for sale for months. Marie was the realtor for it. In fact, the "For Sale" sign had her smiling face on it, a photo that was nearly ten years old. "Let Marie Help You Move In!" the sign proclaimed. Unfortunately, there was bad energy associated with the house. Even though the price was ridiculously low, most buyers wanted no part of it when they found out about what had happened there. The Wilkins family had lived in it until Douglas Wilkins hanged himself in the master bedroom closet in June 2019. The Hatchers hadn't known the Wilkinses except to say hello. Valentina Wilkins, the widow, had sold all the furniture and the family's belongings, and moved to Arizona before the end of summer. The house had been on the market since then, three-quarters of a year. It wasn't selling *before* the pandemic, and it had no chance now. But Marie was doing her best to keep it up to snuff. It was a nice house, but Scott supposed no one wanted a ghost for a roommate.

"Hi, Mr. Hatcher!"

Scott turned to see two boys riding bicycles in the street. He knew that the public schools were all screwed up. The situation differed state by state and county by county, but the Lincoln Grove schools had been closed to in-person classes since March, and virtual classes seemed to be still a "work in progress." Was the school year already over? Scott wasn't sure.

One of the boys had his hand up. Scott waved at Seth Schoenberg, a high schooler with whom he was friendly. The Schoenbergs lived at 506 Marigold, right across the street from the Wilkinses' empty house. The other boy, Don Trainer, was another sixteen-year-old who lived with his folks down at the corner of Marigold and Temple at 500. Scott had no love for Don Trainer. He considered Don a delinquent, a bad apple, a smart aleck, and just plain trouble. In fact, it was well known that Don had been arrested at least twice for minor offenses. Then again, the Trainers often stuck political signs in their yard that were in direct conflict with most of the ones in the rest of the neighborhood. Scott wondered why a good kid like Seth hung out with a bad boy like Don.

"How you doing, Seth?" Scott called. "Hi, Don."

Seth pulled his bike over to the curb and stopped. Don remained in the road, ignoring Scott and pedaling slowly on, looking back at the two as they talked.

"I'm ready to start mowing your lawn again," Seth said. "That is, if you still want me to do it this summer."

Seth Schoenberg had been the Hatcher lawn mower for the past two summers. Scott paid him a reasonable fee, and it saved Scott from having to hire landscapers to do it.

"Yeah, I think it needs it, don't you? That grass is growing like there's no tomorrow. Whenever you want to do it is fine with me, Seth."

"Great, thanks. I'll do it this week. Twenty bucks a mow still good?"

"I'll make it twenty-five. You deserve a raise."

"Thanks."

"How are your folks?"

"They're okay. We're a little worried about Mom, with her working at the hospital and everything."

That's right . . . Harriet Schoenberg was a nurse at NCH Hospital. "I can imagine," Scott said. "I'd be worried too. I hope she's staying safe."

Seth shrugged. "They don't have much PPE."

"I know. Please give my best to her and your dad."

"I will."

Scott gestured to his face. "Shouldn't you and Don be, uh, wearing masks?"

"How come?"

"Well, you live in different households. Social distancing and all that. And your mother works at the hospital?"

Seth shook his head. "Don's been staying home, and I have too."

"What about his folks? Doesn't his dad go to work?"

"It's okay, Mr. Hatcher. We don't get too close to each other. See you soon!"

"Uh, sure, see you."

Seth rode on and joined his friend, and the two of them sped off toward the curve in the road and, Scott figured, the bike paths around Dodge Park. Scott glanced at the Schoenberg house. Seth's father, Mitch, was an accountant working from home these days. Scott and Marie really didn't know the Schoenbergs, but Scott liked Seth a lot.

He walked on.

David Woo was working on the flower bed in front of his house, Number 509. Scott waved at him. Mr. Woo grinned broadly, waved, and said, "Nice day! Nice day!"

"It is!"

Scott smiled to himself. Mr. Woo sometimes had an endearing tendency of saying things twice.

The Woo family was from China and had immigrated to America in the 1990s. David and his wife, May, were in their fifties. Scott wasn't sure how many children they had, but the Woos were now empty nesters. The Woos owned a family business of Chinese takeout restaurant storefronts in the area. Scott thought there were three eateries, but he wasn't sure. The Hatchers had occasionally brought takeout home from the Woos' place in Lincoln Grove's Town Center, and the food was usually decent. No problems there. David and May rarely worked at the restaurants anymore; they had staff who handled everything now, so David was home working on his garden. Luckily for the Woos, takeout restaurants were doing all right during the pandemic.

"Have a good walk! Have a good walk!" the man called out.

"Thank you!" Scott almost repeated the words, but he caught himself. He moved on. Scott didn't know his neighbors on his side of the street beyond the Woo home. However, across the street, next door to the Schoenbergs at Number 508, was the Bergman house. John Bergman and his wife, Rachel, lived there with their son, Thomas.

Rachel Bergman sat at a card table in the yard in the shade under a large silver maple tree. She appeared to be selling something. She waved at Scott, so he decided to cross the road and say hello.

John and Rachel were in their forties, probably closest in age to the Hatchers than anyone else on the block. Scott didn't know them well, but both families always waved at and greeted each other.

One thing Scott had never told Marie was that he considered Rachel Bergman an extremely attractive woman. Maybe she was just Scott's type. She had dark hair, brown eyes, and had a distinctive earth-mother, sixties or seventies hippie look. For some inexplicable reason, he had always been drawn to that sort of woman. Perhaps it was because his own mother had been a flower child.

Interestingly, Marie wasn't anything like that.

"Need any masks?" Rachel asked as he approached the table, staying six feet away.

A variety of colorful homemade masks were displayed in an array. A cardboard stand-up sign announced: $5 MASKS, SUPPORTS WOMEN'S SHELTER CHARITY!

"They're beautiful," Scott said. "You made these?"

"I did. Look, they accordion up and down." She demonstrated how the creases in the fabric expanded when she pulled on one. "They're very comfortable. The money goes to the local women's shelter. You know that domestic violence is on the rise with the pandemic going on? People are stuck at home. You know how it can be."

"Yeah, I've heard." He held out his bare hands. "Sorry, I don't have my wallet on me, or I'd buy one. Look, see, I do have a mask on me. It's not as nice as those, though. I wear it when I go shopping or whatever. Not when I'm out for a walk."

"Of course. Well, I'll be out here a couple more hours, if you find your wallet." She gave him a warm smile.

Scott was tempted to ask if the police had made any progress on the robbery at her husband's Cassette Labs warehouse, but he decided that wouldn't be too cool. Besides, Scott really didn't care much for John Bergman. Sometimes the guy didn't wave back when Scott greeted him. John often gave off the impression that he was a jerk, but Scott had no real proof. Rachel, on the other hand, was always friendly.

"Mom?"

Thomas Bergman, a boy of fourteen, came out of the house.

"Say hi to Mr. Hatcher, dear," Rachel said to him.

Scott found Thomas to be a strange kid. The boy was nice enough, but there was something very *Children of the Corn* about him. For one thing, he never wore T-shirts or shorts the way other kids his age did. Whenever Scott saw him, Thomas was usually dressed, as he was now, in long-sleeved, button-down shirts and black slacks—never blue jeans. The boy always looked as if he were on his way to a Torah study class. Additionally, Thomas's face never seemed to change expressions. Scott wasn't sure if he'd ever seen the kid smile. It was well known that the boy was extremely smart and was on all kinds of honor rolls at school. Word on the street was that Thomas had learned two other languages by the time he was twelve. Nevertheless, the kid was just . . . strange.

"Hello, Mr. Hatcher," the boy said.

"Hi, Thomas. How are you?"

"I'm fine."

Rachel addressed her son. "Why don't you tell Mr. Hatcher what you finished reading?"

"Oh. I read your book, *The Stick Men*. I enjoyed it very much."

"You read *The Stick Men*?" Scott was amazed. It was a novel he'd published a few years earlier that contained seriously adult subject matter dealing with mental illness and drug abuse.

"Yes, sir."

"Well, I'm, uh, glad you liked it. I'll, uh, sign it for you, if you want."

"Oh, I got it as an e-book. Checked it out from the library."

"Ah. Well, that's okay. I like libraries."

Rachel looked at her watch. "With the library closed now, we can only check out e-books. I'm sorry John isn't here to say hello. I was just wondering when he would get home. I didn't think he'd be going to work today, but I suppose he had to."

Scott shuffled his feet. "I, er, I heard about what happened. I'm sorry about that."

"Yeah, I just hope the bosses don't blame John. Well, enjoy your walk, Scott. It's going to be a beautiful day. Oh, and *tonight* the sky will be lovely. The moon was full a few days ago, you know, so it's waning now. But it'll still be bright, and so will a canvas of stars. Mercury is in Gemini, and you know what that means."

Scott chuckled. "No, what does it mean?"

"You'll feel chattier and more social. You'll be all about connecting with people, especially ones you're not close to."

"Is that so? I didn't know you were into astrology."

Rachel smiled, lowered her head a little, and looked up at him. "There's a lot you don't know about me."

Holy cow, is she flirting with me?

"Well, I guess I'll make some phone calls to some friends I haven't checked on," he said. "Thanks!" He gestured awkwardly toward the curve in the road. "I'd better . . . "

" . . . Get going," Rachel finished. "I know. Have fun on your walk!"

"Thanks, be safe. Bye, Thomas."

"Bye, Mr. Hatcher."

Scott moved on, and once he got to the gap in the curve and the path that headed east to the park, he checked his phone again. Still no response from Marie.

It had been a good, sweat-producing hike through the park, then down a couple of side streets, a circle back west toward Temple, and finally a sprint to the end of Marigold and home. Mrs. Kimmelman was no longer in the front yard. The street was empty.

Marie wasn't in the house when Scott let himself inside.

He didn't think she'd *driven* anywhere, but just to cover all the bases, Scott went down to the lower level, opened the door to the garage, and found both of their cars sitting there. Marie drove a white 2015 Chevy Malibu. Scott had a gray 2016 Nissan Altima. Nothing was amiss.

Back in the kitchen, he saw that Marie's purse was on the kitchen table. Her wallet was inside, and it contained her driver's license and credit cards.

Looking at his watch, Scott determined that she'd been away more than two hours since he'd gotten out of bed. Perhaps she'd walked to the Town Center. Maybe she was still mad at him and she just wanted to be away for a while.

Their Mother's Day fight must have been worse than he'd originally thought.

3

Are you still with me?

Now you've met a few of the inhabitants of our little story, and you'll meet a few more soon. It's a rather nice community, wouldn't you say? Neighbors. You know what they're like. You like some of them, and the others . . . well, you know. I suppose what's important is that we all live in enclaves that are congregations of kinship, be they apartment buildings or houses on a suburban or city street. But all is never what it seems. We pretend there's fellowship among our neighbors, but in truth, we all have secrets that we don't want to share—certainly not with our neighbors, and often not even with the significant others who occupy the same living space with us.

For example—you might wonder why Douglas Wilkins hanged himself in the house next door to the Hatchers. No one in the neighborhood could figure it out, and his widow, Valentina, offered no clues except to one other person. She just up and left and moved to Arizona to be near family. What made him do it?

Secrets.

I suppose some secrets are good. For instance, a woman might be happy about learning that she's going to have a baby, but she prefers not to tell the world about it until she's so many weeks along. That's potentially good news that is temporarily kept secret. Or maybe you've been told you're going to get a promotion at work, but they want you to keep it quiet until something or other occurs first. Maybe a Hollywood studio has bought one of your novels and is going to film it—but you have to sit on that information until the studio issues a press release. Those kinds of secrets are nice.

That said, other kinds of secrets are usually dark and sad.

Let's watch our friend Scott for a little while longer before we switch gears and focus on another character in the neighborhood.

Monday, May 11, 2020
11:55 a.m.

Some say procrastination is a writer's nightmare, and yet Scott considered it to be more of a friend. Need to work on that outline of the new novel? Better check Facebook and Twitter first and see if there's something amusing, outrageous, or informative that someone has posted. Don't forget to browse through the news sites. Oh, are there more emails to either immediately delete, mark as "junk," or maybe respond to? Hmm, have you browsed Amazon lately to see if there are any recent reviews of books you've published? Or maybe new releases of books or music you might want? No need to go to a store—Amazon delivers right to your door! Let's see, what's the bank account looking like? Always good to drop in online to make sure there are no unauthorized charges. One can't be too careful these days. The same goes for credit cards.

Scott had indeed been working on an outline, but the motivation had all but fizzled out once the pandemic started. Lately, he just didn't have it in him to create. He hated to be morbid, but he had no intention of leaving behind an unfinished manuscript should he catch the coronavirus and die. Besides, his last few novels hadn't sold well. He could be spinning his wheels for nothing. Had his window already opened and closed at the age of forty-two?

Everything just made him frustrated. All of it. Work, play, the lockdown...

His relationship with his wife hadn't helped either. Before the pandemic, the two of them had their careers to keep them busy and satisfied. Marie was working under the RE/MAX umbrella. There was an office in Town Center she shared with other realtors, but most of the time she had worked from home. Scott had been working for many years as a self-employed writer. For a while, they had been compatible. Looking back over the last ten years, though, Scott could see that he and Marie had stayed married for convenience. But when a couple experienced what they had gone through—and it was not unique to Scott and Marie—there was often discord and sometimes divorce. Things had never been the same since May 2009.

Damn, it's been eleven years...

Scott looked at his phone to check the time. He was surprised to see that it was now a little after noon, so he texted Marie again.

Where are you???

He gave it a minute, then phoned her number. Once again, voice mail picked up, so he disconnected. He'd already left a couple of messages.

Was it time to get genuinely concerned?

Then he remembered her best friend, Cindy. She was a workout companion and someone Marie had known for years through work and other social events. Cindy was happily married and lived in the next town over. Scott had her number in his phone. She and her husband, Jim, were roughly the same age as the Hatchers.

Cindy picked up after two rings. "Scott?"

"Hi, Cindy, yeah, it's Scott. How are you doing?"

"Fine, I guess. I mean, it's like everyone, right? We're doing okay. How about you guys?"

"The same, just trying to get through it all. Say, listen, have you heard from Marie today?"

"No, why?"

"Well, I don't know where she is. She left the house before I woke up this morning. I thought she'd gone for a walk, but she's still not back yet. She hasn't answered her phone or my texts. It's kind of weird."

"Gosh, no, I haven't talked to Marie since, what, last Wednesday, I think."

"Her car and purse are here, so I'm guessing she went on a long walk. Her Mother's Day wasn't very . . . happy . . . so maybe that's it."

"Oh," Cindy paused. "Yeah, I can understand that. You're right. Maybe she just needed some space."

"But with the pandemic and all . . . where could she go? Her mask is in her purse. I don't know . . . I'm considering calling the police."

"Scott, did you and Marie have another fight?"

He hesitated, but Cindy probably knew everything about his and Marie's relationship. She and Marie were tight. "Yeah. Yesterday. She was in a funk about Mother's Day, and I tried too hard to cheer her up. When she snapped at me, I snapped back. We go through this every Mother's Day, I'm afraid. With all the stress that's going on, and all the crap out there, I kind of lost it. Then she lost it. It wasn't pretty."

"I'm sorry to hear that."

"I didn't sleep on the couch, though! We both slept in the same bed. She was—"

Scott stopped and thought about it. He had called it a night before Marie. He must have fallen asleep first. Had she come to bed at all? Was there a depression in the mattress on her side of the bed when he was reaching over for her?

"Scott? You there?"

"Oh yeah, I was just . . . never mind. As I was saying, it wasn't a fight that was any worse than any other battle we've had."

"Did you make up afterwards?"

"Not really."

He heard Cindy sigh. "Look, Scott, I know Marie. She probably needed to step away for a bit. Maybe she called an Uber or a Lyft and went somewhere. Maybe a hotel."

"Without her purse and credit cards?"

"She can use her phone to pay for stuff."

Scott thought about that. "Yeah, I guess you're right. That could be it."

"Try not to worry. I'll give her a call too. If I reach her, I'll let you know."

"Text me anyway, whether you get hold of her or not, would you?"

"Of course. She'll turn up, Scott. Do me a favor, though? Have her call me when she does come in."

"Will do."

"Thanks. Call again if you need to."

"Thanks, Cindy. Talk to you later."

He disconnected and stared at his phone. Maybe that was it. Marie had taken an Uber somewhere. She needed some time away from him.

Do you have a lover, Marie?

It was a question he'd had in the back of his mind for several years. The level of intimacy between them had changed. That was sometimes a sign of . . .

Stop it. She'll be back.

He got up, went to the kitchen, and pulled out from the fridge fixings for a sandwich. He'd read about some folks, and had talked to a few friends, who indicated they'd been gaining weight from being stuck at home. Not Scott. He had lost several pounds. The regular walking, the healthier fare, and not doing takeout or fast-food joints was helping. Scott knew he wasn't a bad-looking fellow. Women often gave him the eye. At five feet eleven with no paunch, and a head full of long black hair with hints of gray, clear blue eyes, and a killer smile, he'd been told he could be a male model if he'd wanted to be. That wasn't a job for him, but his looks and an artistic disposition had provided him with a better-than-average track record with the ladies prior to his marriage.

And after his marriage . . . ?

Scott blocked that thought process and made his sandwich. He then took it outside to the back porch and sat at the patio table that sorely needed replacing. The sun was behind a bundle of clouds, so the air was cool and pleasant. Was it going to rain that afternoon? Not according to the birds chirping and frolicking in the trees and on the wooden fence, or the two squirrels chasing each other back and forth in the yard.

Just as he was about to enjoy his lunch, the moment of peaceful tranquility was sliced to bits by the unbelievably loud shriek of a buzz saw. Scott winced and then peeked through one squinting eye at the backyard behind his. Mr. Blunt, shirtless and his skin glistening with sweat, was on top of the roof of his house and making a racket. The man, who appeared to be in his thirties, had flaming red hair and several tattoos adorning his muscular torso.

Did the guy live alone? Scott had never seen any sign of a wife or kids. He also often wondered if Blunt had obtained a permit from the village to build extensions to his house on his own. As if Blunt could hear Scott's thoughts, the man stopped sawing and looked up. He gave Scott a wave. Still chewing his first bite of sandwich, Scott saluted to his neighbor.

"Is the noise bothering you again?" Blunt shouted.

Scott had politely mentioned it to Blunt once before, suggesting that starting work early in the morning or during the dinner hour might be disturbing to his neighbors. Blunt appeared to take offense and had stared at Scott's nose as if it might make the perfect bull's-eye for a fist. After a few seconds, though, Blunt had grumbled that he would "keep to more agreeable hours." He hadn't, of course, but at that moment it *was* a more acceptable time of day. Scott couldn't very well justify complaining about the noise at high noon.

To answer his neighbor, Scott just waved the question away and gave the guy a thumbs up. He stood with sandwich still in hand and went back in the house. He wasn't in the mood to get into a tug-of-war with Mr. Blunt. Besides, Blunt was built like the Hulk and could be just as intimidating.

A text from Cindy appeared on his phone.

No luck reaching Marie. Have her call me when she comes home!

Scott dropped his sandwich on the kitchen table and suddenly felt very alone.

"Damn it, Marie, where the hell are you?"

4

Now we will shift focus to another character in our tale, someone you've already met briefly. Seth Schoenberg is an old soul at sixteen years old. He's basically a good kid, although he is easily influenced by peer pressure and the need to rebel against the current climate of isolation and boredom.

Seth is a striking, handsome boy. He's way too tall for his age, lanky and thin, with a head of thick brown hair. He resembles the musician Neil Young back when he was just a youngster himself with Buffalo Springfield, but Seth probably doesn't know who Neil Young is. Seth is unsure what he wants to do when he "grows up," but for now he is unwittingly playing the role of the dark, silent mystery man. The girls are going to be all over Seth when he gets to college, and he wasn't doing too badly in high school in that area—until they shut down in-person classes for the rest of the semester and the summer. The problem is that Seth is perhaps too shy for his own good.

Don Trainer, on the other hand, is the athletic, arrogant type without much going on upstairs. He's shorter than Seth, more of an average height for his age, and he likes to puff out his chest and strut around as if he's Mr. Universe. Scott Hatcher is right about

Don Trainer. The kid is trouble. If this were the 1950s, Don would surely be labeled a "juvenile delinquent."

Monday, May 11, 2020
12:35 p.m.

The two boys rode their bicycles through Dodge Park, swerving around occasional joggers, walkers, and folks with dogs. There weren't a lot of people out, though. The heavy foot traffic was usually in the mornings and evenings when it was cooler.

Seth Schoenberg looked forward to his daily bike rides. Even though he had a driver's license now, there was nowhere to go in a car. The arcade in town was closed until further notice, movie theaters weren't operating, and the malls were off-limits. School had shut down for the semester, and it wasn't clear whether it would open back up in the fall. In a way, life was sweet—Seth had no responsibilities other than staying safe, maintaining social distance with what friends he saw, and helping his mom and dad around the house when they asked. Getting out in the fresh air on his bicycle was paradise compared to being stuck in the house during the early spring months when it was still cold in Illinois. Summer was finally starting to show its face. Still, he missed his friends and routine, so staying home was a drag.

He and Don Trainer pulled their bikes to the swing set, even though a yellow "Do Not Cross" tape had been wrapped around the structure by the Lincoln Grove Police Department. Congregating on the playground equipment was prohibited due to the pandemic. Nevertheless, there was no harm in stopping to rest beside the configuration of monkey bars, slides, and swings. For the time being, they were alone in the park. The walkers and joggers had moved on.

"How come you don't carry a mask with you?" Seth asked his friend. His own, one he'd bought from Ms. Bergman, hung halfway out of his shorts pocket.

"Why? We're not going inside anywhere," Don replied. He

shook his head. "Besides, I hate wearing one." He put the kickstand down and got off his bike, went over to the swings, ducked under the yellow tape, and sat on a swing.

"Don, we could get fined if the police see us."

"Do you see any cops?" He pulled a vape pen out of his pants pocket, checked the liquid level, and inhaled, which automatically activated the battery and heated the vapor. "Want some?"

"No, thanks." Seth didn't approve of the habit Don had flaunted for a couple of years already.

"I've got weed if you want. I was saving it for later, though."

"How'd you get it?"

Don snickered. "You know it's legal now in Illinois?"

"Not for us!"

Don waved at him dismissively. "Has that ever stopped us before? You've bought weed."

"From guys at school. We're not at school now. That's why I asked how you got it."

Seth remained on his bike as Don slowly rocked in the swing back and forth, puffing on his vaping device. Seth kept looking around. "There's some lady walking a dog."

"Who cares? She's not going to call the police on us."

"She might."

"We'd be gone by the time they arrive. Relax, dude. You're too stressed out."

Seth laughed. "Tell me about it. Aren't you? This whole thing . . . sucks."

"Yeah. But, hey, at least we're not sitting in Old Man Peeples's American History class. That shit was so boring. His lectures put me to sleep."

"Yeah, me too. It was much easier doing the course online."

"Fuck that," Don said. "I wasn't about to do all that busy work, 'cause that's all it was."

They were silent for a minute, and then Seth said, "You know, I'm really not supposed to be hanging out with you."

"What?"

"Well, with anyone, really. Because of my mom."

"Why, is she sick?"

"No, she's a nurse, remember? She works at the hospital. She's around Covid all the time. She's in a high-risk group, and she could bring it home without knowing it. My dad and I have to be extra careful."

"But here you are."

"Yeah, here I am. If we stay six feet apart, I guess it's okay. Dad knows I'm out with you."

Don took off the backpack he was wearing, put it on the ground in front of his legs, and opened it. He pulled out a soda bottle filled with a yellowish liquid. The top of the bottle was stuffed with a rag, held in place with duct tape. He stood and walked over to a large metal garbage bin that had a swinging lid on top.

"Don, what are you doing? You can't do that here, not *now*!"

"Why not? No one's around."

"It's broad daylight! Geez, you want to get us arrested? Put it away."

Seth had been aware that Don was the vandal responsible for the various trash-can fires in Lincoln Grove parks. On two occasions, Seth had been present when Don had lit and dropped them inside his targets. The first time he'd done it, they'd both been high. The explosion had been louder than they'd expected, and it surprised them so much that they found it terribly funny. The flames that shot out of the can knocked off the lid, and the trash inside fed the blaze. Laughing, they ran like hell and managed to get away before someone phoned the fire department. No real damage had been done except to the garbage bin. The second time Don had done it was in another park, a smaller one closer to Town Center. That time, it had caused a small fire on the grass.

Seth knew it was wrong, and yet it added a degree of excitement to their daily doldrums. Don had been exploding homemade Molotov cocktails on his own over the past few weeks, but he usually did it at night when it was easier to slip away without being seen.

Don stuck the vape back in his pocket and removed a lighter. He flicked it and held the flame near the rag on the bottle.

"Don, don't! Not here! Not now!"

"Chill, dude! Just get ready to ride."

"Wait! Someone's coming."

Don looked up and saw him too. A boy was walking their way. "Who is that?"

"It's . . . oh, it's Thomas Bergman."

"That weirdo? What a ret—"

"Don! No, don't use that word."

Don glared at Seth as if his friend had gone off his rocker. "Well, I'm still going to light it."

"No, don't. Wait."

Don rolled his eyes and said, "Fine." He returned to his backpack on the ground and stuck the bottle inside.

"And don't call him that," Seth said. "The R-word is as bad as the N-word."

"I don't give a shit. It's what he is."

"Don, Thomas is the smartest kid in school. The guy's, like, a genius."

"Then he's a *freak*, and that's what I'll call him."

"Stop."

Thomas Bergman, still dressed in a long-sleeved shirt and black pants, approached them. Before he got too close, he put on a cloth mask that his mother had made. "Hi, Seth. Hi, Don," he said with a muffle.

"Hey, Thomas," Seth said.

"Hey, freak," Don said.

"Don . . . " Seth murmured.

Thomas stood there expressionless.

"You want something?" Don asked.

"I was in the park and saw you," Thomas said. "I came over to say hello."

Don pulled out the vape and gave it a puff. He then offered it to Thomas. "Want some, freak?"

"No, thank you. Besides, your germs have already touched it. Why would I want to put my mouth on that after you have?"

Don turned to Seth. "Mr. Science, here."

"He's right," Seth answered.

"Suit yourself." Don continued to vape.

"You guys doing all right?" Seth asked Thomas.

"Yeah. Are we going to play *Call of Duty: Modern Warfare* tonight?"

"Sure, we can do that."

Don wrinkled his brow. "You play games with this freak?"

"Don, shut up," Seth said. "Thomas and I play games all the time. We've been doing it for years." He nodded at Thomas. "You were, what, about eight when we started playing the first *Call of Duty*?"

"Yes."

"We had some awesome campaigns."

Thomas's eyes fixed on Seth. "We did."

"What happened at your dad's work?" Don asked. "I heard it got ripped off."

Thomas then stared at Don for a few seconds without answering. He then turned back to Seth and said, "My stepfather didn't come home last night. Mom doesn't know where he is."

"Really?" Seth asked. "Wouldn't he be at his office, talking to police and stuff?"

"That's what Mom thinks, but he didn't say anything to her about it."

"Well," Don said through a chuckle, "your mom's crazy, so he probably got the hell out of there."

"Don, Jesus," Seth said. "Come on."

"That's okay, Seth," Thomas said. "I know my mom's not crazy."

"Hey, what happened to that good-looking sister of yours?" Don asked. "Where is she now?"

"Sarah is in Los Angeles with her boyfriend. They're getting married."

"Oh, that's too bad." Don raised his eyebrows at Seth.

"Remember we used to think she was smoking hot?"

"Sarah is my half sister," Thomas explained.

Don frowned. "She is?"

"My mother's first husband was her father."

"And your dad was your mom's second husband?"

Thomas nodded.

"And Mr. Bergman is her *third*?"

Thomas shrugged. "He's my stepfather."

Don looked at Seth. "I told you she was crazy."

"That's enough, Don."

A bulge in Thomas's pants pocket issued a ringtone that sounded like the William Tell Overture. He pulled out his phone and answered it. "Hi, Mom." He listened for a moment. "Okay. Did Stepdad come home?" More listening. "Okay. I'm coming." He hung up and returned the phone to his pocket. "He still hasn't come home."

"Oh, well, I hope everything's okay," Seth said.

Thomas shrugged. "I'm not worried. He's not at home much anyway. See you. I'll text you later, Seth. Bye, Don."

"So long, freak."

They watched Thomas walk to the tree-lined path that headed for their street.

"Jesus, Don, do you have to be so mean?" Seth asked.

"I don't like that kid. He creeps me out. He's right out of a zombie movie."

"Thomas is all right. I admit he's a little odd, but . . . well, he's smarter than you think."

"Well, I *think* he's a freak."

A thunderclap broke above them, and the darkening clouds began to gently issue a sprinkling.

"We better get going," Seth said. "It looks like it's going to pour."

"Hold your horses." Don reached down and got out the Molotov cocktail. "You ready to ride?"

"Don, don't do it."

Don paid his friend no mind. He lit the rag and the flame bloomed quickly. "Holy shit!" He tossed it into the trash can, and then hustled to his bicycle. "Go, go, go!"

Seth was already riding away when the Molotov cocktail ignited. The metal bin muted the explosion, but it was still frighteningly loud. Don howled with laughter, but Seth wanted to disappear.

5

Teenaged boys. I swear, that Don Trainer is going to get Seth Schoenberg in a heap of trouble. Would that be Seth's destiny if people weren't stuck at home, practicing social distancing, and going out of their minds from boredom and worry?

Yeah, probably.

At least Seth is kind to his younger next-door neighbor, Thomas Bergman. As you have seen, Thomas is a unique kid. Yes, maybe he's socially awkward and a bit of a mama's boy, but he's a straight-A student in every single subject. He's good at math, science, history, English, and two other languages. His only problem area is in the physical education department, but he always manages to make an A there, too, because he's never absent and he gets in there and tries. The other boys tease him mercilessly, and he's always picked last to be on teams, but Thomas keeps a stiff upper lip.

These three boys—Seth, Thomas, and Don—will have key roles in our tale.

Monday, May 11, 2020

2:00 p.m.

Seth had made it home on his bicycle just as the sound of fire truck sirens wailed in the near distance. Don had ridden on to his home on the corner of the block. They both felt it was best to disappear inside their houses for a while. Now, a little over an hour after the incident in the park, Seth emerged from his room after checking Twitter to see if anyone had said something about the trash-can fire. It wasn't on the radar yet, but the local news was sure to report it that night.

Leaving his dog asleep on the bed, Seth went downstairs to the middle level, where the kitchen and living room were situated. His father, Mitch Schoenberg, sat with his laptop at the dining room table, munching on a sandwich. A man of fifty, small in stature, long in beard, and big in heart, Mitch was an accountant who, before Covid, had worked in a small firm's office space with two partners in a neighboring town. One of the four bedrooms upstairs had always been his "home office," so that he could get a small tax deduction for "freelance work," but until March, he had never really used it. Now Mitch was always in the room next to Seth's, on the phone, on a Zoom meeting, and staying busy. The man's occasional excursions downstairs for food gave Seth a reprieve from feeling like he lived in a dormitory.

"How's it going, son?" Mitch asked.

"Okay."

"You seem a little tense."

"I do?" Seth guessed that he was still nervous about Don's stunt in the park. "Oh, you know, nothing's normal, Dad. Aren't you tense too?"

"Me? Tense? Nah." The man took a bite, dropping breadcrumbs into his whiskers. "Well, sure, I do worry about your mother. That makes me a little tense."

"I worry about her too."

"I hope you're being extra careful outside. Don't get close to anyone. Wear your mask."

"I do. And I stay six feet from people."

Mitch looked at him. "Who are you seeing?"

Seth shook his head. "Nobody, really. Just Don. I saw George and Lucas the other day at the park." He shrugged.

Mitch took another bite of sandwich and chewed for a moment. Then he said, "I'm not sure what I think of that Don Trainer kid."

Seth let that statement float for a moment. "When does Mom come home today?"

"She has to pull a late one. Probably not until after dark. You know, your mother is a hero."

"I know."

"She's on the front lines."

"I know."

"That means *we're* on the front lines, Seth. It's why we have to be extra careful."

"I know, Dad." He felt his phone vibrate in his pocket. He pulled it out of his shorts and saw that Thomas had texted him. "I'm going upstairs to chat with Thomas on FaceTime."

"How's he doing?"

"I guess okay."

"I'm glad you two are still friends. I know he . . . well, he's unusual."

Seth chuckled. "Yeah." He got up and went upstairs, closed his door, and got on his laptop. It didn't take long to connect with his next-door neighbor on FaceTime. Thomas appeared on the screen. Seth could see the familiar Star Wars and Marvel posters on the bedroom wall behind Thomas.

"Hi, Seth," the boy said in the usual monotone.

"Hey, Thomas."

"Was that Don who set the fire in the park?"

Seth didn't know if he should tell him. "I . . . don't think so . . . "

"Yeah, it was. Actually, I saw him do it."

"You did?"

"I was behind a tree at the edge of the park watching you."

"Oh. Well, then, why did you ask?"

Thomas replied, "I wanted to know what you would say." Seth didn't respond to that. "It's okay, Seth. I know you want to protect your friend."

"Thomas, I don't like it when he does that."

"I know. You can't stop someone like Don."

"I apologize for the way he treats you. He's just . . . I don't know . . ."

"A bully."

"Yeah, I guess he is."

"Why are you friends with him, then?" Thomas asked.

"That's a good question. Because there's nobody else nearby?"

"I'm nearby."

"Well, we're friends."

"You don't hang with me like you do with him."

"Thomas, Don is my age. We're both going to be juniors this fall."

"I bet we don't get to go to school in the fall."

"Maybe not."

Thomas turned his head and said off camera, "Okay, I will." Seth thought he'd heard a muffled female voice. "I might have to get off soon and help my mom with something. We don't know where my stepdad is. Mom is worried about him."

"How long has he been gone?"

"I'm not sure. Mom didn't say. She was talking to two policemen a few minutes ago. They came to the house and talked to her."

"Police? Really?"

"Yeah."

Seth rubbed his chin. "Do you think it might have something to do with the robbery at your dad's work?"

"Maybe. I bet the police will think that. I don't call him my dad because he's really my stepfather."

"I know. Seems like you'd still call him 'Dad,' though."

"I really don't care much what happens to him. He's a bully, too, just like Don."

"He doesn't hurt you, does he?"

Thomas gave a little shrug. "I don't want to talk about it."

"Okay."

"After dinner we'll play *Call of Duty: Modern Warfare*?"

"Sure. Nothing else to do, right?"

Pivoting to a non sequitur, Thomas said, "I saw a light on upstairs in the old Wilkins house."

Seth asked, "What do you mean?"

"Well, the house is empty. It's been for sale for ages."

"Yeah?"

"Every now and then I see a light on upstairs. I can see the house from my bedroom window. It's across the street."

"It's *right* across the street from our house, and I can see it from my room too. I've never seen a light on, though. That place gives me the creeps. I wish they'd sell it or tear the thing down!"

"Maybe Don can burn it down."

"That's not funny, Thomas."

"Ask him if he'll burn it down."

"No, Thomas."

"I think there's a ghost in there."

Seth took a breath. Sometimes Thomas Bergman was indeed strange. "Well, Old Man Wilkins did hang himself in a closet upstairs."

"I've seen shadows in the windows. There are ghosts in the house."

"More than one?"

"Maybe."

Seth cocked his head. "Thomas, I don't know. You don't really believe in ghosts, do you?"

The boy's face had no expression. "I don't know."

Seth thought Thomas was just making up stuff. His imagination was running wild.

"Why do you think Mr. Wilkins hanged himself?" Thomas asked.

"Nobody knows. Well, maybe his wife does, but she moved away fast. I bet it was money problems. Or maybe he was sick. You have to be pretty depressed to kill yourself."

"At least he didn't have to deal with Covid."

"Nope, there is that." Seth laughed.

A woman's voice called out Thomas's name. To Seth it sounded like she was deep in a canyon.

"That's my mom. I gotta go."

"Okay. I'll text you later and we can get on the old Xbox."

"Cool. I still think it would be great if Don burned down the Wilkins house."

"Geez, Thomas."

"Talk to you later."

"Bye, Thomas."

Seth shut down the meeting and then opened Facebook in a new browser tab. He perused some of his friends' pages, but they were all the same. All the postings were of food, political memes, their pets, or selfies in which they were wearing masks. Everyone was bored.

He went to the window and gazed out at what he could see of Marigold Way. The street was empty of people. The rain had subsided, and the sun had returned to reflect off the scattered puddles where the sidewalk dipped in places.

Seth studied the empty house across the street. It had undergone a facelift since Mrs. Wilkins moved out—a new paint job and improved landscaping—but the "For Sale" sign was still there. Seth wondered if anyone would ever move in.

He didn't normally believe in ghosts, but maybe Thomas was right. The house was haunted, all right—with the Ghost of Normal Past.

6

Let's get back to our friend Scott.

As you can probably imagine, he's getting more concerned as the hours tick by. With everything else to worry about—the coronavirus pandemic, the country's political divide, financial uncertainty—adding "a missing wife" to the list would just about make a normal man go bonkers. It would me, that's for sure.

Monday, May 11, 2020

5:00 p.m.

Scott punched the clock, so to speak, once the day was officially late afternoon. He had already phoned several of Marie's other close friends, and, like Cindy, they knew nothing. They all seemed to hint, however, that his wife most likely needed some space for herself for a while. What did they know that he didn't? Had Marie been telling them something about their marriage? She was unhappy? She wanted to leave her husband? What?

Finally, he called the Lincoln Grove Police Department. He wasn't sure if he should dial 911, or just call the headquarters' direct line. Was it an emergency? Maybe it was.

"911, what's your emergency?" the operator asked.

"My wife is missing," Scott said. "I haven't seen her since last night. She doesn't answer her phone or text messages. At first, I thought she might have gone on a hike or something, but now I'm getting worried."

After answering a few more questions, the dispatcher said a patrol car would stop by the house soon. It arrived in ten minutes. Scott thought it must be a slow day for the Lincoln Grove Police.

Two young, uniformed officers came to the door. They both wore masks and appeared to be in their thirties. The name plates identified them as "Sandrich," who was tall and blond, and "Lewis," who was stocky and had a crew cut. Scott let them in, and they followed him to the kitchen. He gestured to chairs, but the men preferred to stand six feet away. Scott sat at the table with his own mask properly covering his mouth and nose. It felt odd to have someone besides Marie in the house with him for the first time since winter.

"Aren't you that *Blaster Bob* guy?" Officer Lewis asked.

"Yes, I am."

"My kid used to like that show."

"I'm glad to hear it."

"You working on another TV show?'

"Not at the moment. Trying to write a novel."

"Ah. My kid never reads books."

"Really? That's too bad. He should."

"She."

"Huh?"

"My kid's a she."

"Oh. Well, maybe she'll like my books, except they're more for grown-ups. How old is she?"

"What seems to be the trouble, Mr. Hatcher?" Officer Sandrich interrupted, steering the conversation to the matter at hand.

"Right," Scott shook his head. "I'm a little nervous and scared. Sorry." He proceeded to tell them the story beginning with waking up that morning. He explained how he'd confirmed that her car was in the garage, her purse and wallet were there in the kitchen, a suitcase wasn't missing, it didn't appear that she'd taken any extra clothes or shoes, and all her prescriptions were still in the medicine cabinet. He'd called and texted her numerous times, checked with several of her close friends, and had come up with nothing.

"She must be wearing her fanny pack," he said. "She always wears it when she goes out walking. She carries her ID, a mask, and her phone in it."

"Mr. Hatcher, you brought up prescriptions," Sandrich said. "Is she taking anything that might cause any disorientation or confusion? Is she on antidepressants? Painkillers?"

"No. Not that I'm aware of."

"How old is she?"

"Forty."

The officer asked for a description of his wife and for a photo. Scott pulled up one of her pictures on his phone and sent it to an email address that Sandrich provided. Sandrich made note of Marie's social media pages, where there was a wealth of photos.

Just as it seemed they were winding up the questioning, Sandrich announced, "Sorry, but we have to ask this question. Have you and your wife had any fights recently? Are you getting along? How is staying at home during the pandemic affecting your relationship?"

Scott sighed. "I'll admit we haven't been getting along very well. We've had . . . some problems. Some arguing. Tension. Seriously, though, I don't think it's anything out of the ordinary from what we were going through before the lockdown. There's no violence on either of our parts, if that's what you're getting at. We would never physically hurt each other."

"When was your last fight?"

"Yesterday."

"What was it about?"

"She . . . gets very depressed on Mother's Day. Nothing can please her, no matter how hard I try. Everything I say or do is wrong. It's just the way it is."

"Why is that, Mr. Hatcher?"

He let out another heavy sigh. "We lost a son to cancer eleven years ago. He was only five. Our marriage hasn't been the same since, but we've stayed together."

After a pause as he wrote in his notebook, Sandrich asked, "Is your wife suicidal at all?"

"No."

"Is there a gun in the house?"

"No."

"And there's no family nearby she would have gone to visit?"

"No. Her mother is in Florida, and she has a sister in Ohio. Marie's car is in the garage."

"Right." He continued to write.

"Is there a way you guys can find her phone? Aren't you able to do that?"

"We can, but we should wait a little longer. We'd have to go to her cell phone carrier and request that they do what's called a 'ping.' Technically you need a court order, but often a phone company will do it if we say the person's life is endangered. Since you say that she's not in danger of harming herself, it doesn't seem to be something we would insist on today. I'd say if she doesn't come home by tomorrow, we would do that."

Scott ran his hand through his hair. "Gee. Okay." He glanced over at the counter. "Oh, her computer is there. You don't need to take a look at it or anything?"

"Not yet, sir. I'd like to ask you another question, though, Mr. Hatcher," Sandrich said.

"Sure."

"Do you know John Bergman, across the street?"

Scott blinked. That seemed to come out of nowhere. "Sort of. Enough to wave hello. Why?"

"His wife, Rachel Bergman, reported *him* missing today too. Since this morning. Does Marie know Mr. Bergman?"

What? What is he implying?

"Not that I know of. I mean, she's like me. We know the

Bergmans, and we wave hello at them when we see them. But we're not friends on a social basis. I mean, we've had friendly conversations with them over the years, but I don't think either of them has ever been in our house, and I'm pretty sure Marie and I have never been in theirs."

"Okay. When's the last time you saw John Bergman?"

"Uh, I don't know. Last week sometime? Not sure. I saw Rachel this morning. She was sitting out in front of her house selling masks she'd made. I stopped and spoke to her briefly."

Officer Lewis cocked his head. "Why were you across the street talking to her?"

"I was out on my morning walk. I was headed that way, saw her, and just went over to say hello."

"Were you aware that her husband was missing?"

"No. She said something like John was at his office. She was waiting for him to come home."

Sandrich continued to write. "She didn't seem alarmed or concerned?"

"Not really. Like I said, this was earlier this morning. It must have been around nine o'clock. Maybe she didn't think anything of it yet."

The officers asked to see Marie's Malibu in the garage, but they didn't examine it. Scott supposed they simply wanted to confirm the car was there.

Sandrich offered a business card to Scott at the front door. "Call us in the morning if she hasn't returned, sir. Try not to worry. Very often we find that spouses can just up and go somewhere when they want to cool off about something. You said you'd had a fight. Maybe she just wants to make you uncomfortable for a little while. We've seen this kind of thing more often than you'd think."

"That's it? I have to wait until tomorrow? I'm not sure I can sleep tonight without knowing what's happened to her."

"Stay calm, Mr. Hatcher. She'll turn up. They always do. This is Lincoln Grove, not Chicago. There's probably a perfectly acceptable explanation for her absence."

With that, the officers got in their patrol car and drove away.

Well, that was unsatisfactory . . .

He went down the front steps to the yard and looked across the street at the Bergman house.

John Bergman? There can't be any connection to Marie, can there?

What the hell?

7

One thing I know from experience is that alcohol is assuredly a self-medicating solution to one's problems, but only in the short term. Extended utilization of the stuff is not recommended, and I don't have to be a doctor to tell you that. Scott Hatcher is not a heavy drinker by any means. Here, though, the circumstances warrant his achieving the condition of being comfortably numb. Whether or not it does him any good is debatable.

Monday, May 11, 2020
8:30 p.m.

The doorbell rang.

Scott opened his eyes, disoriented and seriously drunk. He'd forgotten that he was sprawled on the sofa in the living room. He had asked Alexa to play "soothing music," and the ambient and electronic waves of ethereal moods were still piping through the Bose speakers mounted high in the corners of the room.

The bottle of Jack Daniel's was in front of him on the coffee table. An empty glass stood beside it. He recalled making a badly formed omelet for dinner around six thirty, opening the new bottle of whiskey, and proceeding to down it. He didn't know how many glasses he'd had, but now the bottle was only two-thirds full. For him, that was a lot of booze.

The doorbell rang.

Who could that be?

He managed to sit up, shake his head, rub his eyes, and finally stand. He moved unsteadily to the foyer and made it to the front door without falling.

The doorbell rang again.

"I'm here!" He opened the door to find Lois Kimmelman standing on the porch. She was holding a blue plastic container.

"Scott! There you are! I wasn't sure if you could hear the doorbell over the music. I could hear your stereo through the walls outside."

He stared at her.

"I told Al that the rhubarb casserole came out *exceptionally* well today," she said with a smile. "He said I should bring some of it over to you and Marie. Then he said I should bring some over to Paul and Melissa Justice, and another container should go to the Woos."

The young Justice family lived across the street from the Kimmelmans in Number 502, next door to the Trainers. They had no kids yet. Scott knew them only by sight and name, but rarely saw them outside.

"Al says I should give as much of it away as possible!"

I'll bet he does.

She held out the food. "Won't you take it and try it? I can give Marie the recipe if she likes it."

Scott had the inclination to scream at the woman and tell her to never ring the doorbell again, and to take her rhubarb cass-a-rump and shove it in the out exit. Instead, though, he opened the storm door and accepted the gift.

"Don't worry about returning the container. I've got so many of those things. Marie can use it the next time you two go on a picnic."

Somehow, I don't see a picnic in our future anytime soon.

"Thank you, Lois. I'm sure it's delicious."

"Is Marie here? I'd love to tell her how it's made."

"Marie isn't home right now, Lois."

"Oh?"

"No."

"Okay. Is everything all right? I saw a police car here earlier."

"Everything's fine and peachy keen."

He let the storm door slam shut a little too hard. Mrs. Kimmelman gave him one of those "You're such a kidder!" looks.

"Well, give Marie my best," she gushed. "Let me know what you think of the casserole!"

"Thank you again. Tell Al hello." He started to shut the door.

"Oh, I will. Perhaps you and Marie could come over someti—"

The door didn't slam, but it closed with a satisfying finality. He turned and walked through the spinning foyer to the kitchen. He placed the container on the counter, opened it, and took a deep sniff of the oddly colored mush that resembled a cross between purple pasta and cornbread.

He immediately felt his stomach turn, and he gagged. "Agh! Oh my God, Christ in heaven!" He struggled to stop himself from vomiting, and he was saved only by dumping the mess into the sink, turning on the garbage disposal, and stuffing the horrid nightmare down the drain. He left the container on the counter, stumbled back, and landed hard in one of the dining table chairs.

"Ohhh," he groaned.

He sat there for a while, and then he looked at his watch. It was later than he thought it was.

Marie hasn't come home yet.

Something was definitely wrong.

Scott's phone was on the table. He picked it up to check if there were any messages, but of course there were none.

He eyed Marie's laptop that sat on the counter the couple used as a catchall for miscellaneous stuff—the mail, newspapers, magazines, and junk that had sat there for weeks. He stood, took hold of the computer, brought it to the table, lifted the lid, and booted it up.

Microsoft's welcome screen wanted a PIN.

"Oh crap," he muttered. "What the hell is it?"

He typed her birthday digits, but that wasn't correct.

How many attempts do I get before I'm shut out? Three?

Scott thought about it longer. The day they were married? Unlikely, but he gave it a try.

Nope.

One more chance.

Fuck, there's only one other thing it could be.

He typed four numbers and, sure enough, he was in. The desktop greeted him with a background of the Chicago skyline in daylight. Marie loved the city and had often taken Metra Rail in to have lunch with friends or see a show. Scott had rarely accompanied her. He found driving in or taking the train to Chicago to be more hassle than it was worth. He went to the occasional writers group conference or perhaps a concert when a band he really wanted to see came to town. It was another bone of contention between the two of them. She had wanted him to do more outings with her. Scott had tried to do so, but the venture ultimately ended in cranky bitterness. He blamed himself, but he also thought, *Why should I make myself miserable?* It was a circular butt-kick.

Several folders decorated the desktop. Most of them appeared to be work related. A top folder titled "Marie Hatcher Realty" contained many subfolders dedicated to various properties she repped. Another one had to do with advertising for her company. Scott went to the Documents folder in Users/Marie and found all kinds of subfolders pertaining to his wife's life. One stood out.

Brian.

It had been the date of his birthday that was the PIN to get into the computer.

Even through the alcohol daze, Scott felt a sudden twist in his chest.

Do I open it?

He couldn't help doing so. The folder contained subfolders of photos and documents relating to Brian's birth, illness, and death. Scott opened the Pictures folder and was amazed to find a few hundred stored there. Brian as a newborn at the hospital. Brian's first day at home. Brian as a toddler. Brian at three, four, and five. Brian with grandparents and friends and playmates.

Tears welled in Scott's eyes. He had to close the window.

Resisting the urge to go back to the living room and the bottle of Jack Daniel's, Scott continued to look around the folders in Documents. His mind wandered as he did so.

Brian's death had truly been the end of their marriage. They had only pretended to be husband and wife since then. Scott and Marie were glorified roommates. Friends with benefits. Barely friends with little benefits. She had pursued her own interests, and he his. They sometimes slept in separate rooms—certainly not always, though. He had thought she was in bed with him the night before he discovered her missing in the morning. There was still intimacy every now and then, but only on Marie's terms. A spark of their former love occasionally made an appearance.

Scott then thought of something. He typed "John Bergman" in Windows Explorer's Search box and hit Enter. He watched the scrollbar advance for over a minute, but nothing came up in Marie's files. He tried typing only "Bergman." Again, no results. Scott then opened Outlook to examine Marie's contacts. He searched for variations of their neighbor's name, and nothing came up. No emails, no contact listing, nothing.

"This is stupid," he muttered. There couldn't possibly be a connection between Marie and John Bergman. It was a coincidence that Bergman was also missing. The guy was probably home now. He was in hot water because of the robbery at his warehouse. That had to be the explanation for his absence.

As for Marie, though, Scott had no clue.

He shut down the computer, closed the lid, and placed it back on the counter where it had been. Scott then went to the front door, opened it, and stepped outside. Marigold Way was quiet, illuminated by the two tall streetlamps, but otherwise dark and lonely. The moon was in a waning phase, and the stars were dim. The sky was still cloudy.

"Where are you, Marie?" he whispered.

Headlights appeared at the curve on the east end of the block, coming his way. It was a big black truck he'd seen before many times, a fourteen- to sixteen-foot block-style vehicle that was used by moving companies. White letters on the side proclaimed, "Volkov Trucking," accompanied by a phone number. Scott knew that whoever owned the truck lived on one of the streets that connected to Dodge Park, because he'd seen it parked in front of a house when he was out for a walk. He couldn't remember what street or house, though. As the truck approached, it slowed down. It crept past the empty Wilkins house, and then slowly moved on in front of Scott's home toward Temple Avenue. The head of the shadowy figure behind the wheel was turned toward Scott.

Who are you looking at, buddy?

The truck halted at the stop sign at the end of the lane, and then it turned right onto Temple.

Scott quickly forgot about the truck—the vehicle was a familiar sight in the area and certainly nothing sinister. He didn't think any more about it and went back inside.

He had been too drunk to consider the logic that Marigold Way was a no-outlet street, and that there had to have been a reason the driver had chosen to circle Dodge and Marigold.

8

Ever hear of something called "night terrors"? I suppose they can be a lot of different things, but I think they're nightmares if you're asleep, and anxiety-driven panic attacks if you're awake. Maybe they're hallucinations if your mind tends to visit unknown vistas when the lights are out. Whatever they are, they are none too pleasant. I've had a few of them myself. They can bring a grown man to tears.

Poor Scott Hatcher experiences some of those the first night after discovering that his wife is missing. Is he worried about her? Is he concerned about himself? Does he have powerful feelings of guilt?

Hmm. Guilt. That's a potent emotion. It's something that can persuade the staunchest human to reveal secrets and confess misdeeds. It's the worst. Trust me.

Not sure why I'm bringing that up.

At any rate, those nocturnal terrors do dissipate come morning, when the day is bright and the birds are singing. One is perhaps not exactly absolved of whatever caused the fear, but at least a person can then be calmer and have a firmer grasp of reality.

Tuesday, May 12, 2020
8:30 a.m.

Hungover and feeling as if he'd been hit by a meteor, Scott made a quick breakfast of eggs and bacon to boost his protein level, drank two cups of strong coffee, and then phoned the number on the card that Officer Sandrich had given him.

Marie had still not returned.

He didn't speak directly to Sandrich, but he told the woman at the other end of the line this news. Scott was placed on hold for a moment, and then the woman came back to say that someone would be out to his house shortly.

While he waited for the cops, he checked his phone again for the third time since crawling out of bed, which had literally taken two legs and two arms to accomplish. He wanted to make a note on every day of his calendar reminding himself to never drink as much as he had the night before.

Still no texts or voice messages from Marie.

The patrol car parked on the driveway at 9:45. Officer Sandrich came to the door with a woman dressed in plainclothes, although she wore a badge and a broad belt with a holstered weapon. They both wore cloth masks with the "LGPD" logo on them. Scott found that oddly funny.

Scott opened the door as he placed his own mask over his mouth and nose.

"Mr. Hatcher, good morning," Sandrich said. "This is Lieutenant Pat Dante with the Lincoln Grove Police. She will be taking over the case and has some questions for you. May we come in?"

"Please do."

Scott guessed that Dante was in her middle forties. She was stout but seemed to be physically fit. She had reddish-brown hair down to her shoulders, and she had friendly, smiling eyes.

"Mr. Hatcher, I'm a detective with the police department," she said as they entered. "I'm glad to meet you, although I'm sorry it's under these circumstances."

"Same here. Thank you for coming. Do I call you Detective Dante or Lieutenant Dante?"

"Either one."

"Oh, okay. I like 'Detective Dante' for the alliteration, so I'll call you that, if you don't mind."

"I beg your pardon?"

Scott shook his head. "Never mind. I'm a writer. Pay no attention."

They went into the kitchen, where Scott gestured to chairs that he had already arranged at least six feet apart. Dante and Sandrich sat, and so did he. Dante placed on the table a legal pad and a folder containing papers. She took out a pen. "Mr. Hatcher, I've seen the report Officer Sandrich made yesterday. It's my understanding that you have not heard from your wife?"

"That's right."

"I see. I'm going to ask you some questions, and they may be some of the same questions that Officer Sandrich asked you yesterday. This is routine. All right?"

"Shoot." Flustered, Scott shook his head. "I mean, don't shoot—I mean, uh, sure. What am I saying? Go ahead. Sorry, I had a bad night."

"I understand."

She indeed proceeded to ask the very same questions, so Scott had to go through yesterday's events all over again. They did cover more ground regarding Marie's daily routines. Detective Dante asked him to describe his wife in detail and pressed him on more specifics, such as clothing sizes. He answered the best he could. They went over again what items belonging to her that might be missing from the house. There were more queries about their marriage. Scott repeated what he'd said about his and Marie's relationship, that Marie was not a danger to herself, that she wasn't taking any strange drugs, and that he didn't believe that she could be missing because of a preexisting medical or mental condition.

"Does Marie own a gun?" Dante asked.

"Officer Sandrich asked me that yesterday, too, and the answer is still no."

"Do *you* own a gun, Mr. Hatcher?"

"No. You can call me Scott if you want."

Dante made a few notes on her pad and then said, "All right. Officer Sandrich mentioned this to you yesterday. We have just come from talking to Rachel Bergman, across the street. Her husband is still missing too."

Scott's jaw dropped slightly. "Really?"

"Ms. Bergman is quite upset. I will ask you this again. Is there any connection that you know of between your wife and John Bergman?"

"No. Not that I know of."

Dante nodded, then made a note. "Now. We are continuing to treat these as two separate cases. It is very unusual for two missing persons cases to occur on the same street in the same town on the same day. It's very possible that the cases are connected, though, and the trick is going to be to figure out how. I want you to try to think of what that connection might be. Maybe it's not obvious. Perhaps they know someone in common, a mutual friend or an acquaintance. Personally, Mr. Hatcher, I don't believe in coincidences. I'm not saying this isn't one, but it *is* . . . odd."

"I agree." Scott scratched the stubble on his chin. "I've been racking my brain about it. I don't know what the connection is. If there is one."

"Well, do keep thinking about it. In the meantime, would you be willing to volunteer and hand over copies of your bank statements, tax returns, and investment statements for us to look at? We can get a court order, but it's much easier if you just agree to hand them over."

"I can do that. No problem. I was wondering if you were going to ask me for something like that. I can make copies today. I have a machine here at the house."

"Great. When they're ready, give me a call." She placed another business card on the table. "That has my direct line on it. Use it, please. Call when you have the copies ready, and I'll send someone over to pick them up."

"Okay. Do you want her laptop too?"

Dante held up a hand. "It's not necessary yet. I will want cell phone details, though." She verified Marie's number and the carrier. "We're going to get hold of them and ask for a ping. I don't think we'll need a court order, because I'm going to go ahead and say that Marie is in danger. It will speed things up and cut a lot of red tape. Is that all right with you?"

"Absolutely. How long does it take?"

"We'll know something in a few hours, certainly by the end of the day."

The meeting wound up and Scott walked them to the door.

"Don't hesitate to call if you think of something or, of course, if you hear anything from your wife," Dante said.

"Thank you."

"Any other questions before we head out?"

"Yeah. Do I need an attorney?"

She looked at him without humor. "I don't know. Do you?"

9

What does it mean to be a true friend?

Beyond the obvious things like having stuff in common, what character traits are involved?

I would suspect that a true friend is loyal, helpful, and always there when you need them.

That's another given.

What if a friend does something wrong? Do you protect your friend? Or do you call them out? Do you cover up for a friend? Do you lie for a friend?

Do you keep secrets for a friend?

Tuesday, May 12, 2020
11:30 a.m.

"Go get it, you mangy mongrel," Seth commanded as he threw the tennis ball in his backyard.

Butch, the family's eleven-year-old Dachshund, performed his comical run across the grass, barking repeatedly as if he were saying, "I got it! I got it! I got it!" Because of his wiener-shaped body, his short legs, and his age—which affected the dog's speed—Butch resembled a wiggling sausage as he moved. The barking was an oddity as well. Seth knew of no other dog that would vocally comment on the action while playing fetch.

Throw, bark, retrieve, throw, bark, retrieve. As the boy and his dog repeated the ritual, Seth reflected that it was yet another dull day in Lincoln Grove. Nothing to do, no one to see, no place to go. Seth figured that if there had been no coronavirus, he'd be finishing up his sophomore year in high school. Summer vacation would have been just around the corner. That wasn't going to happen. Junior year was also when parents and students would start the process of college hunting. Seth wanted to go to college, but he had no sights set on any specific institution. He didn't even know what he wanted to be when he "grew up." He was a good enough student with solid Bs, and his attendance record was excellent. The teachers genuinely liked him. The problem was that he had no clue about what kind of career he wanted.

He liked playing video games. Seth thought he might be a good game designer. In his heart of hearts, that was perhaps what he'd like to do the most. His dad wasn't keen on the idea. "That's such a volatile industry," Mitch Schoenberg would say. "I knew people who did it a while back. They jumped around from company to company because the firms would invariably go out of business or lay off people. You want something stable!"

Stable? Look around you, Dad. Tell me what's stable. The world is going to shit, and you want me to do something monotonous and dull while the sky falls around us. Great.

"Hey, Seth."

The voice came from the other side of the rotting wooden fence surrounding the Schoenbergs' backyard. Thomas Bergman was just tall enough to peek over it.

"Oh, hi, Thomas. What's up?"

"I heard Butch barking, so I knew you were out here."

"Yeah, he likes to play fetch." Seth threw the ball one more time and then walked over to the fence. He kept a safe distance, because neither of them were wearing masks.

"My stepfather still hasn't come home," Thomas said. "His car has been gone since yesterday."

"Really? Gee, I'm sorry to hear that. How are you doing?"

Thomas shrugged slightly. "I'm all right. I don't mind telling you that my stepdad and I don't get along very much."

"You've said that. Sorry to hear it."

"The police were here again this morning. The lady detective came and asked my mother questions."

"How did that go?"

"Okay. You want to know a secret?"

"Um . . . "

"They asked Mom if she or stepdad owns a gun. She showed them the lockbox where they keep them."

"Your parents have guns?" Seth was impressed. He'd had no idea.

"Uh-huh. They both do. But my stepdad's gun wasn't in the box."

"It wasn't?"

"Just my mom's. That means that wherever my stepdad is, he's armed!"

Seth didn't know if that was a good or a bad thing, so he said nothing.

"I've been to the range with them," Thomas added. "I've fired both of their guns. I'm pretty good at hitting the targets."

"They take you to shoot *guns*? Are you old enough to do that?"

"If a parent or guardian is supervising, sure. Mom says that all the shooter video games I play have made me good. She believes we should all practice responsible gun ownership and know how to use them properly."

"Wow." Seth saw the Bergman family in a new light. He didn't want to admit that his own family would never have anything to do with firearms.

Thomas then asked, "Do you get along with *your* dad?"

"Sure. He's okay. He's . . . a dad." Seth laughed.

Thomas barely cracked a smile. Sometimes his deadpan expression was unnerving, even to Seth, who had known Thomas for years.

"How long have you guys lived next door?" he asked Thomas.

"Eight years. We moved into the house in 2012. I was six. It was right after my mom married John."

"I remember now."

"We played together a lot in those days."

"Yep."

"You even babysat me for a year or so when you were ten and eleven."

"I can't forget that!"

That almost made Thomas smile.

"You can come over and play with Butch if you want," Seth said.

"I'm not supposed to see you because your mother works at the hospital and I might get the coronavirus."

"Yeah, well, you're right. It's probably not a good idea. I'm not supposed to be in contact with other people either. Sorry."

"You see Don, though."

Seth pursed his lips. "Yeah, I know. But we keep our distance."

"You don't wear masks."

"I'm going to start doing so. I don't think Don will, though."

"He's not a good person, Seth. You shouldn't be friends with him."

Seth bristled at that. "Hey, don't tell me who I can be friends with, Thomas."

"I'm just being honest."

"I know. It's not a nice thing to say, though. But . . . you're probably right. Don *has* been making me nervous lately."

Butch stood at Seth's feet, wagged his tail, and barked at his master.

"Did you ask him about burning down the Wilkins house?" Thomas asked.

"What?"

"We talked about that. How it would be nice if someone burned down the Wilkins house. You said you'd ask him to burn it down."

"I never said that. I told you your suggestion wasn't funny."

"Well, I double-dare him to do it. You can tell him I said so."

"Thomas, geez . . . "

"Oh, it was on the news this morning," Thomas said.

"What was?"

"About the bomb in the park. In the trash can."

Seth shook his head. "It wasn't a bomb. It was a . . . Molotov cocktail. A Coke bottle with gasoline in it."

"That's a bomb."

"Not really."

"It explodes and causes a fire."

"Okay, okay!"

Butch barked again, so Seth picked up the tennis ball and threw it. That helped alleviate his annoyance with Thomas. He was about to walk away, but Thomas took the conversation in a different direction.

"I miss school."

"You do?"

"Don't you? I miss being there, even though other kids make fun of me. But I get better grades than they do."

Seth laughed. "You do! I should get you to do my homework for me sometime. It'd give my teachers a heart attack when I finally get an A instead of a B."

Thomas stared at his friend for a few seconds, and then he said, "I'd do your homework for you, Seth."

Seth thought that was a little strange, so he just replied, "I may take you up on it if we get back to school this fall. I have to go inside now. Talk to you later?"

"Sure. Want to play *Call of Duty: Modern Warfare* again?"

Seth found it funny that Thomas insisted on using the game's complete title. "I'll send you a text."

Inside the house, Seth found his father in the bedroom office with the door open. "What time does Mom get home tonight?" he asked.

Mitch looked up from his laptop and answered, "Dinnertime, for once. She pulled a double yesterday, so we'll get to see her tonight."

"I just saw Thomas outside. He says Mr. Bergman is still missing. The police were there this morning."

Mitch sat back in his chair, a swivel office job that had seen better days. He had "borrowed" it from his real office. "Golly. I wonder if I should call Rachel. See if there's anything we can do."

"What can we do, Dad?"

Mitch frowned and then turned up his palms. "I don't know. I guess not much. We have to be careful and isolate because of your mom."

Seth just nodded, then called to Butch, who stood at his feet. They went together next door into his bedroom. He went to the window and looked out at Marigold Way. There wasn't a soul in sight. The Wilkins house stared back at him, its "For Sale" sign a permanent fixture.

As if on cue, his cell phone vibrated. It was a text from Don.

Cocktails 2night?

Seth wanted to tell him no, but he was going nuts.
He texted back:

Sure.

10

We have come to a point in our tale, folks, when, as they say, the plot thickens.

Let us return our focus to Scott Hatcher, who has successfully overcome the effects of his hangover. Unfortunately, there is still no news from his wife or from the police.

Tuesday, May 12, 2020, 6:30 p.m.

Scott spent much of the day pacing in his house, walking the neighborhood, and browsing online and on social media. He took an hour to make copies of his and Marie's financial statements as requested. A patrol officer came by to pick them up, and then, miraculously, he fell asleep in the comfy chair in the living room at around three o'clock. He was out for the count for two hours.

He hadn't eaten since breakfast, and that had been a meal he could barely stomach. By dinnertime, though, he had felt rejuvenated enough that he had a decent appetite. This time, he grilled some chicken sausages laced with spinach that Marie had bought at Whole

Foods a few days earlier, boiled a cup of Israeli tricolor couscous, and steamed some broccoli. The meal invigorated him even more, and he felt as if he was back in the land of the living.

Then his phone rang. The caller ID read "LG Police." He grabbed it from the table and answered.

"Hello?"

"Mr. Hatcher? Detective Dante."

"Yes. Hello."

"How are you doing? Better than you were this morning, I hope?" she asked.

"I'm okay. Sorry if I was a zombie earlier. Did you get the copies of the bank statements and stuff?"

"I did, thank you. Listen, as this is still a missing person case, I'm calling to tell you that the phone company pinged your wife's cell. Apparently, the device is turned off, or it's not working. Most likely it's the former. However, it does tell us the last place it was before she turned it off."

"And where was that?"

"Your house. Or close to it. Sometimes the GPS is off by a few yards, so it's possible it's outside near your house. Officer Sandrich was there earlier to look for it. Did you see him?"

"I didn't notice. I took a nap."

"He didn't find it. I advise you to look for it on the east side of your home. Next to the house that's for sale."

"All right. That's weird that it would be outside."

"I can't guarantee it is. It may not even still be there. She could have turned it off when she was walking away from the house, and that's why we're getting an odd location for it. But go out and look before it gets too dark. Officer Sandrich may have missed it. Call me back at the number on the business card. That will reach me directly."

"I'll do it now."

He hung up and scratched his head.

Why the hell would her phone be outside?

Scott went out the front door and down the steps, crossed the driveway, and moved to the grass between his house and the Wilkinses place. He took a step and eyed the ground, then took another, and repeated the slow process until he had covered the area. He even went into the Wilkinses front yard and looked around the "For Sale" sign. He crept up to the front porch and noted that Marie's realtor security lockbox was still on the door. Scott was fairly certain she hadn't been in the house to show it to any prospective buyers in quite some time, surely not since the pandemic started.

He made another sweep of the lawns between the two houses, then repeated his search in the backyard. Twenty minutes later, Scott was back in the house. He dialed Detective Dante's number.

"Mr. Hatcher, what did you find out?"

"Nothing. Didn't see a damned thing."

"Well, to tell you the truth, I didn't have much confidence that you'd find it. Wherever Marie is, she probably has her phone, and it's turned off."

"Detective Dante, I hope that's the case. But the phone could be damaged or broken, right?"

"That is a possibility, I'm afraid. Oh, do you have a ring camera on your door or any other video equipment on the house?"

"No, I don't."

"Too bad. Some ring camera videos show a good portion of the front of a house and yard."

"So, what do we do now?"

He heard her sigh. "Mr. Hatcher, I have to advise you to get some sleep tonight and *try* not to worry. I'll check in with you first thing in the morning. If you haven't heard from Marie by then, I will escalate the case into LEADS."

"What's that?"

"The Law Enforcement Agencies Data System. It's a nationwide database where we can plug in information about a missing person. Law enforcement agencies all over the country have access to it, and things can get cross-referenced and such. It's a handy tool. Try to get some rest, Mr. Hatcher. I'll speak to you first thing in the morning to talk about next steps."

"Thank you, lieutenant."

Scott hung up and sat at the table. The news was not good, no matter how Dante tried to spin it.

Having nothing better to do, he went back outside and searched the grounds around his entire house again. He came up with nothing.

It was around seven thirty when the doorbell rang, startling Scott. Since yesterday morning, he'd been jumping out of nervousness whenever the phone or doorbell rang. He rushed to the front door and opened it. A tall blond man stood on the porch. There was something familiar about him, but Scott didn't register who he was. The man had a rather craggy, pockmarked face, a detail that caused Scott to realize that the man wasn't wearing a mask.

"Yes?" Scott asked without opening the storm door.

"Oh, I am sorry to bother you, sir . . . Look, I stand here six feet away." The man spoke with a pronounced Eastern European or Russian accent. He seemed to be younger than Scott, perhaps in his mid-to-late-thirties. Scott liked that Lincoln Grove had seen an influx of many immigrants over the past twenty years—Russians, Eastern Europeans, Indians, Pakistanis, and Asians.

He reached over to a small table that stood in the foyer by the door. It's where he and Marie were keeping their masks. Scott took his and put it on.

The man continued. "My name is Fyodor Volkov. Maybe you have seen my truck in your neighborhood or around vicinity of Dodge Park?" He gestured to the black truck parked in the driveway. It was the same one Scott had seen last night driving past the house.

"What do you want?" Scott asked.

"I live over by Dodge Park on Herndon. It is not far. I am looking to speak to Marie Hatcher. Is she here?"

"No, she isn't. Can I—" He suddenly found it absurd to ask if he could take a message for her. "Why do you want to know?"

"Oh. Sorry. She was supposed to call me yesterday regarding a house. She does not answer her phone. I thought she might be out of town."

Scott was confused. "She was supposed to call you? Why?"

"She is a realtor. Right? I am working with Marie on buying a house."

"Oh. You're a *client* of my wife's?"

"Yes, yes, client. My family . . . I . . . I and my family are thinking of moving from where we live now. We need more room. Third child on the way. Marie said she would get back to me yesterday about a house she had in mind."

Scott found this to be odd. Marie usually told him when she had a potential new client. One of the pleasant things they did do together was follow the sale of a house, which of course benefited them both. Whenever a prospective client became interested, Scott and Marie often placed silly bets on if and when she would close on the deal. She had never mentioned a Fyodor Volkov.

"Well, I'm sorry," Scott said. "She's not here right now."

"When will she return?"

"I don't know."

Volkov's brow wrinkled as if that answer didn't make sense to him. "Really? You don't know when your wife will come home? She is your wife, am I correct?"

Scott wasn't about to reveal any more to this stranger. "I'm sorry, but I'm rather busy right now. If Marie is working with you on a house, then I'm sure she has your phone number and she'll get in touch. I'll tell her you came by." He started to close the door.

"Wait!" Volkov held up his hand. "The house next door is for sale. She mentioned that house. My wife and I would like to see it. Do you have a code to open the lockbox on the front door? Key is inside the lockbox, yes? You give me the code, we look at the house. Easy."

Scott thought that was a *very* weird request. It just wasn't done. "Only Marie can let you in the house. I don't have the code. Sorry."

This time, Volkov's expression was one of serious displeasure. Scott genuinely felt a touch of menace from the man.

"Okay," Volkov said after a few seconds. "Please ask Marie to call Fyodor as soon as she comes home."

"I'll do that. Goodbye." Scott closed the door.

He waited a few seconds until he heard the irritating man descend the stone steps and get in his truck. Scott removed his mask, peeked out the living room window that faced the street, and watched the truck back out of the driveway.

Puzzled and a little disturbed by the man's visit, Scott went to get Marie's laptop, booted it up, punched in the PIN, and then looked through the subfolders in the main Clients folder. There was no "Volkov." He performed a search for that name in the C drive.

After a couple of minutes of a slow scrollbar moving across the displayed window, Scott got his answer.

No results found.

11

Those of you who are parents should probably take note of what I'm about to say.

If you have sons, and you think they're good boys who know right from wrong, think again.

There's a reason that the familiar adage "boys will be boys" has stuck.

Tuesday, May 12, 2020
11:00 p.m.

"Here you go, man," Don said as he dug into his backpack and pulled out a beer can. He handed it to Seth as they sat on the swings in Dodge Park. Their bikes stood a few feet away in case they needed to make a quick getaway.

The moon was behind the clouds, and there wasn't much illumination in the park. They felt relatively safe in the darkness, but Lincoln Grove had curfew rules against being in village parks after ten o'clock, even before the pandemic.

Seth pulled down his mask, pulled the tab, and took a drink. The beer wasn't exactly cold, but he didn't say so.

Don wasn't wearing a mask. He opened a can for himself and chugged it.

Seth wasn't a drinker, but he was ready to get wasted. Perhaps it was because he was angry and frustrated by the whole *thing*. It felt as if his world was collapsing around him, and he was only sixteen years old. Early in the pandemic, his father had said that they were "lucky." They had savings to live on, they had a house, they lived in a relatively safe suburban location away from an epicenter, his mother was still working (albeit in a risky job), and they—knock on wood— were healthy. They would get through it.

Seth wasn't so sure. He tended to be a "glass half empty" kind of guy.

"You're awfully quiet, dude," Don said. "What's up?"

"Nothing." He took another swig.

Don laughed. He drank more of his beer, froze, then whispered, "Don't move, there's a cop."

Sure enough, a patrol car was driving slowly along the road on the north side of the park.

"Can he see us?" Seth asked.

"I don't think so."

"They're patrolling parks more. Because of your Molotov cocktails."

Don laughed. "Yeah."

The car had moved on and was now out of sight.

"Speaking of which . . . " Don reached into the backpack on the ground between his legs. He pulled out a Coke bottle filled with gasoline, its top stuffed with an old rag.

"Don, don't. Not here. Not tonight." Seth looked at his phone to check the time. "Shit, I was supposed to be home an hour ago."

"Dude, it's not even midnight. It's not like we have *school* tomorrow."

"Don't worry, I'm not going anywhere. Fuck it."

"Ooh, a rebel!"

"I'm just saying don't light it here. Let's go someplace else."

"Like where, genius?"

Seth snickered. "You know Thomas Bergman? He suggested that you throw one in the Wilkinses' old house that's for sale." Half kidding, he added, "He said to double-dare you."

Don snorted. "Ha, I should. I hate that place. Nobody's *ever* going to buy it. Hell, I wouldn't want to live in a house where a guy strung himself up. Yuck!" Don finished his beer and crushed the can with one hand, then tossed it out into the grass. "You know, though, that's not a bad idea. Two points for Thomas Bergman, freak that he is. I'll take that double-dare!"

Seth drank the rest of his own beer, also crushed the can, but pitched it toward the metal garbage bin. The can missed the opening in the lid, made a loud BING noise, and bounced off.

"Why don't you wake up the neighborhood, Michael Jordan?" Don blurted and laughed.

Seth laughed too. "Sorry!"

"You know, the Wilkins house is easy to break into. I've done it."

"You *have*?"

"Last December. I went in there and smoked a joint."

"You know who the realtor is? It's the lady that lives next door! Ms. Hatcher."

"Really? Huh. She's kind of a MILF, if you know what I mean."

"I do."

"For that matter, so is Thomas Bergman's mom. If fact, she's even *more* of a MILF. But I still think she's crazy."

Seth rolled his eyes. "Why do you think she's crazy?"

"She wears all that hippie shit, like she's living in the sixties or seventies or something. My mom and dad said she yapped at 'em at the grocery store for not wearing masks. Like she was a crazy lady."

"Come on, Don, your parents *should* wear masks at the grocery store."

"We're not into that, bud. We like having our constitutional rights."

Seth wasn't about to get into an argument with him. "Whatever . . . I think Ms. Bergman is nice. And yeah, she *is* a MILF."

They got on their bikes and rode out of the park toward Marigold Way. It took them only a few minutes. Seth glanced at his house as they rode past. Lights were still on upstairs. His mother was likely home from the hospital, and his dad was still up. They hadn't texted him, though. He figured they trusted their son to stay out of trouble. Alas, he was about to disappoint them, but what they didn't know wouldn't hurt them.

The two of them rode up the driveway of Number 507, the Wilkins house, and parked their bicycles in the darkness between it and the Woos' house. Don put a finger to his lips, and the two boys quietly opened the gate in the rear fence. It creaked a little, but it wasn't loud enough to alert the neighbors. They crept into the backyard. The windows of the family room—the lower floor of the trilevel house—faced the rear and were waist high.

Don tapped a cigarette from a pack of Marlboros that were in his pants pocket, lit it, and took a few drags. "You know what? I've come to like real cigarettes more than the stupid vape. Vape is too sweet or something. This is much better. Want a drag?"

"No, thanks."

Don took a few more puffs. He then whipped out a pocketknife and removed a screen from one of the windows.

"Do you do this a lot?" Seth whispered.

"Break into houses? All the time," Don whispered back.

"Really?"

"Shh." He slid a window open. "Lookie here. Just like I left it last December. No one's bothered to lock it from the inside." He crushed the ember of his Marlboro on the windowsill, and then tossed the remaining three-quarters that he hadn't smoked out into the grass. "Here we go!" Don proceeded to crawl through the window. "Come on."

Seth scanned the yard and reckoned they were safe enough. Besides, it was dark. The only illumination from behind them on Dodge Lane came from the one house with the construction going on in its backyard. The home behind the Hatchers. A floodlight shone over the unfinished structure, but it didn't spill over into the Wilkinses' yard enough to cause a problem. It allowed the boys to see what they were doing, and that was all.

He climbed through the window and was quickly inside.

Many of the houses on Marigold Way and surrounding streets were of the same model and layout. There were often mirror images of each other, side by side. The Wilkinses' house was identical to the Schoenbergs'. The lower level was usually a "family room," the laundry room, and access to the garage. The middle level was the kitchen, dining room, and living room, and the upper floor held the bedrooms.

Seth said, "I can't see a thing."

Don fumbled with his backpack and pulled out his phone. He turned on the flashlight.

"Think we'll meet Old Man Wilkins's ghost?" he asked. "People say there's a ghost in here. Do you believe it?"

Seth suddenly felt creeped out. "No." He took a sniff. "Does something smell funny?"

"Yeah. It's like rotten meat or something. What are all these boxes? I thought Mrs. Wilkins moved out."

Sure enough, the family room was empty except for stacks of cartons. There were at least thirty or forty.

Don held the light closer so they could read the labels.

"N95 respirators, it says."

"What?" Seth moved closer.

"They're boxes of masks!"

"Holy shit, Don. These are the official hospital-grade masks. The ones that are in short supply everywhere!"

"Really?"

"Gosh. My mom needs some of these. She's been reusing her own, and you're not supposed to do that. This is a fucking gold mine!"

"Let's go upstairs to the kitchen," Don said.

Holding his phone, he led the way up a small flight of stairs to the middle level, which was the kitchen, living, and dining rooms.

Every space was filled with boxes still wrapped in cellophane. They approached the ones in the kitchen.

"Medical gowns," Seth said, reading the labels. "AAMI PB70:2012 . . . Level 3 . . . Level 4 . . . Don, these are surgical-strength gowns for hospitals. These are badly needed all over the country!"

"Someone is hoarding this stuff!" Don said.

They went into the living room to look at more piles of stacked boxes.

"Medical gloves," Seth read. "Class I. These are the best you can get. They're for when you do surgery and stuff. And over here are antiseptic wipes. Clorox! This stuff is like gold, we can't find it at the store. Holy shit, Don. We need to get the hell out of here."

"That smell is worse."

"It is. Come on, let's go."

"Nuh-uh." He held up the Molotov cocktail. "I'm going to light this. Whoever's hoarding this stuff has got to be a criminal, right?"

"Don . . . "

"We should mess 'em up."

"What?"

"I'm sick of 2020! Thomas Bergman is right. Let's burn it all up. Burn it to the ground."

"Are you crazy?"

"Yep. Aren't you?" He handed the bottle of gasoline to Seth. "Why don't you do it? I know you want to."

Seth held it in his hands.

Don dug in his pocket, pulled out a lighter, and gave it to Seth. "Aren't you sick and tired of all this? The whole world has gone to shit! Burn it down!"

Seth took a few steps away and faced the longer set of stairs leading to the top floor and the bedrooms.

"Light it, Seth! Your buddy Thomas wants you to!"

Damn it . . . I shouldn't do this . . . but I want to!

Seth flicked the lighter. The flame cast an eerie glow over the space. *Fuck it. Fuck it all . . .*

He lit the rag. It began to burn quickly.

"Throw it, dude!"

Seth tossed it up the stairs. The bottle broke on the landing and the gasoline spread like a virus. It was frightening how the flames swiftly covered the areas where the incendiary liquid spilled.

All the smoke alarms in the house went off with earsplitting high-pitched blasts.

"Let's get out of here!" Seth cried.

They ran back to the kitchen and down the stairs to the family room. They were out the window, into the backyard, and through the side gate faster than they could have imagined moving.

The next thing Seth knew, the two of them were panting, sitting on their bikes in front of Don's house on the corner. Seth was so scared that he didn't remember riding his bike there.

The Wilkins house was ablaze.

Seth's heart pounded in his chest. He truly hadn't expected it to be this bad.

What have I done? What have I done? Oh my God . . . Fuck . . . Shit!

"I better call 911," he said, out of breath.

"No! They'll know we did it!" Don snapped.

"How?"

"They'll figure out that someone broke in and started it. You and I were out riding, what, at eleven thirty at night, and then we call the fire department? We'll be the prime suspects!"

Seth knew Don was right. "I don't care. I'm calling." He pulled out his cell phone.

Don put his hand on Seth's arm. "We weren't in there. Got it?"

"What?"

"In the house! We were never in there!"

"Okay. We were never in there."

"We might get questioned. You have to swear, Seth. If the cops talk to you, you can't say anything about that medical stuff. We don't know it's there. We weren't in there! You won't say anything!"

"I won't."

"Promise?"

"Yeah. You have to promise too!"

"I promise! Geez!"

Seth dialed 911 and reported the fire. The dispatcher asked for his name and he gave it. Then he rode his bike home as he heard sirens in the distance heading toward Marigold Way.

A half hour later, two fire trucks and two police vehicles were in front of the Wilkins house. The fire was catastrophic. Hoses sprayed water on all sides as the firefighters worked to save the structure, but it was clear to everyone who had come out of their own houses to watch that Number 507 would no longer be for sale.

Seth stood with his parents in front of their house watching the flames engulf the upper half of the home. He trembled with fear, visions of prison bars dancing in his head.

The Woos and Scott Hatcher, who lived on both sides of the inferno, had been ordered to evacuate. David and May Woo stood across the street with Rachel and Thomas Bergman next door, keeping a safe distance apart. Scott Hatcher sat on the curb on the other side of the lane, in front of Number 504, with the Smalley family who lived there and almost never appeared outside of their house. Lois and Al Kimmelman stood in their yard.

So far, the Woo and Hatcher houses had not caught fire.

"You're the one who called 911?" Mitch asked Seth.

"Yeah," the boy answered.

"And you were at Don's?"

"Uh-huh."

"You just happened to see the house on fire?"

He hated to lie to his father. "Yep."

"You should have been home earlier," Harriet Schoenberg said. "What were you doing out so late?"

Drinking beer underage and committing arson. "I lost track of time, Mom."

Seth glanced over at the Bergmans. Thomas was looking at him. He subtly raised a hand and stuck his thumb up. Seth went next door to talk to them.

"I've never seen a house burn down before," Rachel Bergman said to him. "Have you?"

"No, ma'am."

"It's a good thing no one lived there!" David Woo said. "Good thing. Good thing."

"I'm the one who called 911," Seth told them all.

"Good for you," Rachel said.

"Yeah, good for you," Thomas echoed. His eyes, lit by the flames across the street, relayed a meaningful subtext to his words. Seth and Thomas shared something unsaid.

Ms. Bergman took Thomas's hand and clutched it. Her son turned his head to look at her, and his mother gave him an encouraging smile. "Yes, Seth, did the right thing, didn't he, Thomas? We should be thankful for him."

Thomas returned his gaze to his friend. "Yes. Thank you, Seth."

12

Do you ever have one of those mornings when your sleep is interrupted by a loud noise and it scares the bejesus out of you? Then it affects the rest of your day? You spend it grumpy and anti-social, and you feel like crap? And it only gets worse from there?

Scott Hatcher's about to have one of those mornings.

Wednesday, May 13, 2020

9:05 a.m.

"WHAT?! WHAT?!" he screamed, jolting in bed and punching the air above him with his fists.

The phone continued to ring and vibrate on the nightstand next to him.

Where was he? What was happening?

Then reality hit him like a semi-truck as he recognized the room. His bedroom. In his house.

Scott had been heavily into a dream in which he was leaping over the neighborhoods around him in single bounces, like Superman could do. It was a common dream, but this one had felt exceptionally realistic.

The phone continued to ring.

He grabbed it. "What? Hello?"

"Mr. Hatcher?"

"Yes? What?"

"Sorry, did I wake you?"

He looked at the digital clock that was also on the nightstand. 9:05.

"Who is this?"

"Sorry, it's Detective Dante with the Lincoln Grove Police Department."

Oh, right.

"Oh, sorry, Lieutenant Dante, I . . . I didn't get much sleep last night. I . . . the phone woke me out of a . . . I'm sorry, what . . . how can I help you?"

"I'm sorry to wake you," she said. "I can imagine what your night was like. I've been ringing your doorbell. We're outside your house. I need to speak to you. Are you able to come to the door?"

Oh shit . . . I have to pee and put on some pants . . .

"Uh, can you give me a minute? I need to . . . I just woke up and . . . you know . . . "

"We'll wait."

He hung up and rushed into the bathroom. When he was done, he quickly threw on yesterday's jeans, pulled off his sleep shirt, and replaced it with yesterday's T-shirt, which featured an image of the late Frank Zappa sitting on a toilet and a caption above it that read: "Phi Zappa Krappa."

Scott ran downstairs and opened the front door. Detective Dante and Officer Sandrich stood on the porch.

"Sorry to barge in on you like this," Dante said through her mask. "Good morning."

"Nice shirt," Sandrich muttered.

"Come in," Scott said. They hesitated, and then the light bulb went on in his head. He reached over to the table, grabbed his mask, and put it on. "There we go. Sorry."

"It's all right." They came in and moved past him to the kitchen where their meetings usually took place. "What time did you finally get to bed?" Dante asked.

"Four? The firefighters finally told me and the Woos we could return to our houses around three thirty, I think it was. But I probably didn't fall asleep until around six. It was a stressful night. How does it look out there in the daylight? From what I could see last night, the house was destroyed, but the walls were still standing."

"It's a big, blackened arson crime scene," Sandrich said. "The whole structure will have to be demolished."

"Geez. Do you know how it started?"

"That's not what we're here to talk about, Mr. Hatcher," Dante said. "You'd better sit down."

He did. "What? Is it about my wife?"

"I'm afraid it is."

Just those words alone caused a sudden sinking in Scott's chest. "I guess . . . I guess you'd better tell me, then."

Both officers took chairs and sat. "Mr. Hatcher, around the time the firefighters told you it was safe to return to your home, they also began to explore the interior of the house next door. They found the charred bodies of two people in one of the upstairs bedrooms."

Scott heard his own gasp of breath. "What?"

"A man and a woman. They were on what appeared to be the remains of an inflatable mattress. They were not wearing clothing and were covered with a blanket."

Scott's heart felt as if it might burst out of his chest. "And the woman was . . . ?"

"Scott, I won't lie to you. We don't know who they are yet, but we believe it's quite possible that they are indeed Marie and John Bergman."

"*What?*"

"Everything is burned. What personal items they had in the room with them are completely charred to bits, including two cell phones. The phones appear to have been deliberately broken—the screens are smashed and the devices are completely useless. That's a mystery. We're still investigating. Again, I want to stress that the victims have not been identified."

"So, it's possible the woman is *not* my wife?" Scott asked.

"It's possible, but, like I said, it's looking like that's not the case. I'm sorry."

Scott was stunned. He sat back in the chair and put a hand to his mouth. He felt tears in his eyes. "Marie . . . and *John Bergman*?"

"There's something else," Sandrich began.

Dante held up a hand at her partner.

"What?" Scott asked.

Dante continued. "There was a handgun in the room. Guns can survive fires like this, although it will forever be unusable. A Smith & Wesson M&P9 Shield. It was in the male victim's hand. On preliminary examination, it was determined that the man had been shot in the head twice. The woman once. Autopsies will be performed today to find out more, but it appears to have been a murder-suicide. The man shot the woman and then himself. We're still trying to figure out how he shot himself twice, but he did."

"Maybe," Sandrich said.

Again, Dante held a hand to keep him quiet.

"I think what Officer Sandrich is implying is that we're still investigating. It is indeed true that there have been suicides in which the person fired once, it didn't do the trick, and they fired again. Even head shots. Hard to believe, but it's happened. That said, some crime scenes can be staged. One big question mark is the arson itself. Who started the fire? Did the two victims start the fire themselves? Did they start it and then kill themselves? If so, why? Did he shoot her first, then start the fire, and then shoot himself? Again, why? If they started the fire, and they *are* your missing wife and the missing John Bergman, were they hiding in the house since Monday morning? *Why?*"

"It's obvious," Sandrich said.

Dante shot him a look and he turned away with a frown.

"I . . . I can't believe it," Scott said. "I just can't believe she would . . . do . . . something like this . . . " His head was spinning.

"There's another thing, and it raises even more questions."

"What's that?"

"The house was full of stolen PPE."

"Stolen what?"

"PPE. Personal protective equipment. Hospital masks, gowns, gloves, hand sanitizer, antiseptic wipes. Stacked in every room in the house, still in sealed cartons. It was all over the news. The robbery of this top-grade merchandise from the warehouse of nearby Cassette Labs."

"I . . . I remember reading something about that. Oh my God, John Bergman worked there."

"That's right. Now, unfortunately, all that PPE is ruined. PPE that was sorely needed here and around the country. I guess what I'm trying to say to you, Scott, is that there seems to be a lot more to this case than we ever thought when you and Ms. Bergman reported your spouses missing. There are a lot of questions that need to be answered."

Dante stood, and so did Sandrich. Dante pulled some literature out of a folder she carried and placed the papers on the kitchen table. "Officer Sandrich and I need to get back to the station. We have a lot going on this morning, as you can imagine. We'll be speaking further. I'm leaving these pamphlets with you. It's information about grief counseling, in case that's something you want to look into. I know this is hard. We're going to get to the bottom of this, I promise you."

Scott clenched his fists. He kept staring at the floor, breathing deeply and heavily. The tears wanted to come, but he couldn't manage to cry.

"I want to know . . . " he said.

"Want to know what, Scott?" Sandrich asked.

"I just . . . I want to know . . . what you find out."

"Of course," Dante said. "I'll be back in touch after the autopsies are performed. We may have some of those answers then. Are you going to be all right?"

Scott didn't respond.

"Scott? Mr. Hatcher?"

He snapped out of his daze. "Huh? What?"

"Are you going to be all right?"

"Yes. I . . . I don't know. I think so."

He kept it together until he saw the officers out the front door and made it back upstairs to his bedroom.

Then he fell facedown on the bed and screamed into his pillow.

13

The folks who live on Marigold Way, and Dodge Lane by extension, are in shock. Nothing like the events of May 12, 2020, has ever happened in their neighborhood—unless you count the unsavory suicide of one Mr. Douglas Wilkins in the same house. Is Number 507 cursed? Or is it simply a pocket of bad luck? If this were a horror movie, it would be about the time in the tale when some wise old man to whom no one pays attention—he might even be someone like me—would intone, "Oh, it was built on ancient burial ground," or some such nonsense to scare people.

The fact of the matter is that none of the houses on Marigold Way were built on a burial ground, no UFO crashed there in the 1940s or '50s, and no mysterious radioactive fog enveloped the neighborhood on a stormy night long ago. I suppose one could argue that the devil has made more than one appearance at Number 507, depending on one's beliefs. I'm not going to go there, though.

Now *boogeymen* are a different story. There are boogeymen in real life. They're not make believe. Boogeymen are indeed bad people who can be at least one of these things: selfish, greedy, lascivious, malevolent, sociopathic, paranoid, and desperate. Some boogeymen have all those traits.

By Thursday of that week in May, the citizens of Marigold Way—those who speak to each other—are gossiping and sharing all kinds of conspiracy theories about boogeymen and the devil and adulterous spouses who commit murder-suicides and arson. Maybe a few folks are considering the ancient burial grounds . . . who knows?

As a result of all the prurience, Scott Hatcher stays indoors all of Wednesday, May 13. And now it's a new day . . .

Thursday, May 14, 2020
9:10 a.m.

Scott had no problem answering his cell when it rang that morning. He had been up since seven, had considered going for a walk, but decided against it. He didn't want neighbors watching him and pointing fingers. There goes the cuckold. There goes the poor man whose wife cheated on him right next door. There goes the man who may or may not be a suspect in a few crimes. There goes the man whose name is listed as a Notable Resident of Lincoln Grove on Wikipedia. There goes *that man*.

"Hello?"

"Mr. Hatcher, it's Detective Dante. I hope I didn't wake you again?"

"Not today. I was . . . I was expecting to hear from you."

"Right. Can you come to the station for an interview?"

Scott didn't like the sound of that. "An interview?"

"Mr. Hatcher, we need a videotaped interview. It's part of the investigative process. It's routine, sir."

"Am I . . . am I a *suspect*?"

"You know the phrase, so-and-so is 'wanted for questioning?' This is like that. We just want to ask you some questions, many of the same ones we already asked you, and get it on videotape. Believe me, Scott, it's routine."

"Do I need a lawyer?"

"Only if you want one. The thing is, we need you down here within the hour, so if you've already engaged an attorney, he or she would have to get here as soon as possible. We can't have any delays. You can come in voluntarily. Otherwise we'll have to send a patrol car to pick you up, and I don't think you want that."

Scott rubbed his brow. He knew he had nothing to do with what had happened next door. He was a totally innocent man. That was the truth, so what could happen to him? He would answer their questions, and they'd turn him loose. He wanted to cooperate. He wanted to know the facts about what had occurred just as much as the police did.

"I'll be there in fifteen minutes."

"Thank you, Scott. See you soon. Don't forget your mask."

They sat in a sizable conference room at the Lincoln Grove Police Department, located in the minimalist "downtown" of the village. Detective Dante and Officers Sandrich and Lewis were on one side of the table, all three wearing masks. Dante looked as if she was the one not sleeping much, as her eyes were puffy. Scott figured that the nature of the case had brought on a level of stress to which the staff of the little department was perhaps unaccustomed.

Scott sat opposite them, but they had placed his chair a few feet back from the table. Another officer to whom Scott had not been introduced was operating a video camera that stood on a tripod behind the trio of interrogators.

"Please remove your mask now, Mr. Hatcher," Dante said. "We want your entire face visible for the video interview. I think we're far enough apart."

Scott did so and held the cloth item in his lap.

There were some preliminary tests of light and volume, and then they began. Scott was asked to state his name, birth date, and where he resided.

Officer Lewis then went over to a small table that was to the right of Scott, where a cloth covered something. Lewis removed the cloth to reveal objects inside four clear plastic bags. Lewis then moved away.

"Mr. Hatcher, do you recognize any of these items?" Dante asked. "Don't pick them up, just look."

All the items in the baggies were black and charred, but Scott knew what they were. He couldn't help but sigh sadly.

He pointed. "That's Marie's fanny pack, the one she'd wear when she was out of the house. I can still see a little of the red flower design there on the corner. It looks like hers." He moved on. The next piece was a mangled, broken piece of hardware. "I think that's Marie's cell phone. I admit it's hard to tell for sure." He stood and bent over closer to the third object. "Is that her driver's license? It's so burned, but there's a piece of the picture still visible. Yes, I believe that's Marie." The fourth item was a coin purse that was not too severely damaged. "And that's Marie's too."

"There was a ten-dollar bill and six ones inside it, plus some loose change," Dante said.

"That sounds about right. She didn't keep a lot of cash on her. We both tend to use debit and credit cards when we go to the store these days."

"Mr. Hatcher, the coroner wants Marie's dental records to compare to the . . . uh, victim's teeth. Who is her dentist?"

Scott told her. "So, it's still not certain it's Marie?"

"Your ID of those objects gets us to about 99 percent sure. The coroner wants the records to make it a hundred percent. He likes to cross the *t*'s and dot all the *i*'s. A pretty big confirmation we have is that John Bergman's car, a 2019 BMW, was in the garage of the house."

"Christ, why didn't you tell me that before?"

When Dante didn't answer, Scott gazed at the objects for a few more seconds and then returned to his seat. Dante proceeded to ask many of the same questions that she had asked when Scott had reported Marie missing. He answered everything and felt as if he had done so honestly and truthfully.

Then Dante got more personal. "Mr. Hatcher, were you aware at all that your wife might be having an affair?"

He thought about it before answering. "I have suspected it over the years since our son died of a rare cancer. Our relationship changed after that. There have been times when she spent a weekend in Chicago or some other city. A realtors' convention or a ladies' outing in Vegas with her friends, or whatever. I never confronted her about it. But I could tell. I have no proof, though. Well, until now."

"What about you, Mr. Hatcher? Have *you* ever had an affair?"

He hesitated. "I . . . once."

"Would this be with Diana Keyes?"

Scott winced. "I see you've been using Google. Diana Keyes is an actress who was on the television show I created, *Blaster Bob*. We . . . had a short fling in 2005. Fifteen years ago. It was nothing, really. Unfortunately, the tabloids had photos of us together at events, so there was speculation and gossip in the media. I told Marie it was all nonsense, but I don't think she believed me. I'll admit that I've been in denial that it happened, but it did. I was in LA at the time. I was caught up in all that show business *stuff*."

"There has been nothing since then?"

"Nothing."

"Okay, pivoting back to Marie. What do you know about John Bergman?"

"Like I've told you before, we barely know the Bergmans. We know them by name and sight. They live across the street. We wave at each other. Sometimes we've stopped to speak. When they first moved in . . . When was it, seven or eight years ago? We had them over for drinks to welcome them to the neighborhood. I remember that now. I wasn't sure if they'd ever been in our house before, but I do recall that get-together now. I've never been in their house. I don't know about Marie."

There were a few more questions, and finally Dante indicated that the interview was over. The whole thing had lasted approximately a half hour. The cameraman shut off the machine.

"Can I ask a question?"

"Yes, Scott."

"Have you determined whether what happened was indeed a murder-suicide?"

"There will be more eyes examining the crime-scene photos and evidence. Someone from the FBI is coming tomorrow because of the arson component and the stolen medical equipment that was in the house. You will need to do this all over again for them, I'm afraid."

"Really?" He noticed that she hadn't answered his question.

"Yes. I'm sorry."

"Couldn't we have waited and killed two birds with one stone?" He winced again. "Sorry, that came out wrong."

"We needed our own interview. There's a lot of bureaucracy involved in a case like this. That reminds me—we *will* want to look at your wife's computer. Can we send someone over today to pick it up? I should have asked you to bring it. My apologies."

"That's all right."

"You're free to go, but please don't leave town. We'll contact you soon about the FBI interview and if we get any more concrete news from the coroner."

"Can't I . . . see her? Couldn't I identify the body?"

Dante shook her head. "We're sparing you that indignity. I'm afraid there's not much to identify, sorry to say."

Scott swallowed. "Geez."

He was let out into the lobby of the station, where Rachel Bergman and her son, Thomas, were sitting and waiting. Ms. Bergman was apparently next to be video interviewed.

His eyes met Rachel's. She looked a bit shell-shocked. Nevertheless, she nodded slightly and gave him a hint of a smile.

Her expression said: *We now have something in common, don't we?*

"Hello, Mr. Hatcher," Thomas said.

"Hello, Thomas. I'm sorry for your loss. You, too, Rachel."

Rachel bowed her head. "Thank you. I'm sorry for yours too."

Incongruously, Thomas asked, "Mr. Hatcher, is Seth Schoenberg going to be mowing your lawn this summer?"

"Thomas . . . " Rachel murmured.

Scott blinked. "Uh, I think so. Why do you ask?"

"Oh. If he doesn't, I wanted to give it a try."

Rachel raised her head and her eyes locked into Scott's again. He could see that even she was somewhat amused by her son's non sequitur.

"Well, as it stands now," Scott replied, "I've already committed to Seth. But if something falls through, I'll let you know, okay?"

"Sure. Thanks."

Officer Sandrich announced, "Ms. Bergman, we're ready for you."

Rachel stood and addressed her son. "You'll be all right waiting out here for a while, Thomas?"

"Yes, Mom. I brought a book to read." He pulled it out of a backpack that was at his feet and revealed it to Scott.

The Dangerous Alibi by Scott Hatcher, which was published in 2010.

"I got it used on eBay," Thomas explained.

"Oh," Scott said. "I . . . I hope you enjoy it." He watched Rachel walk across the lobby and go with Officer Sandrich through the door marked "Authorized Personnel Only." Scott had to get out of there quickly. He couldn't take it anymore. He said goodbye to Thomas and left the station, dazed and confused.

14

By the end of the day, the media outlets have the fodder for gossip. The suburban Chicago papers run the story about the arson and the two bodies uncovered in the burned-out remains of 507 Marigold Way. Then it's on the six o'clock local television news. The victims' names are not revealed because the police have not released their identities. However, social media is a different matter. Someone from the block posts to Twitter that Marie Hatcher and John Bergman committed a murder-suicide and burned down the house she was trying to sell. Other Twitter members make the connection to Scott Hatcher, creator of *Blaster Bob* and author of several less successful books, and Scott becomes a viral joke about cuckolding. Other tweets link John Bergman to the robbery at Cassette Labs. At least one news organization reaches out to the medical company for comment, but the PR department has so far not issued one.

By eight o'clock in the evening, Marie Hatcher and John Bergman have become the Bonnie and Clyde of Lincoln Grove—illicit lovers in a robbery scheme involving coveted personal protective equipment, making their crime the most heinous thing imaginable, given the situation in the country.

The mainstream media has no choice but to reveal the victims' names coming up on the ten o'clock news.

Thursday, May 14, 2020
9:00 p.m.

"Oh man, this is so hilarious," Don Trainer said as he took a drag off his cigarette. "To think this is happening on our street. They're going to make a movie about it someday, you watch!"

Seth and Don sat in the swings in Dodge Park, their bicycles parked nearby, as usual. While Don was having a grand old time with what was happening, Seth was feeling progressively worse. He didn't sleep at all the night of the fire. He'd been certain that the police would come to his home and arrest him. His parents would be shocked and disappointed. He'd go to jail and miss the rest of his high school years. His life was going to be ruined.

But Wednesday passed and nothing happened. He was able to finally sleep, and then the shit hit the fan on social media a few hours earlier on Thursday. Now everyone in the world knew about the fire and the adulterous couple that had been burned to a crisp in one of the bedrooms.

If only I'd known they were up there . . . !

Seth had repeatedly turned it over in his head since the news about the bodies came out. If Marie Hatcher and John Bergman had been alive upstairs, wouldn't they have heard him and Don making noise? They couldn't have been asleep. It wasn't even midnight when it happened. *Were they already dead when he lit the Molotov cocktail and tossed it to the top-floor hallway?*

"Man, oh man," Don said, shaking his head and laughing. "They were cheating on their spouses right in the same neighborhood. Classic!"

"I don't think it's very funny, Don," Seth managed to say.

"Why not?"

"Don, do you think they were alive when we were in the house?"

"Huh?"

Seth explained his thought process. Don exhaled the tobacco smoke and shook his head. "I don't know. We were being quiet."

"No, we weren't. Outside we were, but not inside. Once we had crawled through the window, we spoke in our normal voices. Anybody else in the house would have heard us."

"So then they were already dead!"

"And that's what's weird! It means we burned up a crime scene that was already there. Don't you see the kind of trouble we could be in? If the cops find out it was us that—"

"Relax! If they haven't caught on to us yet, I don't think they will. What's to connect us to that house?" Don took a drag, exhaled, and added as an afterthought, "Besides, what do you mean, *us*? You're the one who lit the fuse."

"Hey!" Seth barked. "I'm not taking the rap by myself. You were with me. It was your Molotov cocktail. You pressured me into it!"

Don turned and looked at his friend. With the sun nearly set, darkness covered up the fierceness in the boy's eyes. "Nobody twisted your arm, bud. And wasn't it Thomas Bergman's idea?"

"He wasn't there. You know I was just joking about him saying we should burn down the Wilkins house. And he meant that suggestion for *you*, not me."

"Why would he do that? Does he know about me and the other park fires?"

"He suspects."

"Did you tell him?"

"The other day when you lit one here, he was watching us."

"He told you that?"

"Yes."

Don seethed. "That little creep. I'm going to bash his brains in. I'll make sure he stays quiet."

"Don't bother him, Don. It's not worth it. You hurt him, and it *will* come out that you're the park arsonist, and if that happens, you'll get linked to the Wilkins house."

"And you with me."

"Yeah, probably so." Seth stood and moved toward his bike. "And another thing—uh-oh."

"What?"

"Look."

Don followed Seth's gaze, and they both saw a figure standing some fifty yards away in the dim blackness. His shape was a silhouette outlined by the beam of the streetlamp behind him at the eastern edge of the park.

"Who is that?" Don asked.

"I think it's Thomas."

"Is he watching us?"

"I think so."

"That creepy fuck." He shouted. "Hey, idiot!"

"Don! Don't!"

"What's wrong with you?" Don yelled again.

Thomas didn't move. He stood on the combination foot/bike path running through the park.

Don got up, put on his backpack, went to his bicycle, and saddled up. He kicked back the stand and took off on the path toward his prey.

"Don!" Seth got on his own bike and pedaled after him.

Thomas held his ground. The bike was coming at him, picking up speed. It would collide into the boy in six seconds.

"Don!"

It was a game of chicken, except that one player was stationary. All Thomas had to do was step to the side and into the grass. The bike would then zoom past him on the pavement.

Four seconds.

"Don! Stop!"

Don emitted a war cry that split the air over the park. If the oncoming bicycle didn't scare the strange kid, then the banshee yell would.

Thomas remained still.

Two seconds.

Seth pedaled harder, but Don was thirty-five yards ahead of him. One second!

And then Don choked! He swerved into the grass, lost control, came dangerously close to a thick tree, and forced a wipeout to avoid a collision.

All that time, Thomas never moved.

Don rolled in the grass, jumped up, and strode toward the younger boy. He was hopping mad.

"You little freak! Look what you made me do!"

"I didn't make you do anything," Thomas calmly stated.

Seth pulled up to them at that instant. "Don, stop!" He got off his bike and stepped between them, holding up his hands. "Don, stay back."

"He's an idiot! He wouldn't even move out of the way! He made me crash!"

"Don, you're the one who rode at *him*!"

Don roughly shoved Seth in the chest, knocking him back.

"Hey!" Seth blurted. "You shit!" He held up two fists—but he had never been in a fight in his life.

Don, on the other hand, was well versed in brawls. He assumed a boxer's stance and taunted, "Come on, Seth, do it. Take a swing. I dare you."

As they were standing closer to the edge of the park, the illumination from the streetlamp cast a golden glow over Don's face. From Seth's perspective, the distorted features, the display of anger and menace, and the burning eyes all combined to exhibit the mask of a demon.

Seth lowered his fists. It was a lose-lose situation.

"Ha. I thought so," Don said. He turned to Thomas. "You little creep. How does it feel to have your dad cheat on your crazy mom with a fucking *neighbor*? Too bad he got all burned up. Serves him right. I bet the two of them looked like a barbecued pretzel! Ha!"

"Don, geez . . . " Seth muttered.

"He was my stepfather," Thomas said with unnerving calmness. "Not my dad."

Don stopped laughing and suddenly looked disgusted. "You are really weird." He swiveled and stormed toward his fallen bicycle. He picked it up, got on, and began to ride away. "So long, assholes."

Seth and Thomas watched him go along the path toward the curve between Marigold Way and Dodge Lane, and his form disappeared into the darkness after he left the light of the streetlamps.

"Why are you his friend?" Thomas asked.

"I don't know," Seth replied. "I don't think I am anymore." He realized he was trembling from an adrenaline rush. He took a deep breath and let it out slowly. "Are you okay?"

"Sure. Are you?"

"Yeah."

"I'm going home," Thomas said.

"You want me to walk with you? I can walk my bike."

"Nah, that's okay. You ride your bike. I want to walk alone."

"Okay." A few awkward seconds slipped by, and then he said, "See you later."

Seth got on the bicycle and started pedaling. When he reached the edge of the park, he looked back.

Thomas hadn't moved.

15

Can you imagine what your life would be like during the coronavirus pandemic if you didn't have the internet? There's no question that computers keep folks working in "these uncertain times" (God, I hate that phrase) with the Zoom technology and such. Computers and phones also keep most of us sane. You keep connected with others by email and social media and all that.

Think back to the 1918 influenza. World War I was coming to an end, and America had to deal with a damned influenza that no one knew how to fix. There was no internet or Zoom or computers then. There wasn't any television. Some people had radios. Movies were in their infancy, but there was a dip in attendance at the time. Maybe in those days folks didn't depend so much on that interconnectivity that is an important part of our lives today. I still bet it was tough, though.

Don't you find it odd that it's exactly a century later and humankind is going through it again? Is it a coincidence? Happenstance? Or is it . . . destiny? (Cue the eerie music.)

There are all kinds of conspiracy theories about the coronavirus out there, and with a big fat thanks to our friendly technology tools—the computers—these crazy suppositions spread like, well, viruses.

Technology can be used for other nefarious things too. Have you ever received one of those creepy emails that say you're locked out of your bank account or your credit card and you need to sign in to validate your credentials? Doing so, of course, means someone else can steal your password, and then you're really screwed. It's a hack job. The scams are everywhere.

Computer criminals are having a field day in the age of Covid.

I'll leave you with that tidbit as we join our pal Seth at home.

Thursday, May 14, 2020
11:30 p.m.

Seth received the email at 11:20 with an invitation to join Thomas on FaceTime at 11:30.

His parents had gone to bed. Harriet Schoenberg appeared more haggard and worn out with each passing day. His father constantly intoned that she wasn't paid enough for the risks she was taking. "You should all get hazard pay!" he'd grumble. Seth's mother was usually too exhausted to tell him to shut up. Every evening it was the same round of conversations, unless his mother was working a night shift. Then it was just him and his father. They generally stayed apart. If Mitch Schoenberg wasn't working in his little bedroom office, he was watching television downstairs.

Tonight, though, the adults had hit the hay at ten o'clock, leaving Seth to his own devices. He tended to stay up late anyway and not get up until nearly noon the next day, especially since school had shut down. He figured that chatting with Thomas on FaceTime was better than getting lost on social media, which had become cesspools of misinformation, political arguments, and photos of bad haircuts.

Seth signed on, and Thomas greeted him with a simple "Hey."

"Hey. Are you all right?" Seth asked.

"Yes. Why wouldn't I be?"

"Just making sure. I'm sorry about what happened earlier with Don. The guy can be a real ass sometimes."

"Only sometimes?"

Seth laughed. "Maybe more than that." He pushed away the levity and added, "I'm sorry about what he said about your dad. And your mom."

"My stepdad. Thanks."

"Yeah, your stepdad. Sorry, I don't know why I can't get that through my head."

"It's okay. A lot of people think he's my real dad."

"Have you talked to your sister?" Seth asked.

"My half sister, you mean?"

"Yeah."

"Sarah's in Los Angeles with her fiancé."

"I know. Have you talked to her?"

"No. Mom has. She talked to her last night to tell her what happened. Sarah and my stepfather didn't get along. She moved out as soon as she graduated from high school three years ago."

"I guess the possibility of her coming to visit is out of the question?" Seth asked.

"With the coronavirus? No, I don't think so. Would *you* get on a plane?"

"Maybe if I had to."

"That's how I feel," Thomas said. "But it's probably not a good idea."

"No, probably not. Is Sarah on Facebook or Instagram?"

"Yeah, why?"

"Just wondering what she looks like now."

Thomas's eyes widened a bit. "You're one of those guys who thought she was hot?"

Seth felt his cheeks flush. He smiled. "Yeah, I guess. You don't mind, do you?"

"No, I understand. All the boys liked her. Some girls too."

Seth didn't want to ask what he meant by that.

"Sarah doesn't get along with our mother much either," Thomas added. "She's going to get married and live her own life. That's what she said last time she was here."

"How come they don't get along?" Seth asked.

"Sarah didn't want Mom to marry John. That's the main thing. She'd already gone through a stepfather before him—*my* real dad."

"Where is he now?"

"He's on the East Coast somewhere."

"Do you talk to him?"

"No. He's a shit too."

"Really?"

"I *don't* want to talk about him."

"Okay, sorry."

There was a pause in conversation. Seth looked around his room, but Thomas kept his eyes on his webcam, creating the illusion, Seth thought, that Thomas was beaming gamma rays from his pupils at Seth through the monitor.

"How's your mom handling all this?" Seth finally asked.

"Okay. I mean, it's hard, you know. We were at the police station this morning. She had to answer a bunch of questions."

"Where were you?"

"Sitting in the lobby of the police station. We saw Mr. Hatcher there too. They asked him a bunch of questions before my mom."

"I guess you have to expect that. They have to rule her out."

"My mom didn't do anything, though."

"Of course, she didn't," Seth agreed.

At least she didn't start the fire!

"The FBI is coming tomorrow," Thomas said. "She'll have to answer *their* questions too."

"Really? The FBI?"

"Because the FBI investigates arson cases. And there's all that PPE that was in the house. Stolen from my stepdad's warehouse. That's a federal crime."

"I guess so. Geez."

"Hey, Seth, did you know I'm good at hacking?" Thomas asked, inexplicably pivoting to a completely different topic the way he tended to do.

"Hacking? You mean computer hacking?"

"Yeah."

"Tell me more."

"I've been learning how to do it for several years now."

"Thomas, you're, what, thirteen?"

"Fourteen."

"How are you learning?"

"I'm teaching myself. I'm good at computers. You didn't know I could program?"

"I knew you could a little, from school. What kind of hacking do you do?"

"So far I've hacked into Johnson High School. I can change someone's grades if I want to."

"*What?*"

"I hacked into Ubisoft, Blizzard, and Rockstar Games. To get codes and cheats. It's fun."

"Thomas. That's . . . You know if you get caught, you could get in a shitload of trouble?"

"I know. But I don't. I'm telling you because you're my friend. Maybe my only friend."

Seth didn't know what to say to that.

"You won't tell anyone, will you?"

"No," Seth answered. "But you need to be careful."

"I've hacked into Don's computer," Thomas whispered. "It was easy."

"Don't do that, man."

"I might see what's there. It'd be fun."

"Geez, Thomas."

"Hey, did you know there's a man who lives near here who's connected with a local organized crime group?"

"*What?*"

"Yeah. He lives near the park. You've seen his truck. It's a big black truck with the windows painted over. It's says 'Volkov Trucking' on the side."

"I *have* seen that truck!"

"The guy who drives it is a gangster."

"How do you know?"

"I hacked into his company. I've seen his emails."

"Thomas, you have not."

"I have. My stepfather was doing business with him."

"*What?*"

"It's true. I think that's what all this arson and murder stuff is all about. My stepfather and this guy Volkov were selling medical supplies and drugs to the black market."

Seth's jaw dropped. "You can't be serious!"

"I am."

"Have you told . . . Does your mom know this?"

"No."

"You should tell her. The police should know. Do *they* know?"

"They don't know anything."

"Then you need to tell them!"

"But Seth," Thomas said, "If I told them, then they'd want to know how I know. I'd have to admit I'm a hacker. Then *I'd* get in trouble."

"Jesus, Thomas, I don't want to know this either. Don't say anymore!"

"This Volkov guy actually works for someone else. A bigger boss. I don't know his name yet, but I'm trying to find out."

"Thomas, you have to stop this!"

"On Mr. Volkov's emails, the guy has a nickname."

"What is it?"

"Scoutmaster."

"*What?*"

"Yeah. The boss of the mob is called Scoutmaster."

"You're pulling my leg."

"I'm not, Seth. Don't tell anyone."

"This is nuts, Thomas."

"What I can't figure out, though, is who would want to burn all that PPE? Maybe it was a competitor. Whoever did it wanted to get rid of the merchandise so Scoutmaster and Volkov couldn't profit from it."

Seth's head was spinning. Was Thomas making all this up? Was it real?

Thomas's eyes narrowed slightly. "Unless . . . you got Don to do it like I suggested."

In a moment motivated by feelings of guilt and a sudden braggadocio, Seth asked, "Thomas, if I tell you a secret, will you promise not to tell a soul? Not your mother, not the police, not *anyone*?"

"Sure, Seth. I just told you some secrets."

"Yeah, you did, so I'll tell you one."

"So, what is it?"

Seth took a breath. "I know who started the fire in the Wilkins house."

"You do?"

"Yeah."

"Was it Don? I thought he would do it if he was pushed into it."

Seth stopped. He blinked and felt his mouth go dry.

"I won't tell anyone," Thomas said. "I promise."

Seth nodded. "Yeah. It was Don," he lied.

16

In Thornton Wilder's play, *Our Town,* deceased characters make an appearance in the third act as . . . well, they're ghosts. They're sitting in chairs on the stage, and these are meant to be their graves in a cemetery. They each say something about their lives or people they knew or whatever. When the living characters come to visit the departed, they don't see or hear the dead. On the other hand, it's long been a trope in fiction that ghosts can see and hear those who are still alive. The spirits sometimes visit the living and leave signs of their existence.

Does that really happen?

It's one of those mysteries of life and death that supposedly you'll know the answers to after you've crossed the threshold.

I think at this point we can all accept that the two bodies in the Wilkins house were once the vessels of Marie Hatcher and John Bergman, even though the county coroner has yet to confirm this. In our tale so far, we have never met Marie, and I can tell you that we won't meet her as long as I'm telling this story. That doesn't mean her spirit doesn't exist . . . somewhere.

Perhaps my musings make you wonder. Can Marie see and hear Scott the same way those characters in *Our Town* can observe their remaining loved ones? Can any of the folks who are long gone drop in and pay a visit?

I am certain they can, just the way I can believe that microscopic germs can wreak havoc on the entire world in a few months. I don't mean to get all existential on you, but anything's possible, folks.

Friday, May 15, 2020
8:15 a.m.

The noise of a buzz saw woke Scott Hatcher. At first, he was disoriented and didn't know where he was, an all-too-common occurrence as of late, but that quickly passed, and he became angry.

Mr. Blunt was at it again before nine o'clock in the morning.

Scott pulled the extra pillow over his head to muffle the din. It didn't help much.

Then came the hammering. The never-ending cycle—saw, hammer, saw, hammer . . .

The anger segued into a heavy sadness. Scott had been dreaming about Marie. She had been there in the house with him. They were in the kitchen and working together to create a dinner from scratch the way they used to do in the early days of their marriage. It was one of the few fun things they shared for a few years. Marie would wash and chop the ingredients for salad, and Scott did the meats and vegetables. Sometimes the space became cramped, and they might have to avoid colliding into one another, but that was part of the adventure.

When Scott was about to place into the oven a casserole dish or a tray of stuffed mushrooms—he couldn't remember now what it was—Marie looked at him and said, "Our neighbor is raising a ruckus again."

It was a phrase she had often used. "Raising a ruckus." She had borrowed it from actress Debbie Reynolds, who sang a song called "Raise a Ruckus Tonight" in the movie *How the West Was Won*, which Scott and Marie had seen together in 70mm at the Music Box Theater in Chicago. Marie had liked the alliteration. In those days when the relationship was good, she'd hint that they'd go to bed and "raise a ruckus tonight."

Now fully awake, Scott threw the pillow across the room and cursed aloud. He got out of bed, put on pants, and stormed downstairs to the kitchen. He opened the sliding glass door that led to the patio and backyard. In his bare feet, he strode across the grass to the rotting wooden fence—it desperately needed replacing—and yelled to his rear neighbor.

"Hey! Mr. Blunt!"

The hammering stopped. Blunt, who was shirtless and wearing shorts, his muscular and tattooed body already glistening with sweat, looked up. He was by himself, attaching plywood to the roof of his house.

"Mr. Hatcher! Good morning!" he called out. The intonation was not friendly.

"I've asked you several times. Can you not do all this so early in the morning?"

"And I've told you several times. It's the best time of day. It's not too hot!"

Scott closed his eyes tightly and opened them again. "I don't know if you've heard or not, but my wife *died* a few days ago, and it's hard enough getting sleep. Your sawing and hammering do not help. Please!"

"Not my problem, man! I have to get this done."

What did he say?

"Did you hear me?" Scott yelled back.

"It's daylight, Mr. Hatcher! I'm going to do man's work." With that, the guy had the audacity to start hammering again.

What was he implying? That I'm not a man?

Scott couldn't help himself. "You better watch out!" he yelled. "There's an arsonist on the loose. Your house could be his next target!"

Blunt stopped pounding. He put down the hammer and stood up straight. He resembled an elevated Roman statue, superior to everything at his feet. "Are you threatening me?" he growled.

Scott simply slumped a little and looked at him in disbelief. It wasn't worth it. *Damn him.*

Without responding, he turned and went back to the patio, opened the sliding door, and went inside. Scott thought he heard Blunt say, "Yeah, I thought you'd back off."

He's just a bully. He probably picked on kids smaller than him.

Scott continued to curse the man under his breath as he made coffee and booted up his computer. He'd already handed over Marie's laptop to the officer who had come by to pick it up yesterday. At the time, a news van was parked outside his house, hoping to catch a glimpse of the cuckolded widower-possible-suspect. After the interview at the police station, Scott had stayed indoors all day. It was a jungle out there. He hoped today would be different, and that some other sordid scandal would occupy the news.

There were anonymous nasty emails in his inbox. "Did you kill them, Hatcher?" "Where there's smoke, there's fire!" "Hey, Hatcher, what's Diana Keyes up to now?" Crap like that.

His social media pages were also bombarded with disgusting comments. Only a few were notes of sympathy. He did have some fans who seemed to care about what he might be going through. But why had people become so . . . antagonistic? One would think that the presence of a global pandemic would bring people together in kindness, but *NOOO!*

The news outlets offered nothing more to the case. A piece in the local paper online stated that the police were still investigating the "suspicious fire and deaths" at a Marigold Way house in Lincoln Grove. Photos of Marie Hatcher and John Bergman accompanied the article.

"You bastard," Scott said to the picture of Bergman.

He stayed at the kitchen table for the next hour, surfing the web and listening to Blunt's symphony of sounds. Then his cell phone rang. He recognized the caller ID as Marie's sister, Louise.

Scott answered. "Louise?"

"Hi, Scott," the woman said. He had not spoken to her since the news broke. She lived with her husband in Cincinnati. Or was it

Cleveland? He never could remember. Louise was three years older than Marie.

"Hey, Louise." He sighed audibly.

"I heard the news. My God, Scott, why didn't you call me?"

"I was going to today, Louise. Honest. Listen, the police still haven't really confirmed it's Marie. We think it is, but the death certificate hasn't been signed yet."

"Really? The news says it's her! Her picture is online!"

"I know. The media jumped the gun. If you read those stories carefully, they say the police still haven't confirmed the identities of the bodies."

"What do *you* think, Scott?" Louise sounded more angry than bereaved.

"I think it's her."

"So, what, she was having an affair with that guy she died with? What was going on?"

"Louise, I don't know. It was all a surprise to me too."

"Really? I don't believe it. How can you not know? *How can you not know?*"

"Louise," Scott cradled his head in his hand, set the phone down, and put her voice on speaker. "You do understand I'm the injured party here?"

"You? My sister is fucking *dead*! And *you're* the injured party?"

That got Scott's blood boiling again, just after he had calmed down somewhat following the altercation with his neighbor. "Yes, Louise, I am! Your sister was cheating on me with a man who lived on our *block*! It looks like she may have been involved in criminal activity beyond that! The goddamned FBI is coming in today to look at it. And I knew nothing—*nothing*—about it! So please spare me your indignation."

She was quiet for a bit, and then Louise said, "All right, I'm sorry. I'm just upset. Mother is upset too. Have you called *her*?"

Scott rubbed his temples. "I was going to call her today too. Look, it's been a terrible couple of days. I just found out on Wednesday.

Marie went missing on Monday, and the police told me not to worry. Then that fire happened Tuesday night and I found out on Wednesday morning that she was in the house. I've barely had time to comprehend it myself, much less talk to anyone."

"But we're *family*!"

Right. Family that Marie wanted little to do with. How often had Marie and Louise seen each other in the past five years?

When Scott didn't say anything, Louise asked, "So, is there going to be a funeral? What's happening?"

"Louise, I don't know anything yet. Her body is still with the coroner. Besides, there's a pandemic going on, you know. There aren't any funerals happening."

"You can have one with less than ten people!"

"In some places, yes. I don't know what I plan to do yet. How about I let you know when I do."

"Please."

"Are you and Bill doing all right, otherwise?"

"We're fine. Staying safe, but Bill goes to work. I worry about that."

Scott couldn't remember what Louise's husband did for a living. He realized he'd never liked Louise and Bill. Marie's instincts were right in that regard.

"Well, I have to go now. Thanks for calling. I'll call Lilian now."

"You do that. Take care." She hung up.

What, no "goodbye?"

Scott dreaded what he was about to do now. *Might as well get it over with.*

He found Lilian Dinkins in his contacts list on the phone, and then he dialed. Marie's mother lived alone in Florida somewhere. Boca Raton? Fort Lauderdale? Somewhere like that, where wealthy retirees resided.

When the woman answered, Scott told her who he was.

"Oh, Scott, I've been wondering if I should call you or not. I'm so distraught I don't know what to do!"

"I'm sorry, Lilian, I really am. It's all so . . . tragic."

Scott thought Marie's mother was okay, although she was an

alcoholic and could sometimes be a mean one. He'd liked Carroll Dinkins, but Marie's father had died of a heart attack ten years earlier, not long after Brian had passed away. That had caused another fissure in Marie's emotional stability. Scott always suspected that it was Lilian's drinking that pushed Carroll over the edge.

"I can't believe it, Scott," the woman said, obviously starting to sob. "My baby girl . . . I can't believe it . . . "

"I know, I know."

"How . . . how did it *happen*?"

"Lilian, the police are investigating. The FBI is coming in today. It's a big mess. I hope they'll figure it out and find out who was responsible for this."

"Well, did *you* do it?"

That threw Scott. He blinked. "What?"

"I mean, I can understand you being the jealous husband and wanting revenge and all. I want to know if you killed my daughter!"

"Lilian! Come on. *I* didn't do it! I can't believe you'd say something like that!"

"Oh, I know, I'm sorry. I'm just so upset."

"Well, I am too."

"It's just that they always look at the spouse, you know. Nine times out of ten, it's the spouse."

How do you know?

"I had nothing to do with it, Lilian. I'm still in shock from the news." He proceeded to tell her the same thing he'd told Louise.

"Well, I don't think I'd try to get on an airplane to fly up there for a funeral, Scott," the woman said. "With everything that's going on, you know."

"I don't blame you. There won't be a funeral, I can pretty much guarantee that. Perhaps we can have a memorial service together when all this Covid stuff is over."

She seemed to accept that, and Scott said his goodbyes. He promised to be in touch, even though talking on the phone to Marie's relatives was not pleasant.

He needed to reach out to someone who was at least empathetic to what he was experiencing. Scott searched his contacts for Rob Chadwick's number and hit Dial. Rob was a friend since college, one of his buddies, and someone who had gone through a divorce because his wife had also cheated on him.

"Is this who it says on my Caller ID?" Rob answered with surprise.

"It is," Scott said.

"What's up, man? Long time no speak!"

Rob lived in one of the western suburbs of Chicago and was a patents attorney.

"Have you not heard about what happened in Lincoln Grove?" Scott asked.

"No, man. What happened?"

"I guess you don't follow the news. My wife was having an affair with a neighbor, and they were both inside a house that she was selling when someone decided to burn it down. She's dead."

"*What?*"

Scott told him everything he knew.

"My God, man, I'm so sorry! Are you okay? Is there anything I can do?"

"Thank you, yes, I guess I'm sort of okay. Still in shock, I think. I feel like Marie is here with me, though, watching and listening. I dreamed about her this morning. You think she's trying to tell me anything?"

"Gee, I don't know, Scott."

"The whole thing is so . . . weird. And embarrassing too. You should see my social media pages. The crazies are out in full force. People are just so cruel."

"Oh, I know. Don't pay any attention to them. You can close down your pages, you know. Or at least deactivate them temporarily."

"Hm, maybe. But from an anthropological standpoint, the response to my *tragedy* is kind of interesting. It's like people don't have anything better to do during a pandemic."

"Right."

"Listen, Rob," Scott said, "Maybe there is something you can help me with."

"What's that?"

"Do you know any defense lawyers? Someone who won't cost me an arm and a leg who might, well, take on my case?"

"Oh shit, Scott. Do the police think you did it?"

"Not yet, they don't. At least they haven't said anything. But you know how it is. You've watched TV before. They always suspect the spouse. With the FBI coming today, I think they're going to grill me harder. I may need a lawyer."

"You didn't start that fire, did you?"

"Rob! No!"

"Hey, I had to ask! Sorry. Of course you didn't!"

"And no, I didn't shoot my wife and her lover either! So, let's forget that line of thought, okay?"

"Sorry."

"So, how about it? Do you know someone?"

"As a matter of fact, I do. I know a guy. Harry Edmonds. Criminal defense lawyer in Chicago."

"He already sounds expensive."

"They're all expensive, bro. But I think you may want someone good, right?"

"Yeah."

"Let me give you Harry's number. Great guy."

Scott jotted down the contact, and then he talked with his friend a few minutes more before he'd had enough. The next call went to his literary agent. He kept the exchange short—he just warned him that there could be some bad publicity attached to his name. He again related the squalid tale and told the agent about the attacks on social media. Luckily, his agent was in New York, and he said that he'd "heard it all." He expressed his condolences, offered words of encouragement, and basically said not to worry about the PR. "Everything passes," he said. "Next week, no one will remember it. I'm very sorry for your loss, Scott." That was it. Scott wondered why the man hadn't asked how his novel was coming. He figured it was because his agent didn't feel it was appropriate, or that he didn't care. Scott sighed. The agent probably couldn't sell it now, anyway. The virus was wreaking havoc on everybody's livelihood.

After all the phone calls, Scott thought he might go back to bed. Mr. Blunt had tapered off with the construction cacophony. However, before he could get too far up the stairs, the doorbell rang.

Now what?

Scott reversed course, went into the foyer, and peeked through the peephole. He wasn't about to blindly open the door with news camera crews stalking him.

The distorted figure through the fisheye lens was Thomas Bergman. The boy was dressed in his trademark long-sleeved shirt and black pants, as if he'd been wearing a suit and removed the tie and jacket. He did have on a mask.

Scott put on his own mask and opened the door. "Thomas?"

"Hi, Mr. Hatcher."

"Hi."

The boy didn't say anything.

"Can I help you?" Scott asked.

"May I come inside?"

Scott stuck his head out and scanned his immediate view of the street. No news crews. No reporters.

"Where's your mother?" he asked the boy.

"At home."

"Uh, sure, come in, I guess."

Thomas entered and walked straight into the kitchen to sit down.

Gee, make yourself at home.

"What can I do for you?" Scott asked again.

Thomas had a worried crease in his brow. He placed his arms on the table and locked the fingers of both his hands together.

"Is something wrong?" He sat down across from Thomas.

"I didn't like my stepfather. I'm glad he's dead."

That surprised Scott. He didn't know what to say.

"I bet you would be a good stepfather," the kid continued. "I like you."

What the hell . . . ?

"Thomas," Scott began, "I . . . thanks, but . . . I don't understand why you came over to tell me this."

"No reason. I just wanted you to know that."

"Uh, thanks."

Thomas looked around the kitchen. "It wouldn't be bad living here. Maybe I could come and keep you company."

What a fucking bizarre thing to say.

"Thomas, I don't think that's . . . possible. Does your mother know you're here? You know, she probably needs you to be with her."

The doorbell rang again.

"Uh, excuse me a second," Scott said. He stood and went to the peephole in the front door.

Rachel Bergman stood on the front porch.

17

Some of you might be thinking that we haven't really seen much of Rachel Bergman so far. Well, allow me to rectify that. It wasn't an oversight. It's because I'm the storyteller here, and I can tell the tale any way I choose!

Since I left you hanging earlier, I won't take up your time with my meanderings. Let's pick up at the front porch where we left off.

Enter Rachel Bergman.

Friday, May 15, 2020

10:50 a.m.

Scott opened the door. Rachel wore a bright, cheery sundress, a broad brimmed hat, sandals, and sunglasses. She looked as if she were going to the 1967 Monterey Pop Festival instead of down the block to a neighbor's house in the year 2020. For someone in mourning, she was stunning.

"Hi, Rachel," he said.

"Scott, sorry to trouble you. Is my son here?"

"He is."

"Oh my God, I hope he's not bothering you."

"Not at all."

"Thomas?" she called.

"It's okay, he's right inside." Scott knew it was clumsy, but he asked, "Would . . . would you like to come in?"

"Mm . . ."

"Or . . . I could go get him . . ."

"No, I'll come in for a minute, if it's all right."

"Uh, sure. Please."

A mask hung wedged in the belt at her slim waist. She put it on her face, removed her sunglasses, and came inside. Scott led her to the kitchen, where Thomas was still sitting.

"Thomas, what are you doing here?" she asked him. "Are you bothering Mr. Hatcher?"

"He's not bothering me," Scott answered. "Although I admit I'm not entirely sure why he came to visit. Not that I mind! It's okay, really."

"I just wanted to talk to Mr. Hatcher," Thomas said. "Is that bad?"

"Well, Thomas," Rachel said, "Considering what happened this week, I'm not sure it's a good idea."

"Why not?" Thomas asked. "You both lost your spouses. Who says you can't be in solidarity about this?"

Scott was astonished by the kid's mature demeanor. He turned to Rachel and said, "He's right, you know." He shrugged.

Rachel's eyes smiled as she shook her head. "I guess."

"Would . . . would you like some coffee?" he asked.

She hesitated, but then said yes.

"It'll be just a sec." He went to the sink, filled up an electric kettle with water, and got a can of ground coffee out of the fridge. "I make it with filters and a cone, drip style," he said.

"So do I, actually," Rachel responded. She sat at the table next to her son.

There was silence for a moment, and then Scott said, "I . . . I'm sorry for your loss."

"I was going to say the same thing," she replied. "I suppose this *is* a little awkward."

He stood at the counter while he waited for the water to boil. "Hey, you know what? It shouldn't be awkward. *We're* the collateral damage here. Maybe we should compare notes, so to speak."

Rachel nodded. They waited in silence as Scott made the coffee. "You want something, Thomas?" he asked.

"Do you have grape juice?"

"No, I'm afraid not. I don't think I have any soda either. Sorry. Oh, I have orange juice. How's that?"

"Sure."

Scott poured a glass of OJ and handed it to Thomas, and then he brought a hot cup of coffee to Rachel. He really didn't want to talk about his wife and Rachel's husband in front of the boy, so he said, "Er, Thomas, I have a big flat-screen TV downstairs in the family room. I have Netflix and Disney+. Maybe you want to go watch something while your mom and I talk?"

Thomas looked at his mother. Rachel gave him a slight nod, and he said, "Okay."

Scott said to Rachel, "Be right back." He then led Thomas down the stairs and set him up with the TV and the controller. He also showed him a collection of DVDs and Blu-rays on the shelf that Thomas was welcome to play if he wanted.

Back upstairs, Scott sat at the table across from Rachel. "I think that'll keep him amused for a little bit."

"Maybe," she answered. She moved her mask a little from around her lips whenever she sipped the coffee, and then immediately recovered her mouth. "Now if you had an Xbox and some games, that might do it for hours."

"That I don't have. How old is he?"

"Fourteen."

"He seems so much older."

"Yes, he does. I don't want it to sound like I'm bragging, but Thomas is what they call one of those 'gifted' children. His IQ is scary high. Sometimes I'm flabbergasted by some of the things that come out of his mouth. I'm afraid he has a hard time at school. Kids make fun of him. He's often the victim of bullying."

"I'm sorry to hear that."

"I tell him it's because the other kids are jealous," she said. "He's so much smarter than anyone else his age. We've been talking to the people at Johnson High School about an accelerated path to graduation. Seriously, he makes straight A's in everything. Thomas can get up in front of the class and write out a complicated math equation on the whiteboard that even the teacher can't do. I don't know where he gets it. *I'm* not that smart, and I'm terrible at math! His father, well, he was just . . . a bum. Ha, sorry. I'm talking too much. I'm a little nervous."

"No, you're not," Scott replied. "Talking too much, I mean. It's okay to be nervous. I am too. Anyway, that's fascinating about Thomas. He's a kind of genius, isn't he?"

"He is. Thomas is just . . . a unique kid. As you say, he's very much ahead of himself in years and intelligence. My daughter—I have a daughter, Sarah, who lives in California—she isn't anything like him. Thomas and I . . . well, we have a good relationship. We're close. I don't know what I'd do without him. Especially . . . now . . . "

Tears came to her eyes. Scott jumped up to grab the tissue box on the kitchen counter. He handed it to her. "Here."

"Thanks," she took one and sniffed as she wiped her eyes. "Sorry."

"It's quite all right. I understand."

"It's all so . . . unreal."

"I know what you mean."

After a few seconds of silence, Rachel asked, "How was your interview with the police?"

He shrugged. "I just told the truth. What I don't like is having to repeat my story over and over. I guess we're going to be talking to the FBI soon?"

"That's what they told me. I agree with you. Saying the same thing repeatedly is tedious. Do they really think I'm going to change my story?"

They sipped their coffee around the masks. Scott kept wanting to look at her, but he forced himself to avert his eyes. He had never been one to believe in auras, but he could swear Rachel Bergman had one. Or maybe it was just the sunlight streaming in through the sliding glass doors?

"Scott . . . It's all right if I call you Scott?"

"Sure. I think we're past the Mr. and Mrs. stuff."

"Scott," she started, "Do you . . . do you believe that John and Marie killed themselves?"

He puckered his lips and exhaled with exaggeration. "I've thought about that a lot since I learned the news. I have to say, I can't imagine why they would. I'm totally mystified by the whole thing."

"Me too."

"Did you . . . did you know about their affair?" he gently asked.

Rachel cocked her head. "I think I did. No, that's not true. I *know* I did. I knew he was seeing her. I didn't *want* to believe it, but I knew it."

"For how long?"

"Months. Since at least fall of last year."

Scott turned toward the sliding door and gazed at the backyard. "Wow."

"You didn't know?"

"No." That was when he realized that there was no noise coming from Blunt's backyard. He stood and peered beyond the top of his fence.

"What are you looking at?" she asked.

"Oh, my neighbor back there. He's building all that stuff and makes a lot of noise. I guess he's on a lunch break right now."

She stood too. "Oh my. What is it?"

"It's like he's building a second house in his backyard that's attached to his main house. Does the village allow that? Is the main house not big enough for him? He lives alone!"

"Maybe he's putting in a bowling alley."

Scott laughed at that. "Maybe! Or a movie theater."

They returned to their seats.

"I'm sorry," Rachel said.

"For what?"

"That I didn't tell you about their affair. I probably should have."

"No, I can understand why you wouldn't. It wasn't your place to do that."

"I would hope that you'd have told me if the situation was reversed."

"Yeah. Maybe. I don't know."

"I didn't do anything about the affair because John and I . . . well, we didn't have . . . a proper marriage for years."

"Really? The same is true with Marie and me. I may not have known about the affair, but I always suspected she kept secrets from me."

"That's what it's all about, isn't it? Secrets? John had plenty of secrets."

More silence.

"You want more coffee?"

"No, thanks. Scott . . . "

"Yeah?"

"If it turns out that Marie and John were . . . killed . . . by a third party, who do you think might have done it? Would you have any kind of clue?"

"No. I've thought about that too. I know *I* didn't do it!"

She emitted a single laugh. "Well, I didn't either."

"I believe you."

"I believe you too."

"It probably has something to do with all that PPE that was in the house. The robbery at your husband's business. Don't you think?"

She nodded.

"What kind of plot were they involved in?" he asked rhetorically.

"I think John was mixed up in some things that were over his head."

Scott nodded with exaggeration. "I should think so!"

"I trust the police—or the FBI—will figure it out." She slapped her palms on the table. "I'd better collect my son from downstairs and get out of your hair."

"You're not in my hair."

She shook her head. "We should go. It . . . it wouldn't look good for me to be seen here. You know how it is."

"At least the camera crews are gone."

"Thank God. They were in front of my house all day yesterday."

"Look," Scott said. "Maybe we should exchange phone numbers? Would you want to keep in touch? Compare notes going forward? We could text each other?"

"I'd like that."

He fetched a notepad, and she gave him both an email address and her cell phone number, and he did the same for her. Then Scott walked her to the foyer. She called down the stairs, "Thomas! We're leaving!"

They heard the TV shut off. The boy appeared and ascended to their level. "I was watching the governor's briefing on the coronavirus."

Scott looked at Rachel with astonishment before turning to Thomas. "*That's* what you were watching? No Marvel superhero movies or anything like that?"

"Nah. I've seen all those. I'm interested in what's going on in our community," Thomas answered.

Rachel laughed as Scott shook his head. "Thanks for the coffee."

"You're welcome." He opened the door and they stepped out. Once they were six feet away, Rachel removed her mask and said, "The moon is in Pisces. It means we can have great sensitivity and perceptiveness of our surroundings. You may feel insecure, but we should wait and see what happens." She gave him a warm smile. "Thanks again."

Scott removed his mask. "You're quite welcome."

Was it his imagination, or did she linger on the porch longer than was needed? He could swear there was something in her eyes that beckoned to him, as if she were telling him that they should see more of each other. And the whole astrology thing . . . what was *that* all about?

He finally shut the door as Rachel and Thomas turned and tra-versed the short path from the porch steps to the empty driveway.

Scott could feel his heart thumping.

What the hell just happened?

18

I believe humans are born with the capability of working and playing well with others, being smart about science and politics, and coexisting peacefully. The problem is that humans make mistakes. They're fallible, they take too many gambles, they're greedy, and too often they just don't think. Human beings are the most self-destructive creatures on the planet.

I'm not sure why, but I'm reminded of an old movie I saw back in the day. The premise was that in the future, humans are the savages and apes have ascended to be the dominant species on the earth. I remember thinking it was good entertainment but total nonsense.

Now I'm not so sure that it isn't beyond the realm of possibility.

Oh, sorry for the tangent. I've been known to go off on them every now and then. I suppose I should have stated the disclaimer upfront, but I forgot. Opinions are mine and mine alone. The author and publisher of this book accept no responsibility for any viewpoints expressed by the commentator. To wit, ergo, de facto, caveat emptor, and a hey-nonny-nonny-and-a-ha-cha-cha!

Friday, May 15, 2020

3:30 p.m.

Seth Schoenberg wiped the sweat off his face with the bottom half of his old and faded *Rise of the Planet of the Apes* T-shirt, and removed the grass catcher bag from the lawn mower. He opened the large paper recycling bag and dumped the cut grass into it. The Hatcher lawn had sorely needed mowing. Seth knew he probably should have begun the summer's work at least two weeks earlier, but it didn't happen. The tall grass in the lawn had begun to seed. Mr. Hatcher had phoned him to say, "If you still want the job, you'd better come do it. It's becoming a jungle out there!" Having nothing better to do, Seth agreed. He rolled his own family's mower across the street and worked on both the front and back yards for an hour.

Now he was done.

Scott Hatcher stepped outside his front door, pulling on his mask. "Looks great, Seth! Thank you!" He held up a twenty-dollar bill and a five. "I'll just place this here on the steps under the flowerpot so it doesn't blow away."

"Thanks, Mr. Hatcher!" Seth called out.

"You need any water?"

"Nah, I'll get some at home. Thanks, though."

Scott went back inside, and Seth finished up by dragging the full recycling bag to the side of the house. Mr. Hatcher would take care of placing it on the curb on the next trash pickup day. Seth rolled the lawn mower onto the sidewalk and prepared to cross the street as the mail truck glided by and stopped in front of the Hatcher mailbox. Seth said hello to the postman and received a friendly reply.

Life goes on, Seth thought, rolling the mower across the street toward his house.

Keeping busy had helped alleviate the painful feelings of guilt Seth had been experiencing since the fire. Nights were particularly bad. Several times he had sat up in bed with tears rolling down his face. He prayed to God to forgive him, he paced his room, he surfed the internet for sites that offered advice, and he waited for the sun to rise. Seth usually felt better during daylight hours, but he wasn't sure how long he was going to be able to live with the remorse.

If only he could tell someone . . .

He hadn't spoken to Don since that night. Don had sent a couple of texts wanting to know if they could get together, but Seth merely replied, "Can't." Seth had no desire to hang out with Don anymore. He'd had enough of Don's bullying, nihilism, and politics that were the antithesis of his own. The way Don treated Thomas Bergman was especially mean. While Thomas was not a particularly *close* friend of Seth's, he'd known the kid since the Bergmans had moved in next door, he *had* been Thomas's babysitter for a short time, and he had enjoyed playing games online with his neighbor for years. Yes, Thomas was a strange boy. The clothes he wore were incredibly dorky, he sometimes spoke as if he were a robot, and he displayed an air of superiority that could be annoying. But Seth, who had no siblings, felt oddly protective of Thomas.

Inside the house, Seth stopped in the kitchen to drink a full glass of cold water. He was about to run upstairs and hit the shower, until he noticed his father sitting alone in the dining room without his laptop and quietly staring at the wall.

"Dad?"

When his father didn't answer, Seth moved closer behind him. "Dad?"

"Huh?" Mitch jumped a little and sat up. He turned. "Yes? Oh, Seth. My God, you look like you've taken a shower with your clothes on. Take those sweaty things off."

"I just mowed Mr. Hatcher's lawn."

"Oh? How is he doing? Did you speak to him?"

"Just a little." He went around the table so that his father wouldn't have to turn his head to talk. "He seems okay. I don't know, really."

Mitch shook his head. "Terrible thing that happened. He must feel so . . . I don't know . . . betrayed. And Ms. Bergman too. She must feel awful. Did you see all the news trucks yesterday?"

"Yeah. They're not here today, though."

"That's good. I was afraid they'd try to grab and interview any neighbor they saw outside."

"What are you doing? How come you're sitting in here?"

Mitch sighed. "Oh, I don't know. Just didn't feel like working. Taking a break." He creased his brow and looked directly at his son. "To tell you the truth, I'm worried about your mother. She had to go to the hospital really early this morning."

"I heard the garage door open."

"Sorry if it woke you."

Seth shrugged. "Doesn't matter. I was awake."

"You're not sleeping well?"

"Who is?"

Mitch laughed a little. "Everybody's on edge. Everyone I talk to feels as if we're all on a precipice. It's a test for the human race, you know."

"Who's in charge of the test, Dad?"

Mitch smiled wryly. "We don't go to temple very often, do we? Well, not as much as we probably should. You know, our synagogue is doing some of those online services. Maybe we should join in tonight. It's Shabbat."

"When does Mom come home?"

Mitch shook his head. "Not sure. It's a double shift." He took a breath. "She told me that she was exposed to Covid in a bad way yesterday. She had her mask off, and a patient was behind her, a nurse was helping him walk in the hallway. He coughed, and she said she felt the spittle on the back of her neck. She immediately went and washed off, but she said there is absolutely no way the doctors and nurses and aides can be totally safe. The hospital is *packed* with patients. They insist she still has to work and can't quarantine. She's deathly afraid she'll get it. I am too."

Seth felt a pang of anxiety bubble in his chest. Mixed with the guilt that was already residing there, the emotion grew until he uttered an involuntary sob.

"Try not to worry. I know it's hard. If you feel like crying, it's okay. I've cried."

Seth just nodded.

Dad, I burned down the Wilkins house.

He didn't say it aloud. Instead, he muttered, "I'm going to take a shower," and went upstairs.

19

Okay, folks, it's time to get serious and advance the story with some revelations. I'm just going to keep my mouth shut for a while and allow events to unfold. Grab a glass of your beverage of choice and settle in. Things are about to get interesting.

Friday, May 15, 2020
5:30 p.m.

Scott opened his fridge and pondered what he could fix for dinner. His appetite had been erratic since Monday. One day he couldn't eat, but the following day he was able to get some food down and be satisfied. The next day he was back to having a dead stomach. Nothing appealed to him. Today was like that. He knew he should try to eat something to keep up his strength, but he had no idea what sounded good.

Was this grief?

He was well aware that he had not exhibited the kind of sorrow and tears that should have been a natural reaction when one has lost a spouse. Yes, he was sad and had cried a little in private. The shock of learning what had happened to Marie was indeed palpable. And yet, Scott wasn't "going to pieces," which was something a normal person might be expected to do.

Maybe I'm not normal.

For most of the day he had been questioning his relationship with Marie and examining moments in their life together that might have served as turning points. There were many. The sex-filled trip to Hawaii where he had proposed. The wedding in 2003, which was held at the Chicago Botanical Gardens. Brian's birth in 2004. The mess with Diana Keyes. Brian's death. Marie's addiction to tranquilizers, and her struggle to break free of them. Brian's death. His own addiction to alcohol, and his struggle to sneak bottles into the house after being given an ultimatum. Marie selling her first house. Brian's death. The sale of his first novel, which had taken three years to write and three weeks to disappear from Barnes and Noble. The arguing. The humiliation. Brian's death.

Was he upset that Marie was gone? Yes, of course. But was he upset *enough*? How does one measure that? Would the police notice? Was he supposed to be acting like a wreck? He wasn't. Just that morning, he'd had the widow of the man who had been having an affair with Marie, and who had died with Marie, over for coffee. Who does that?

Scott closed the refrigerator door and went to the pantry. Not much there to get him salivating either. Maybe a bowl of cereal would suffice. He reached for a box of Cheerios that were likely stale—and the doorbell rang.

He closed the pantry and made his way to the front door, grabbing his mask off the little table and putting it on as he opened the door.

Uh-oh. I should have looked through the peephole first.

It was the guy with the black truck. No mask.

"Oh, hello, sir, it's me again," the man said. "Fyodor Volkov. You remember I came by earlier in the week?"

"What do you want?" Scott asked with no hint of friendliness.

"May I come in and speak with you? Some business to discuss, please."

"No. I don't know if you've heard, but my wife is dead. I don't know what kind of business you had with her, but it's probably over. Have a nice day."

He started to close the door, but Volkov moved forward to touch the storm door. "Wait! Yes, I know about Marie, I am sorry!"

Scott hesitated. "Move back, please."

"Did she leave an envelope for me?"

"What?"

"Marie Hatcher—she surely left an envelope of some kind for me?"

"What? No, she didn't. I don't know what you're talking about. The house next door is obviously not for sale anymore, and now it's a crime scene. Whatever realty business she had with you, it's over. Now I'd like to be left alone, sir. Goodbye."

Volkov pointed a finger at him and appeared quite agitated. "Do not close the door!"

"Go away or I'll call the police."

Volkov quickly opened the storm door and moved to come into the house anyway. Scott pushed the front door to shut it, but Volkov pressed his body hard against it, keeping it ajar.

"What are you doing?" Scott yelled. "Get away!"

"I must talk to you!"

The man was strong. Scott couldn't shove the door closed. It was a stalemate for a few seconds, and then, inexplicably, Volkov began to cough. His body broke away from the door, and he gasped for breath.

Scott backed away, horrified. "Are you sick? Do you have the virus?"

Volkov shook his head. He coughed again and took a deep breath. "Is asthma. I promise. Is asthma. I am sorry."

"You tried to force your way into my house!"

"No, no, I'm . . . I apologize. I . . . your wife . . . left envelope . . . "

"No, she didn't." Scott looked past Volkov to the street, where a Lincoln Grove police car was pulling up in front of his house against the curb. "Oh, look, the police are here, just in time."

Volkov turned to see them and made a face of consternation. "I am sorry to bother you. Forgive me," he said as he left the porch and went quickly to his truck, which was parked in the driveway. As he started to back out into the street, Detective Dante and Officer Sandrich exited their vehicle and began to walk up to the house across the lawn.

Scott stood in the open doorway.

"Who was that?" Dante asked through her mask as she ascended the few steps to the porch.

"Some guy who lives nearby. He tried to come in my house!"

"He did?"

"He said he had some realty business with Marie. He kept saying something about an envelope that Marie might have left for him."

Dante looked at Sandrich. He raised his eyebrows. "Interesting," Dante said to Scott. "May we come in? We have something to discuss."

"Sure."

Once they were in their usual positions in the kitchen, Scott asked, "Do you know that man or his business? Volkov Trucking?"

Dante shook her head. "We don't know every business in Lincoln Grove."

"I think he lives near Dodge Park on one of those streets over there. He came by the other night . . . when was it? Monday? I've lost all track of the days. Yeah, I think it was Monday night. He came to the door looking for Marie. He said she was showing him houses. He even asked about the one next door. It was still standing then. He said that she'd told him about it, and he wanted to view it."

"And you don't know anything about that?" Dante asked.

"No. And Marie usually told me when she had a new prospective buyer she was working with."

"What was his name?'

"Volkov. I . . . now I can't remember his first name. He said it. Something Russian or Eastern European."

"We can look up Volkov Trucking," Sandrich said. "We'll find out who he is."

"Thanks."

Dante and Sandrich then looked at each other and back at Scott.

"Should I sit down?" he asked.

"That might be a good idea," Dante answered.

He did so, but they remained standing.

"Mr. Hatcher, the coroner has completed his work, and we have the FBI in town to look at the case," Dante said.

"Uh-huh?"

"Special Agent Eugene Carlson. He was examining the evidence for most of the day. He and the coroner put their heads together, and we now have some news. First of all, I'm sorry to say that the victims in the house were indeed your wife and John Bergman. Their dental records confirm both."

Scott slumped in his chair. "I . . . I was expecting that."

"You were?" Sandrich asked.

"Well, you guys had more or less confirmed it already. You said John Bergman's BMW was in the garage of the Wilkins house. What more proof do you need?" When they didn't respond, he said, "It doesn't make it any easier, though."

"No, I suppose not," Dante admitted.

"What else?"

"There's a question as to whether the crime scene was staged prior to the fire. Unfortunately, the condition of the scene makes it near impossible to determine for certain. We hope the FBI will have the means to shed some light on this conundrum. It could very well have been a murder-suicide, or a double suicide, which is what it looked like. It's also possible that Marie and John were murdered by a third party. If that is the case, then we're not certain what the sequence of events was. Both were shot in the head with John's handgun, a Smith & Wesson. Ms. Bergman has identified the gun as belonging to him. John was shot twice in the head, your wife only once. The gun was in John's hand. We believe their deaths occurred quite some time prior to the fire. The coroner cannot determine the time of their deaths because of the condition of the bodies. We can only guess. Since your wife and Mr. Bergman both disappeared last Sunday night, it's reasonable to believe that the crime occurred in the hours before daylight Monday morning. You testified that you had gone to bed before your wife on Sunday night. She must have left your home and met Mr. Bergman in the house next door after you were asleep. What exactly happened next, we don't know."

Scott's mouth was open as he gazed at the two police officers. It was too mind boggling to fathom.

"Mr. Hatcher?" Dante asked.

"I . . . I don't know what to say." He trembled with a slight sob, and then caught his breath. He swallowed and cocked his head. "Hold on. I don't understand. How does the fire fit in? The arson. If someone killed them on Sunday night, why would he burn them up on Tuesday night? Why wait two days?"

"We don't know," Sandrich answered. "That's the big hitch in the third-party murder theory. It's quite possible those two crimes were committed by different perpetrators."

"But it makes no sense!" Scott said. "I'm a *writer*, and this makes no sense!"

"Scott," Dante said, "We're going to need you to come in again tomorrow to speak with Agent Carlson. It'll be another video interview, like before. He's going to want to hear your story from you directly. He may have additional questions. You can bring an attorney if you wish. Depending on how the interview goes, you may be subject to a search warrant for your house, your car, your computer, and, well, anything we deem necessary."

Scott felt a surge of apprehension in his chest. "You think I'm a suspect?"

Dante held up a hand. "It's routine. You know we have to look at everything."

"Is the same thing happening to Rachel Bergman? Is she being interviewed by the FBI too?"

"We can't comment on that."

"I suppose you'll be talking to all the neighbors now."

"Scott, it's—"

"—routine, yeah, I know."

"Can you be at the station at ten o'clock?"

Scott nodded. He felt deflated and defeated. Was he now going to have to prove his innocence? Was he going to have to pay attorney Harry Edmonds the retainer that his pal Rob had mentioned? It was beginning to look that way.

"If you've done nothing wrong, Scott," Dante said, "then you have nothing to worry about."

"Yeah, well, I've done nothing wrong, but I'm still worried. It's one thing to lose a spouse and lose her *in this way*, and then have to go through the horror of realizing you're a suspect in a murder."

"Don't think of it that way. We don't know if it's a murder. We're just questioning you. Gathering all the facts. I'm sure you know this, but you are not to leave town. Please stay put."

Scott almost laughed. "I'm not going anywhere. We're in the middle of a pandemic."

"See you tomorrow, Mr. Hatcher," Sandrich said, and the two officers left the house.

Scott now knew what his dinner would be. He went to the pantry, grabbed a bottle of vodka, and set it on the table. He took a glass from a cabinet, filled it with ice from the fridge dispenser, and sat.

He then dialed the number for Harry Edmonds.

20

A May rain can be lovely in the Chicago area when it's just a brief downpour in the middle of warm, bright sunshine. Isn't it strange how that sometimes happens? It'll be sunny one minute, and suddenly there are some clouds in the sky and you get a little rain—but the sun is still shining! Then, just as magically, the rain stops and the sun continues to cast its beams over the freshly dewed grass and pavements. It's almost as if the earth needed its sweat washed away and Nature obliged. Then, everything smells all fresh and clean. Weird, huh? I'm no weatherman, so don't ask me to explain how it works. But I like it.

Nature has a mind and will of her own, doesn't she? Nature doesn't give a hoot in hell about what we humans are doing on the planet. She doesn't care if we have plans for an outdoor wedding, a vacation flight across the country, a Super Bowl, or a beach party. If she wants to rain or snow or throw us a hurricane or tornado, she's going to do it. Weather can ruin many a well-intentioned event if it's supposed to be held outside.

Which brings up a question . . . Is the coronavirus a thing of Nature? Does it fall in her jurisdiction? It's arguable, but I don't think so. It's not under her control. Nature pays it no mind. The weather is going to be whatever Nature decides it is on a given day, regardless of whether the tiny, insignificant humans on the earth are happy and playing . . . or sick and dying.

One thing's for sure. The rain isn't going to wash away the virus.

Saturday, May 16, 2020
12:10 p.m.

Seth Schoenberg rolled his bicycle out of the garage and over a puddle of water that always seemed to collect in a slight dip in their driveway. He had meant to get out of the house an hour earlier, just after he'd gotten out of bed. The sun was shining, and the day promised to be beautiful. He threw on yesterday's clothes, went outside . . . and it was raining! One of those strange phenomena was happening when the sun shone as the sky poured. Seth went back in and waited it out. Now being outside was even better. He *loved* to ride his bike after a rain. The sound the tires made zipping through a puddle was music to his ears, and the smell in the air was certainly what it might be like in heaven.

He rode toward Dodge Park. The wind rushing against his face did wonders to alleviate the continuing tidal wave of guilt that coursed through the middle of his torso on a near-constant basis. Bedtime and the hours between midnight and six were torture. His sleep was erratic and a source of additional anxiety. He'd read somewhere that his health could be severely compromised without a good night's sleep, and the coronavirus *loved* that shit. He was afraid that his immune system, even at sixteen years old, was weak and a sure target for the disease. Sometimes he felt woozy, or his throat was scratchy, or he had aches and pains . . . all supposed symptoms of Covid. These things freaked him out. Seth would spend way too much time online reading about symptoms, which did more to increase his anxiety level than his lack of sleep.

Luckily, he could get outside and ride a bike. It was a miracle cure. He felt *great* now, and he wished he could take off cross country on the bicycle. To him, Lincoln Grove had become a claustrophobic, oppressive corner of the world, and Seth would give anything just to go somewhere else.

Hell, I'd even go back to school.

Seth spent the next half hour riding through the park and up and down the side streets around it. Very few people were out and about aside from the occasional sightings of yard workers, dog walkers, and another kid or two playing in their own yard.

It was as if the world had died and only a small number of survivors were left.

Seth circled the park and then headed back. Instead of turning right toward Marigold Way, he went left to speed down Dodge Lane. He slowed, though, when he saw the black truck with the words "Volkov Trucking" painted on the side. It was parked in the middle of the block on the north side of the street between houses 502 and 504.

This was the truck Thomas Bergman had told him about. The guy who owned it was supposedly a mobster. Was it true?

What was the truck doing on Dodge Lane? He knew that whoever owned the truck lived on one of the streets that spun off the park. He'd seen it parked in front of a house. What was the name of that street? Hayden? Hordern? No . . . Herndon. That was it. Herndon Lane.

Seth was about to ride by until he saw the truck's owner come around the front of the vehicle to the driver's side. Volkov himself. He must have been in front of the truck, where Seth couldn't see him. Then another figure appeared on the street. Seth came to a full stop, and then he quickly pulled over to the side of the road, made a U-turn, and rode back toward the park.

Don Trainer, on his bicycle, had turned onto Dodge Lane from Temple at the end of the block and was riding toward Seth.

Seth didn't want to be seen, but something held him back. He slowed when he got to the curve and turned his head to look. Don had just passed Volkov and waved at him. Volkov waved in return and then got into the truck, started it, and drove off toward Temple Avenue. Don kept riding toward him.

It was too late for Seth to get away. Don had already seen him, so Seth stayed put.

"Hey!" Don called.

Seth raised a hand.

Don rode up to him. "What are you doing here?"

"Just out riding." Seth couldn't help himself. He pointed toward the end of Dodge Lane, where the truck was turning right onto Temple. "Do you know that guy?"

"What guy?"

"The Volkov Trucking guy."

"Oh, him. Not really. I met him yesterday."

"Why were you waving at him?"

Don frowned. "Why do you care?"

"I was just curious."

"I don't know, I might start working for him. I'm looking for a summer job. I saw the truck yesterday over on his street, whatever it is, by the park. I thought, what the hell, so I stopped and asked him if he needs any help with anything. I said I could do deliveries or work in his warehouse or something until I can get a commercial driving license. Then I can be a trucker!"

"What did he say?"

Don shrugged. "He said maybe. He didn't need anyone. I wanted to ask him about it again just now, just to show him I'm still interested, but I didn't get the chance. He drove away. I wonder what he was doing here."

Seth nodded. "Is it safe?"

"What do you mean?"

"From the virus. Do you wear a mask if you work in the warehouse?"

"I don't know! Who cares? It's a *job*. I'd make some money! It's probably not going to work out anyway. Jesus."

Seth hesitated, then said, "He doesn't seem very nice."

Don made an ugly face. "What are you talking about?"

"I've heard that guy is, like, a gangster. He works for a mob."

"What? You're nuts, Seth. Where did you hear that?"

Seth naturally didn't want to reveal his source. "I don't know. I don't remember."

Don rolled his eyes. "Yeah, right. You don't know shit. And you hang out with creepy idiots. See you around."

With that, Don rode away.

Seth watched him go, realizing that they'd been within six feet of each other without masks.

Shit.

There was nothing he could do about it now.

Seth wondered if Don had any feelings of guilt regarding the Wilkins house.

Nope, probably not.

He didn't think Don was capable of feeling guilt.

He began to pedal around the curve and saw Scott Hatcher power walking toward the park.

"Hi, Mr. Hatcher!" he called and waved.

The man waved back and kept walking.

Seth rode on home. The encounter with his former friend Don, which is how Seth now thought of him, had dampened the euphoria he'd felt just a little while earlier.

21

We'll just shift the focus over to Scott at this point. No need to complicate things. I could have shown you Scott's interview in the police station with FBI Special Agent Carlson, but those G-Men are so secretive! Ha ha, not really, I'm just messing with you. The following scene neatly summarizes it, and Lord knows I don't want to be repetitive!

Saturday, May 16, 2020

1:05 p.m.

Scott waved to Seth Schoenberg as the kid rode by on his bicycle and hollered, "Hi, Mr. Hatcher!" Scott liked Seth and thought he was a good kid, but why did he have to hang around that awful Don Trainer, who had ridden by a minute or so earlier *without* waving?

Out for his first walk in days, Scott felt better than he had in a while. Since Wednesday he had not wanted to show his face in the neighborhood. Too many whispers and pointing and gossip. It was uncomfortable. Even today as he power walked down Marigold Way toward the curve, David Woo just looked at him. No wave and no "Hello. Hello." Nothing. Just a stare. *There goes the cuckold and possible murderer*, the man must be thinking. Scott figured, though, that if he didn't start getting out of the house again, then he never would.

The fresh after-rain air was lovely. It wasn't too hot yet, but the sun was shining, and the grass and puddles glistened in reflection. The park would be wet, but not the footpaths. As he got to the conduit between the houses on the curve that led to the park, Scott thought back a few hours to his meeting with the FBI agent.

It had taken place in the same conference room at police head-quarters. Only Special Agent Eugene Carlson and Scott's attorney were in the room with him. However, there was a large dark rect-angular window behind Carlson in the space, and Scott was certain that it was a one-way glass. He'd seen it a million times before in movies and television shows. Other law enforcement people were assuredly behind the glass, listening to and watching the interview. He suspected Detective Dante and Officer Sandrich were back there.

The attorney, Harry Edmonds, had met him at the station on time. It was their first face-to-face meeting. Edmonds was in his fifties, had a head of longish white hair, and was fit and handsome. He exuded wealth too. Even on a Saturday morning, Edmonds was dressed in a sharp summer suit that made him look like a model from *GQ*. Scott had arranged to meet with him twenty minutes prior to the scheduled interview so that they could go over the retainer agreement. Scott had written him a check for $10,000, which was in no way an easy thing for him to do. He'd had to move some money around from savings and retirement to pad his checking account. Edmonds would bill by the hour, of course, starting that morning. Scott hoped there wouldn't be too many more interviews after this one, or else that $10,000 would be eaten up quickly.

Edmonds seemed to be a nice enough guy. He wore a cloth mask that matched his suit, and Scott and Edmonds greeted each other by bumping elbows. They sat in the lobby to discuss terms in seats a few feet apart, a chair with a "please do not sit" sign between them. Their conversation went smoothly, and then Officer Sandrich called them into the conference room.

Agent Carlson was a young man, in his late thirties at the most. He, too, was decked out in a standard FBI uniform—a dark suit, a mask to match, and crewcut. Scott thought the man probably wore sunglasses everywhere he went outdoors . . . just because.

The interview had gone well, although Scott felt that Carlson had treated him with malevolent suspicion. The agent was especially intent on asking about Marie's finances and if she had any other accounts besides the ones Scott had indicated. He answered the same questions about his own movements on the weekend prior to Marie's disappearance, and everything he could remember about hers. He repeated the embarrassing revelations about his fling with Diana Keyes, and his nagging beliefs that Marie had been cheating as well over the years. He reiterated his not knowing anything about John Bergman.

Carlson asked Scott point-blank if he had anything to do with Marie's disappearance. He answered, "No." He was then asked if he was involved in the arson that burned down 507 Marigold Way. Again, Scott replied no. Then came the question Scott had specifically been expecting. "Can you verify your whereabouts on both Sunday and Tuesday nights?"

Ah, the old alibi quagmire. Scott had no alibi for either night and he said so. There was a pandemic going on. He wasn't going anywhere. He was staying at home. Social distancing. Scott asked if perhaps the agent could check with his phone carrier and confirm that his device was at home at those times. Or look at his laptop browser history for date and time stamps. The agent made a sour face and wrote down some notes. He didn't say whether he believed Scott or not.

Not once did Harry Edmonds make a comment or advise Scott not to answer something. Afterward, Edmonds told him that the interview had been quite routine. Unless the police found something incriminating against him, then Scott probably had nothing to worry about. He should cooperate with any search warrants. "If you ever have a question or concern, don't hesitate to call my cell number. Now that you're a client, you have 24/7 access to me." Good to know. The only lawyer he'd ever had that much communication with dealt with intellectual property contracts.

The whole thing had taken a little over an hour. Interestingly, when Scott had first arrived at the station to meet Edmonds, Thomas Bergman was sitting alone in the lobby. His mother was being interviewed. Scott had sat apart from Thomas and exchanged small talk. A masked Rachel had emerged from the "Authorized Personnel Only" door to collect her son. She had greeted Scott with a "Hello" and an eye roll that indicated, *Whew, it's a relief to get that over with!*

Now, out for his walk, Scott put all that behind him. He circled the park twice, then went up and back one of the side streets. He began his return to Marigold Way and passed the intersection of the park and Herndon Lane. The black truck with "Volkov Trucking" painted on its side sat in a driveway in front of the third house from the corner.

Right. I remember now. That's where that guy lives.

Scott had seen the truck before in that spot. He wondered why Volkov wanted to move to a new house. Or did he really? It was all very strange.

As Scott returned around the curve to Marigold Way, he noticed Rachel Bergman out in front of her home, collecting items from her mailbox. He kept walking on her side of the street and waved when she looked up at him. She remained standing at the end of her driveway and waited for him to approach. He stood a respectful distance away.

"How did it go for you this morning?" she asked.

"All right. How about you?"

She shrugged. "Same old, same old. All the same questions. He was a little more intimidating than Detective Dante."

"I agree with you there!"

"But I take it you survived? They didn't arrest you and haul you away in handcuffs, obviously."

Scott laughed. "Not yet. Have you given up on selling your masks?"

She looked doubtful. "I'm not going to sit out here exposed to the world for a while. The news trucks the other day really freaked me out."

"I don't blame you. That was scary."

There was a moment of feet shuffling, and then Rachel asked, "Would . . . would you like to come in for a cup of coffee? My turn, this time."

Scott hesitated, then scanned the neighborhood. David Woo was no longer in front of his house. No one else could see them unless they were watching out a window. It seemed discreet enough.

"Okay," he said. "Thanks, although I'd probably prefer something cold to drink."

They walked to the house, and she let him in. He put on the face mask that he'd been carrying in his pocket, and she did the same when she got inside.

"I can make you iced coffee, if you like."

"That sounds great."

They passed through her foyer and into the kitchen. The layout was the same as Scott's house. "All these homes are exactly alike, aren't they?" he asked rhetorically.

"Pretty much," she said as she opened cabinets and started filling the kettle with water. She got a pitcher out of the refrigerator that was already filled with coffee and poured him a glass with ice dispensed from the fridge. "A lot of them flip-flop, you know, like mirror images. Then every three or so houses you get a different design. Number 510 next door has three bedroom windows in the front instead of two."

Thomas appeared at the top of the stairs leading down to their family room. "I thought I heard someone."

"Say hello to Mr. Hatcher, Thomas," Rachel said.

"Hello, Mr. Hatcher."

"Hi, Thomas. How are you?"

"Good. I'm playing an old *Donkey Kong* game downstairs on a PlayStation. It's *really* old."

"I may have played that in my lifetime."

"You know what, Mr. Hatcher?"

"What's that, Thomas?"

"I like that my name begins with the letter that's right after the first letter of *your* first name."

Scott blinked, not quite comprehending.

"You know," Thomas explained. "Your first name begins with *S*, and my name begins with *T*!"

"So they do. Huh!" Scott smiled.

Thomas nodded. "I just thought that was interesting. Okay, I'll leave the two adults to talk and I'll go back to my game." With that, he was gone.

Scott chuckled a little and sat at the kitchen table. There was a pile of pamphlets for grief counseling, many of them familiar to Scott.

"I see we have the same reading habits," he said, indicating the literature.

Rachel allowed herself a slight laugh. "Yeah. Do they do you any good?"

"I haven't touched them."

"Me neither. How . . . how are you holding up?"

She remained standing by the counter. He couldn't help but look her up and down. She wore tight blue jeans and a T-shirt with the Rolling Stones logo of the mouth and tongue on it. She appeared much younger than she really was.

"Oh, I'm doing all right, I guess. It's hard, you know."

"Yeah. I know." He sipped the drink. "This is great iced coffee."

"Thanks." She sat across from him with her cup of hot brew. "I don't mind telling you. John and I were probably going to get a divorce. There is no love lost between him and me. I'm sorry he's dead, you know, but I'm also furious with him. I'm afraid my body is not allowing me to grieve as much as I probably should. It's just not inside here—" She patted her sternum. "—to feel much sorrow. Is that wrong?"

"I feel exactly the same way," he replied. "The same is true of Marie and me. We were just roommates in the same house. I mean, we were friends and we got along most of the time, but the intimacy was gone. I'm not feeling the grief either. I'm afraid it might look suspicious to the cops."

"That FBI agent asked me about my relationship with John. I told him the truth." She shrugged. "So sue me."

"The same thing happened at my interview. I don't think they can sue you. Maybe throw you in jail, but not sue you!"

That broke the ice more, and they laughed together.

"They're also digging into my private stuff," she said. "My bank records, my emails, my texts."

"Mine too."

"I don't mind telling you. I think John was involved in that robbery at his warehouse. The brass at Cassette Labs have hired their own investigator, and he wants to talk to me too. It makes sense. John had the security codes for the building. He ended up dead where the stolen goods were hidden. He probably did it."

"And it appears Marie was in on it too. I suppose it was her idea to supply the empty house to store the stuff in."

"But did somebody kill them? And why? Or did they commit suicide together?"

"I'm pretty sure the cops are leaning toward the latter, but there's that possibility of a third-party killer. How was John shot twice? I have no idea," Scott said. "And if it's that, why burn the house down two days later? Makes no sense to me."

They sat without speaking for a minute.

"Are you from here?" Rachel asked.

"Yes. I grew up in Chicago. I went to college in New York, though. I thought I wanted to be an actor, so I got into Juilliard. That didn't work out, so I moved to Hollywood and was there for some time and started writing. I met Marie there—she's from Chicago, too, but was going to college at UCLA—and eventually we came back here in 2004. She hated LA."

"Why was she there?"

"She graduated in 2002 and got a job in retail. It wasn't long before she had a head-honcho job with Guess. She lost it, though, and she wanted to come back to the Midwest. Then she got into real estate. What about you?"

"I'm from Santa Fe, New Mexico. There's not a huge Jewish community there, but it's good enough. That's where I grew up. I spent some of my young adult years in Sedona. I guess that's where I got into New Age stuff, or whatever you want to call it."

Somehow that didn't surprise Scott.

"I met my first husband, Sebastian, in Sedona," she continued, "and that's where Sarah was born. He died in a freak accident, though, and I went to Boulder, Colorado. I married Thomas's father, Franklin, there. Then he got a job in the Chicago area, so we moved to Evanston. But things went south. Franklin was a mean drunk. We divorced rather quickly, and he went east. I think he's in Delaware. Eventually I met John. Things were pretty good for a while. We moved out here to Lincoln Grove. John adopted Thomas, which is why he's got John's last name. But I guess John was more interested in being a crook and adulterer than an honest and faithful husband and father. I was done having children, and I think he also resented that. He wanted one from me. As a result, he and Thomas didn't get along. He was downright abusive. Not physically, but psychologically. He couldn't accept the fact that Thomas was . . . different. And Thomas would never call him 'Dad.' It was always 'Stepdad' or 'Stepfather.' That drove John a little nuts, and so they stopped relating to each other. I had many fights with John about that. And now, here we are!"

Scott decided he could tell Rachel about the millstone that had destroyed his marriage to Marie. "We had a son."

Rachel raised her eyebrows.

"His name was Brian. He contracted a rare brain cancer in 2009 when he was four. He passed away at the age of five, eleven years ago. I think that's what ultimately sent our marriage down the tubes. Nothing was the same after that."

"I understand. I'm so sorry. That's terrible."

"Thanks."

"I know of many couples who don't survive the death of a child. You poor thing. I can see the melancholy in your heart."

"My heart?"

"Yes." She smiled. "I can see it."

"That's quite a talent."

"I'm talented in a lot of things, Scott."

"I bet you are."

Her eyes subtly widened at that.

A few more seconds of silence passed. He looked at the watch on his left wrist. "I should be going before the neighbors start a new trending hashtag on Twitter about us."

That made her laugh. "Don't go because I said I could see what was in your heart. I'm just an old hippie, and I can say some strange things sometimes."

"I'm *not* a hippie, and I can say some strange things sometimes too!"

She placed a hand over his. Scott almost instinctively jerked it away because of social-distancing guidelines—no touching!—but the softness of her palm and fingers felt nice. He didn't move his hand.

Rachel gave it a gentle squeeze and he felt a spark of electricity.

"Would you . . . like to chat later this evening? On Zoom, or Skype, or FaceTime?" he asked.

She smiled broadly. "I'd like that."

22

The heart wants what it wants.

At least that's what poets and romanticists have led us to believe over the centuries. They've given us the impression that love generates in the heart, right? But does it? What is it about the heart that is the Love Generator?

I'll bet you'll say it's because we feel it in our chests. Whenever we have those first pangs of a new relationship with someone, we feel all wobbly and fuzzy in the upper chest, that space between the lungs and behind the sternum. By the same token, if we have what they call a "heartbreak," that is, a breakup or a fight with a loved one, we feel pain in the same spot. So, I suppose it's natural that human beings over the years have likened the emotions related to romance to the heart.

What if I told you, though, that it's really all in the *mind?*

When we are attracted to another person in, ahem, *that* way, the brain releases chemicals into our bloodstream called dopamine and oxytocin. These are *drugs,* folks, and we become addicted to them. The more intimate we become in a new relationship, the more wacko we get because of those drugs. Yes, dopamine and oxytocin produce physical effects—you know, heavy breathing, palpitations, flushing skin, and . . . ahem, *other* physical reactions. There's also a lot of adrenaline involved, and *that* affects the heart muscles too. So, yes, we do feel all these things in our chests, but it's because the brain is the instigator.

Heartache works the same way. When those drugs are cut off, we experience withdrawal. Withdrawal is painful. We feel those unpleasant feelings in our chest because the heart is suddenly deprived of those feel-good drugs, dopamine and oxytocin.

That brings us to the term "crime of passion." You know what that is. It's when someone does something bad because of the *withdrawal* of those chemical reactions that begin in the brain and are felt in the heart. Crimes of passion occur all the time, don't they? Unfortunately, the term somehow whitewashes and romanticizes the reality of an act that is likely violent and messy.

But I guess "crime of dopamine and oxytocin" doesn't sound as elegant.

Saturday, May 16, 2020
10:30 p.m.

For most of the day, Scott was thinking about Rachel Bergman. He couldn't get her out of his head. He couldn't understand it. They barely knew each other. The two times they'd had coffee together amounted to a little over an hour.

He was supposed to be in mourning, full of grief, and making final arrangements for his murdered wife. The coroner's office had earlier in the day released Marie's body to the funeral parlor that Scott had to hastily approve. A cremation was to take place tomorrow.

"Really, a cremation?" he'd asked the funeral director, Mr. Samuels. "She's *already* burned to a crisp!" Samuels was obviously shocked by the statement. Scott hadn't meant to sound tactless or make a sick joke. It was just the way his thought process worked.

Nevertheless, it was decided that cremation was the best way to go. There would be no service. No one was having in-person funerals. The urn would be placed in what was called a columbarium located in Lincoln Grove's only cemetery. Scott had informed Marie's sister and mother of his decisions. They weren't happy, but given the situation with Covid, they weren't in a position to argue. Neither of them wanted to travel to attend any kind of funeral anyway.

It had all been accomplished over the phone. Scott chose the urn, electronically signed forms, paid with a credit card, and he was done.

How did it make him feel?

Up to that point, he'd felt mostly numb. Scott had attributed this to shock, but now he wasn't so sure. There was no question that he would never in a million years wish harm on Marie. What happened to her was truly horrible. He felt terrible about that. It was the sequence of events leading up to it that stuck in Scott's craw, and he was already beginning to look back at the marriage with a kind of contempt he never knew was bubbling inside of him.

He had come close to sliding into a deep depression that afternoon. Scott pulled out the vodka and had one glass with ice. It was tempting to keep going and get ridiculously drunk again. He was afraid, though, that he might become destructive and break some of Marie's things.

Then he remembered the upcoming Zoom date with Rachel, and that made all the difference. She took over his thoughts, and he felt better. By dinnertime, Scott had put the unpleasantness with the funeral home behind him.

Am I a bad person?

Scott even looked in the bathroom mirror and asked the question aloud to himself.

"Society" would think so. "That Scott Hatcher—his wife isn't even cold in the ground, and he's already got designs on someone else!"

Yes, there were twinges of guilt brewing inside, but he also had that fuzzy warm feeling in his chest that he never thought he'd experience again. It was the sensation of *infatuation*. He knew intellectually that these emotions were caused by biochemistry. Hormones, or whatever they were. The wonder of it was that it felt *good*. Naturally, his reaction was to move toward the source of that pleasure.

Hence, he allowed visions of Rachel Bergman to swim in his brain.

During the evening hours, he debated when to set the Zoom meeting and send the invitation. Was eight o'clock too early? Was eleven too late? Scott had no idea what time Rachel usually got ready to go to bed. He finally settled on ten thirty and sent her the Zoom link. He guessed that Rachel's son would maybe be out of her hair then, so she could have some privacy.

He had another glass of vodka shortly before the call to loosen him up and ease his nervousness. Scott sat in the kitchen, signed on to Zoom, and waited for her to show up.

Rachel was only one minute late.

Scott let her into the meeting, and her lovely features occupied one-half of the gallery view of the Zoom interface.

"Hi there!" he said.

She smiled. "Hello!"

"All good to chat? I hope it's not too late for you?"

"Oh, no, I don't go to bed until around midnight these days. Are you having trouble sleeping too?"

"I think we all are. With all the crap that's going on . . . "

He noted that she had a glass of red wine and was sipping it. Scott held up his glass of vodka. "I see we both came with appropriate props. Cheers."

"Cheers. Can't do without this prop at night. So, what did you do all day?"

He told her about dealing with the funeral home and his plans for Sunday. "I'm not looking forward to it."

"I still have to make all those arrangements," she said. "Part of me just wants to forget that he's lying in the morgue. What's left of him isn't my husband. That sounds so crass. I'm sorry."

"No. I understand. Believe me, I understand."

"I imagine I'll go the cremation route too."

Scott looked past her at the room she was in. "Where are you?"

"Oh, this is the master bedroom. My bedroom." She moved over slightly to reveal the end of a king-sized four-poster bed. "Now, I don't know if you can see the mess. I've been going through John's clothes, his chest of drawers, and other places where he might have hidden something."

Scott did see piles of clothing on the floor in the dim lighting behind her. "Why are you doing that?"

"Well, Scott, think about it. John must have stolen that stuff from his warehouse for *money*. If that's so, then where is it? What did he get out of the crime? So far, I can't find any trace of new money deposited into our accounts."

"Maybe he had an account somewhere that he didn't tell you about."

"That's what I'm thinking."

"Or maybe he hadn't been paid yet. Remember, the stuff was just sitting there in the house. Maybe he wasn't going to get paid until after it had been transported to wherever it was ultimately going."

She nodded. "That's a possibility too."

"I've been wondering the same thing. What was Marie getting out of it? She surely wouldn't risk her freedom for the sake of . . . " He swallowed and hesitated.

"What?"

"Well, a *man*. Knowing Marie, she had to have been in it for the money."

"Have you been looking for it too?"

"Yes, but I haven't been going through her stuff yet. There's no indication of extra money in our accounts, and we shared them. She had her own retirement account, and that hasn't changed. It's all very strange, isn't it? Why did they kill themselves? Or, worse, why were they killed? And why was the house burned down before getting the goods out of there? I wonder if the case is too complicated for our little Lincoln Grove police force. They haven't searched my house yet. It's weird, isn't it? It's like they don't know what to do."

She laughed a little at that. "Don't forget, the FBI is involved now too."

"And you think they're any smarter?" He rolled his eyes and they laughed more freely. "I mean, I keep waiting for someone to show up with a search warrant. I don't think they know what they'd be looking for. And you know what? I think they know we're innocent of any wrongdoing and figure searching our houses would be a waste of time."

"That would be a relief, wouldn't it?"

Scott rubbed his brow. "Everything is so . . . *mad*. The world has gone completely mad. And we have too."

After a pause, Rachel said, "Don't criminals like this have offshore banking accounts? You always hear about those things. I don't know much about them, do you?"

"Not really. I had a character use one in a novel of mine, but I really had no idea how they worked. I faked it and no readers noticed or complained."

"All I know is that you can access your money from anywhere in the world," she said. "You have a key code or PIN to get into your account, and then you can transfer funds to your real checking or savings account. You always hear about drug cartels using them, so they're good for hiding your money from the government. Where are those offshore things, anyway? The Bahamas?"

Scott answered, "Yeah, the Cayman Islands, Belize, and some of the other dodgier island destinations. They protect money like it's the secret to eternal youth."

"Isn't it?"

More laughs. The alcohol on both sides was doing its job.

"I have to go to John's office soon and pick up his personal belongings," she said. "His bosses have already cleaned it out and packed everything in boxes. I wish I could have done it. John might have hidden a clue there."

"Didn't the police go there and search his office?"

"Yes. They did. As far as I know, they found nothing. They gave Cassette Labs the all-clear to empty the office and get rid of his stuff."

"That was fast."

"Yeah."

"Where is Thomas, by the way?" Scott asked.

"In his room. Probably playing a video game or reading. Two of his favorite pastimes. Funny, he doesn't seem to have problems sleeping. He stays up until midnight, too, and he gets up on time for his virtual classes, which appear to be petering out as the semester finishes. That reminds me. How would you like to come over for dinner tomorrow night?"

That surprised Scott. "Really?"

"It was Thomas's idea, actually. I asked him, 'What about social distancing?' and all that. He sensibly replied that we could sit on opposite sides of the table, and that this would be the accepted amount of space between us. Besides, we haven't been seeing anyone. It hasn't quite been a week since I was with John, and I can't vouch for *him*, but I'm pretty sure we're safe. It's really up to you, Scott. I'll understand if you don't want to."

"No, no, I think I do want to. That's very kind."

"Thomas really likes you. He said so. Maybe we can all be friends, despite what happened to our families."

"Um," Scott hesitated. "You know, the police might not like how it appears."

"Hey, if we're not guilty of anything, then there's nothing they can do about it, right?"

"I guess not."

"I mean, there's no law against survivors of murder victims getting together. And besides . . . " she drifted off, looking away, pondering what to say next.

"What?"

"Nothing."

"What, Rachel? It's okay, you can tell me."

"Well . . . I was going to say that . . . I enjoy talking to you. I've been thinking about you."

Scott thought his heart just skipped a beat, although he knew that it was really the effect of brain chemicals surging through his chest.

"I . . . I feel the same way," he said. "I've been thinking about you too."

She gave him the smile that he liked so much.

For the next half hour, they talked about their individual histories, their desires, and their dreams.

After signing off Zoom, Scott had to admit that he was attracted to Rachel Bergman and that he felt no guilt about it. In fact, he was convinced that his interest in her was what was keeping him from that "going to pieces" scenario that might have been expected of him.

Something Rachel had said had got Scott to thinking. Marie had been a partner, or at least had aided and abetted John Bergman with his crime. Had Marie hidden something in the house that was a clue to the money she was possibly paid? Like Rachel, perhaps he should start going through Marie's clothes and drawers and cubbyhole storage spaces. He didn't know what he'd be looking for, but it would give him something to do.

He wasn't tired. The chat with Rachel had invigorated him. He decided to start on the cleanup. Scott went upstairs to the master bedroom. He looked around and asked himself where he should start. He eyed the bathroom, which was still half hers, and shrugged.

He went in, turned on the light, and started picking up the many toiletries and makeup items that were sitting on the countertop by the sink. He dropped them into the trash can. Nail polish, files, mascara, tweezers, toothbrushes, toothpaste, dental floss, combs, brushes . . . It wasn't long before the medium-sized trash bin was full. Scott picked it up and took it downstairs to empty it in the big Waste Management trash bin in the garage. He grabbed a yard waste recycling bag and brought it back up to the bathroom to continue the chore.

The medicine cabinet was the next target. It was full of over-the-counter drugs and vitamins and bandages and other items that one would normally find in such a spot. Scott knew that prescription drugs should be properly disposed of, so he took those, one by one, opened the childproof caps, and dumped the pills into the toilet. He got to the antidepressants—Lexapro—and poured those into the bowl as well.

A flash drive dropped into the water with the pills.

Scott stared at it for a few seconds, then acted quickly, reached in, and scooped it out. He shook it, but the thing was very wet.

"Holy shit," he gasped.

Would it still work? How should he dry it?

Scott went downstairs to his computer and searched online for advice about what to do if you got a flash drive wet. Following the instructions, he buried the thing in a jar that he filled with dry, uncooked rice, and he planned to let it sit for twenty-four hours.

It wasn't like Marie—or anyone, really—to store a flash drive in a bottle of pills . . . unless it was to hide something.

23

Can you keep a secret?

If your best friend, or your spouse, or your sibling told you a secret about someone else, would you be able to hold it inside? What if the secret would change lives? That knowledge becomes weighty. It can even be a weapon.

I know from experience that a lot of people can't keep a secret. Probably most people! There's an old saying that if you want something to be a secret, then don't tell anyone else about it—keep it to yourself! And if three people know a secret, then it's no longer a secret.

And that, my friends, is just common sense.

Sunday, May 17, 2020
2:30 a.m.

Seth couldn't sleep.

He recalled a dumb joke his Dad had once told. "I feel awful. I slept like a salad—I was tossing all night long!"

That was what was going on. Seth couldn't keep still. After kicking the sheets off the bed and punching the mattress a couple of times out of frustration, he sat up and turned on the nightstand lamp. He noted the time and sighed. He'd been known to stay up later; it was just that he genuinely felt tired. It was his *brain* that wouldn't shut up.

Concern about his mother was part of it. Earlier, after dinner, she had started crying at the dinner table. She was experiencing so much stress at the hospital. His dad told her that if she wanted to resign, he'd support her decision.

"Are you kidding?" she blustered. "They *need* me! There are people *dying*! The ICU is full!"

Seth's father apologized and said he was only trying to help her see options. For the millionth time, he told her how proud he was of her, and that she was one of the heroes. Nevertheless, she had gone to bed upset.

Seth spent the rest of the evening watching television and avoiding his parents. He still felt awful about the fire at the Wilkins house. The less he had to face his mom and dad, the less he felt the guilt.

Now, in what he'd once read was near the "hour of the wolf"—the wee hours of the morning when most living things in the time zone were supposed to be in dreamland—Seth was wide awake. He thought he might as well get on his phone and see who else was up.

It never changed. Facebook was the usual deluge of political rants, misinformation about Covid and arguments for and against the falsehoods, and the occasional photo of a pet or a home-cooked meal. The new trend was profile pictures of people wearing masks.

Seth saw on the newsfeed that Thomas had shared a news story about an upcoming video game, and the time stamp was just a few minutes earlier. Seth used Messenger to ask him, "Are you up?"

A few seconds lapsed, and then Thomas replied, "Yes."

"Want to FaceTime?"

"Sure."

Seth quickly tapped the video icon to call Thomas on Face-Time. Within seconds, they were looking at each other, each wearing headphones. While Seth wore an XL T-shirt to bed, Thomas was decked out in real pajamas. They appeared to be silk.

"Can you hear me?" Seth asked. "I have to talk quietly."

"Yes. Me too. You can hear me all right?"

"Sure."

"So, how come you're up?" Thomas asked.

"Just couldn't sleep. What about you?"

"Same thing."

"What's going on in your house these days?"

Thomas considered the question.

Seth picked up on his hesitation and said, "That's not a good topic, sorry. You guys must be going through a bad time."

"No, no," Thomas answered. "I was just trying to decide what I should tell you. But you're a friend. Maybe my best friend."

Seth wasn't sure if he was flattered by that, but he accepted it. "Thanks."

"My mom has been rummaging through my stepdad's stuff. All day. Picking through his clothes and searching his cabinets and bathroom and everything. She's looking for something."

"What?"

"I don't know. Something to do with the robbery of all that medical equipment. She thinks he was involved."

Seth nodded. "Well, considering he was in the house . . . "

"I know. She's probably right. It's weird to think I was living with a criminal."

"Is your mom okay?"

"She's a little freaked out by everything. I hope she doesn't send me away somewhere."

"Where would she send you?"

Thomas shrugged. "I don't know. Nowhere, really. If I have to go anywhere, I'd want to go to California to see my half sister, Sarah. But she doesn't have room for me, and with Covid going on, it wouldn't be cool. I'm not going anywhere. Mom needs me here."

"Didn't you say your mom and Sarah don't talk?"

"They don't, normally. And because they don't talk, I don't talk to Sarah much either. I haven't seen her in three years."

That didn't sound good to Seth. It was likely that Sarah wanted nothing to do with the family.

"Hey, Seth, can you keep a secret?"

"Uh, yeah?"

"I want to show you something. Watch this." Thomas pointed his phone camera at his laptop screen, then opened a Windows Media Player video file.

Seth's jaw dropped when he saw the images on the screen. It was a video of Don Trainer, captured on a phone from perhaps thirty to fifty feet away, possibly from behind a tree. He lit a Molotov cocktail and tossed it into a metal garbage can in a park. Don quickly exited the frame as the camera stayed on the trash bin. BOOM! Flames erupted from the top of the can, and then the video stopped.

"Whoa," Seth said. "Did you shoot that?"

"I did."

"When?"

"A couple of weeks ago. I have another one, too, from this week. It was at Dodge Park, and you were with him. Remember? At first you could be seen in the video, but I edited it so that you're not in it. Only him."

Thomas opened another file, and Seth watched the incident he had witnessed that past Monday. It appeared as if Don was alone in the park. He lit the rag, threw it into the bin, and ran. BOOM!

"Wow, Thomas," Seth said. "That's some serious shit."

"I know. I figure if Don bothers me again, I can just forward these to the police."

"I can't believe only a week has passed since that day."

"I know. Time goes fast, but it goes slow at the same time. Isn't that weird?"

"I know what you mean."

Thomas asked again, "Oh, can you keep another secret?"

"Sure."

"I saw people in the Wilkins house garage a few nights before the fire. That Volkov Trucking truck was in the driveway. It looked like people were unloading boxes from the truck and bringing them through the garage and into the house."

"What? Really?"

"Yeah."

"When was that? What day?"

Thomas thought about it. "Friday, May 8. Well, technically, it was Saturday, May 9, early in the morning."

"Holy shit, Thomas, why didn't you tell me this before?"

"I don't know. I didn't think about it at the time. After the fire, I remembered."

"You should tell the police."

"Hmmm, I don't know."

"Did you see that Volkov guy there?"

"Yes. Him and another guy I've seen in the neighborhood. He lives around here somewhere. I don't remember where. Looked like he was giving the orders to Volkov and the other two. You know what I think now? I think that guy is Scoutmaster. You know, the mob boss."

"Really?"

"Yes."

"Whoa. Who were the other two?"

"Oh, I didn't say? My stepdad and Ms. Hatcher. They were in the garage that night too."

24

The world of online banking can be a quagmire of security issues. It can be complex and intimidating.

It can also be a tool for criminals.

Sunday, May 17, 2020
10:15 a.m.

After he'd gotten up, brewed some coffee, and fried an egg, Scott checked the jar of rice that contained Marie's flash drive. He dug the device out and examined it. It seemed to be perfectly dry.

"Here goes nothing." He held his breath as he booted up his laptop and stuck the flash drive in a USB port. He opened the drive and revealed its contents.

There were two folders. One was titled "Pics" and the other "Stuff."

Scott opened "Pics" and was met with dozens of photos. He sorted the thumbnails by "Date Created."

The dull pain in his chest increased as he gazed upon the images.

Early photos showed Marie with John Bergman in Chicago at various locations. There were groupings dating back nearly a year and moving forward. A restaurant, Wrigley Field, the Art Institute, a hotel room, another restaurant, Michigan Avenue . . . Several other pictures revealed them in the woods somewhere in front of a log cabin, and a couple of selections of Marie inside what appeared to be that cabin, standing at the kitchen sink and sitting on a couch near a fireplace. The most recent collection was from Marie's trip to Jamaica the previous January, just before Covid hit. It was supposed to have been a trip with fellow realtors for business and pleasure, and she had specifically told Scott that she was going "with the girls."

There were no other women in the photos. They were just of Marie alone, of John Bergman alone, and a few with them together that they had managed to get by likely asking a passerby to shoot.

The pang of this new heartbreak hurt worse than knowing that his wife was dead.

Scott carefully studied every photo as he made comments and asked questions in his head. *What were you thinking in this shot, Marie? I'll bet you weren't missing me. Oh, you two have a glow around you in this one—did you just finish having sex? Nice bikini, Marie—when was the last time you wore one in front of me? Ah, nice photo of you two at . . .*

Wait.

The picture of Marie and John on the street had a vendor behind them selling T-shirts with "Cayman Islands" verbiage. Pennants, baseball caps, and those cheap decorated dinner plates. All with "Cayman Islands" or "George Town." Scott knew that George Town was the big major city in the island group.

Marie hadn't gone to Jamaica at all. She and John had visited the Cayman Islands.

Scott closed that subfolder and opened "Stuff." Inside were a handful of Word documents and PDFs. He opened a PDF titled "Seashell."

It was a statement dated January 17, 2020, from Seashell Bank in George Town. The name on the account was marked "Private," as was the holder's address. It appeared to be a savings account, and there was a balance of $10,000.

Marie must have opened the account when she was in the Cayman Islands in January.

Another PDF was a copy of the offshore banking account agreement. This one clearly had her name on it, with the instructions to keep the document safe if she wished to keep the account anonymous and private.

A third PDF was another bank statement, this time from First Lincoln Bank in Lincoln Grove, a small local outfit. Both Scott and Marie had separate checking and savings accounts at a completely different bank, each in their own names. From the looks of the statement, though, Marie had a checking account at First Lincoln that Scott didn't know anything about. The name on it was Marie Dinkins Hatcher, with her maiden name added in the middle. There was $100 in this new one, probably the opening deposit, which was made on February 3, 2020.

The Word document was something she had typed herself, Scott guessed. It was titled "MH." It consisted of only two lines:

USER: MH001009002008

PW: Brian04*09

A third line was a URL address.

It was Marie's username, password, and the address to log in to her account.

*Brian04*09.* Their son's birth and death years.

Scott copied the URL and pasted it in his browser. A page for Seashell Bank opened with username and password fields.

He did so, and—

Uh-oh.

He was being asked to answer three security questions.

Okay, let's give it a go.

The first question: In what city did you meet your spouse or significant other?

Scott knew that one! He typed in "Los Angeles," and pressed Enter. Bingo.

Second question: What is your father's middle name?

Scott had to think about that one. He knew it. What was it? He drummed his fingers on the table. *Carroll Dinkins, Carroll Something Dinkins, Carroll . . .*

He typed "Wayne."

Bingo.

Third question: What is the first name of your first boyfriend/ girlfriend?

Scott stared at the screen. He knew this. Marie had talked about that guy a lot. He was her high school boyfriend. She had lost her virginity to him. It was some dorky name, too, like Norbert or Manfred or Shylock. *What the hell was it?*

He typed "Norbert."

INCORRECT RESPONSE. YOU HAVE ONE MORE TRY BEFORE BEING LOCKED OUT OF YOUR ACCOUNT FOR SECURITY PURPOSES. PLEASE TYPE YOUR ANSWER CAREFULLY. CASE-SENSITIVE!

He was stumped. He couldn't remember it.

Scott got up from the table and paced the kitchen. "Who was your high school boyfriend, Marie?" he asked the room.

Then he got an idea.

Scott turned and ran up the stairs to the guest bedroom where a lot of their books were stored on shelves. He scanned them.

There!

Her high school yearbook. Scott pulled it out and thumbed to the section at the back where friends wrote phony platitudes like, "You're the *best*!" "Will miss you *SOOO* much this summer!" "Best of luck to you at college!" "I know you'll be the toast of the campus!" He kept turning the pages, scanning the entries, and finally found it.

Nearly half a page of badly written pseudo-poetry and maudlin words that clearly indicated that the guy knew Marie was going to break up with him over the summer and that she was making a mistake.

It was signed Delbert Lockwood.

Delbert. I wasn't even close!

Scott ran downstairs and typed the name into the computer. He was in. It was then easy to maneuver to Marie's account.

His jaw dropped.

The balance in the Seashell account was now $510,000! In fact, $500,000 had been deposited into the account on Monday, May 11. The day Marie had disappeared.

Scott's hand trembled as he tried to find out more details about where the money had come from, but none of that was available. It had been a wire transfer. That was all he could glean.

Whoever had sent the money must have done it on that Friday, Saturday, or Sunday, possibly, and then it showed up in her account on Monday. Was it the payment for the robbery? Was that just *her* share?

"Oh my God," he said. He found that his forehead was perspiring.

The final piece in the folder was a photo taken of a piece of paper on which someone had drawn a flowchart. A handwritten heading proclaimed it as ROUTE 66. A few sentences were written below: "To transfer from Seashell to home bank. Pull TO drop-down menu and select 'Route 66.' Hit "Transfer,' then confirm it, and that's all there is to it! Money goes on this journey we set up." Lines were drawn to indicate the connections from there. "Seashell Bank -- Ocean Breeze Bank (Belize) -- Chase (New York) -- First Lincoln (LG)."

Scott thought about that. If he understood it correctly, Marie had the ability to transfer funds from the offshore account in the Caymans to her private checking account in Lincoln Grove at the touch of a button. The money made a roundabout trip, routing through Belize and New York before landing in Illinois. John Bergman had obviously helped her set it up. Scott figured that John most likely had a similar arrangement for his own share of the money.

Wow. Just wow.

He sat back in his chair and pondered all this information. It was almost too much to comprehend.

$510,000.

Scott had already gone over Marie's estate details with the police and his attorney. She had a will, drawn up while Brian was still alive, that clearly stated that Scott was her primary beneficiary. She had never changed it.

Surely . . . *surely* . . . as the widower of the deceased customer, he would be entitled to whatever money landed in this Lincoln Grove Bank account.

"Hello?"

"Rachel? It's Scott."

"Hi there."

He was still sitting at the kitchen table in front of his laptop. He had spent the last hour digging deeper into Marie's accounts and had learned a few things.

"Can you talk?"

"Sure."

Scott proceeded to tell her about finding the flash drive buried in the pill container, and that the information on the drive led him to Marie's offshore account. Rachel had gasped at the news. He continued, "I'm betting that John had a similar account set up, probably at the same bank. Are there any pill bottles in John's medicine cabinet? Have you looked there?"

"No, I haven't. That's a good idea. Wow. Unbelievable."

"I know, right?"

"Hey, do you . . . do you want to come over and help me look?"

"Uh . . . "

"I just . . . I think you might have better ideas of *where* to look. My mind just doesn't work that way. I would have never thought of that."

Scott thought, *What the hell? Why not?*

There was one hitch. He had to go to the funeral home for Marie's cremation and interment of the urn.

"Are we still having dinner?" he asked.

"Sure, if you're up for it."

"Why don't I just come over then and help you?"

"That would be fine. Six thirty? Is that all right?"

"I'll be there."

They hung up, and he got up from the table. He happened to glance into his backyard through the sliding glass door that led to the patio, and he saw that Mr. Blunt was sitting on the roof of his ever-growing structure. It appeared as if Blunt was looking right at Scott, peering into the kitchen.

Is he spying on me?

Scott opened the sliding door and stepped outside. As soon as he did so, Blunt stood and turned. He held a hammer in his hand and started to bang on something on the roof. Scott didn't move. He stood and watched his neighbor. After a few seconds passed, Blunt looked over at him, and then he quickly turned his head back to his project. BANG-BANG-BANG-BANG.

He was *spying on me! That was a guilty "I'm going to cover up by pretending to be working" look.*

"Mr. Blunt?" Scott called, walking a little into his yard. BANG-BANG-BANG. "*Mr. Blunt!*"

The man pivoted his head and stopped hammering. "Are you calling me?"

"Yes."

"What do you want, Mr. Hatcher?"

"Were you . . . I'm sorry, but were you . . . spying on me?"

Blunt frowned and wiped his brow with a bare arm. "What?"

"I think you heard me."

"Spying on you? What are you talking about?"

"Just now. You were sitting there and watching me in my kitchen."

Blunt set the hammer down and stood. "No, I wasn't. I was not looking at you."

Scott had nothing to go on but what he'd seen. Had he been mistaken? Was he imagining things?

"It looked to me like you were."

"Man, you're paranoid. What's the matter, are the cops putting pressure on you? Do they think you're the one who killed your wife and her *lover*? Leave me alone, I'm busy here." The man picked up the hammer and went back to his work. BANG-BANG-BANG.

Scott couldn't fathom the insensitivity of the guy. What a horrible thing to say. Maybe it was time for Scott to move from Marigold Way, not only to leave behind the sour memories of his marriage and the ghastly thing that had happened to Marie, but also to get away from the asshole who lived behind him!

He turned and went back inside, stormed up the stairs, and proceeded to shower and shave. When he was fresh and clean, Scott felt a little better. After he dressed in a suit for the first time since the beginning of March, he grabbed his mask and opened the garage door. Marie's Malibu and his Altima greeted him expectantly, or so he imagined. He patted the Malibu and muttered, "Sorry, Chevy," and for a fleeting moment he wondered how much money he could get for selling it.

Scott got into the Altima and checked his phone for directions to the funeral parlor. He started the car, backed it out of the garage, and steeled himself for something he never in a million years thought he'd be doing.

25

I've heard tell that there are three things that can change a person's character. The first would be the embracing of a religion. That doesn't concern us here in this story. I'm not saying that none of our characters are religious—it's just that whatever they believe in a spiritual sense has no bearing on their actions in the tale. Besides, what human beings don't know about the afterlife could fill a bottomless pit.

The second and third things are more relevant. These are love and money. People can become blithering idiots when it comes to affairs of the heart. By the same token, they can become stupid as hell when it comes to money. The prospect of either seems to turn off the common-sense switch. More often than not, our prisons are filled with persons who committed crimes in the name of love or money. Or both.

I've heard that money can't buy you love. I suppose the reverse is true too.

Sunday, May 17, 2020
2:00 p.m.

Everyone wore masks at the "funeral," such as it was, and it went as well as it could. Scott felt surprisingly emotionless during the proceedings. He was surprised to see Detective Dante there—the only other attendee. Scott hadn't bothered to tell Marie's friend Cindy about it. Dante asked him in the funeral parlor's lobby if he minded her presence. He didn't see why not, but then he figured it was part of her investigation into the murders and arson. She wanted to see how *he* behaved at his wife's funeral.

Scott didn't cry, but he exhibited a solemn, pained demeanor that he thought would have been acceptable in most civilized venues. British people often displayed "stiff upper lips" and all that, so why couldn't Americans?

When it was all over and he was presented with the bronze-colored urn, Scott did find that he'd temporarily lost his voice. He had to whisper, "Thank you," to the funeral director. The urn was placed in a box, and then he had to drive to the cemetery in Lincoln Grove for the interment. Detective Dante followed, not in a police car, but in her personal vehicle. The funeral director met them there, and Marie's ashes were placed in a compartment in the columbarium. A plaque was on order and would mark the space within two to three weeks.

Keeping an adequate six-foot distance from him, Dante expressed her condolences and asked Scott if he was all right. He nodded without speaking, but then managed to thank her for coming. He then asked if there had been any progress in the investigation.

"I can't comment right now, but I'll be in touch, maybe as soon as tomorrow," she replied.

"I hope you figure it out," he said.

"That's my job," Dante said. She said goodbye and left him to his thoughts, which, unknown to her, were all about the upcoming dinner at Rachel's house in a few hours.

At 6:25 p.m., Scott, now dressed in shorts, a T-shirt, and sandals, grabbed his mask and went out the front door. Lois Kimmelman was in front of her house, using a watering can on the flower beds. She heard him shut the door and lock it.

"Oh, Scott, hello!" she called.

Scott inwardly sighed. "Hello, Lois. How are you and Al doing?"

"We're good, we're good." She set down the can and walked to the edge of her yard. "The question is how are *you* holding up? Are you okay?"

"I'm all right, thank you for asking."

"I've been meaning to bring over some food. I know you've probably been having a hard time with . . . with Marie . . . "

Scott held up his hands. "It's okay, Lois, thank you, but I'm managing. You don't need to bring anything."

"I have a cabbage and spinach casserole I made last night. Al said he was willing to sacrifice his portion for you, bless his heart, so I saved some. I was going to bring it over today, but I can run in and get it now, if you want."

Scott knew perfectly well why Al had made that suggestion. "Please, Lois, I don't want it. I appreciate it, but Al deserves to have your culinary delights, not me. He's *your* husband. I have to go, Lois, I'm on my way somewhere."

He took off across his driveway and walked in front of the burned shell of the Wilkins house. Someday soon the village would come and tear down what was left. Incongruously, Marie's "For Sale" sign was still in the yard. Scott stopped and attempted to pull it from the ground, but the post was too tightly buried. He gave up and almost crossed the street there, but he saw that David Woo was in *his* driveway unloading groceries from his SUV. Scott waved at him, and the man called out. "Oh, Scott! Oh, Scott!" Woo placed a bag back inside the car so he could talk. Neither man wore a mask, so they remained a few feet apart.

"Hi, David, how are you all? I hope your house didn't get damaged the other night," Scott said.

"No problem. Your house is okay?"

"As far as I know."

"Good, good. I, uh, wanted to tell you . . . "

"What is it, David?"

Woo lowered his voice and looked around as if he didn't want anyone else to hear him. "May and I heard a noise next door last week. At night. Late. We were asleep. Woke us up. I looked out the window." A bedroom window on the side of the house did overlook the Wilkins structure. "People were going in and out of the garage. Men. I saw Marie with them. She's the realtor, so I thought all was okay."

"Yes, she was the realtor. When was this, David?"

He frowned. "Weekend before the fire."

"Friday? Saturday? Sunday?"

Woo looked confused. "I do not know."

"Did the police talk to you?" Scott asked.

Woo nodded with vigor. "Yes. We talked to the police."

"Did you tell them this?"

"Yes. I told them."

"Good. That's probably something they should know. Thank you for telling me."

Woo shook his head. "Terrible business. May and I are sorry for you."

"Thank you, David. I appreciate it." Scott gestured across the street. "I was just heading over to . . . to talk to Ms. Bergman about the . . . case. See you later."

Woo's expression of bewilderment replaced any response he might have uttered and repeated.

Scott crossed the road to Number 508. He turned back to see that David Woo hadn't moved. He stood staring at Scott in disbelief. Three doors down, Lois Kimmelman was also still standing in the same spot in her yard, watching him. Three houses down from Rachel's side of the street was 502, where Paul Justice was in his driveway. He, too, stood with hands on hips, gazing at Scott.

Fine, let them gossip.

He walked up Rachel's driveway and rang the doorbell. Scott's nervousness returned. It was as if he were a single man again and about to go on a date.

Well, it's true . . . I am *single again!*

The door opened and there she was. Besides the mask on her face, Rachel was dressed in a tight black leotard that looked like something she might wear while working out, with a bright flower-print skirt at the waist. She was barefoot, and her legs appeared to be bare under the skirt. Scott couldn't stop his eyes from jumping to her cleavage and the clear, white skin of her neck.

"Happy Sunday," she said. Above her mask, her eyes crinkled from her smile. "Come on in."

Scott donned his own mask and stepped inside. "Thank you. Nice to see you."

"You too." She led him into the kitchen, where Thomas was sitting at their table, a pencil in hand, and working on the *Tribune*'s crossword puzzle.

"Hello, Mr. Hatcher," the boy said.

"How are you, Thomas?"

"I'm fine. Working on this puzzle. Do you know an eleven-letter word that starts with an 'i' and ends with 'ive'? The clue is 'heartless.'"

"Hm." Scott looked over Thomas's shoulder at the paper. Thomas pointed at the empty squares. "I'd say that might be, hm, 'insensitive'?"

Thomas wrote the letters in. "That works. Thank you, Mr. Hatcher."

Heartless. Insensitive. Scott experienced an involuntary shiver. He covered up the sudden spasm in his torso by reaching around the back of his neck and rotating his head.

"Is your neck bothering you?" Rachel asked.

"Yeah, I guess I slept on it funny." The moment had passed. "I'm all right."

"Oh—we're having pasta with a red sauce, mushrooms, and black olives. I didn't know if you're a meat eater or not."

"I am a meat eater, but that sounds great just like that."

"We sometimes do the pasta with ground chicken or turkey. But not tonight."

"I can't wait."

Rachel looked at Thomas and gave him an eye signal to get the hell out. He subtly nodded, picked up the paper, got up from the table, and started to leave. "I'll be downstairs," he said.

When he was gone, Scott said quietly, "He didn't have to—"

Rachel shook her head. "We have things to talk about." She jerked her head toward the stairs. "Let's go up to my computer." Scott hesitated. "It's all right. Detective Dante and her sidekicks aren't up there watching us."

"How do *you* know?" he asked facetiously, but he followed her to the top floor anyway.

The bedroom was a mess. Men's clothing was all over the floor, draped over furniture, and on the four-poster bed. The lights were on in the master bathroom, which was relatively large (the Hatcher house had nothing like it), and toiletries and other items were splayed on the counter.

"I went through the pills and vitamins and other stuff in the medicine cabinet, and in the drawers . . . I even emptied out toothpaste from the tube," Rachel said. "Nothing. No flash drive."

"Wow. Your husband had a lot of clothes."

"They're all going to Goodwill unless you want something. Although I think John's size is larger than yours."

"Rachel, I don't think I would want to wear John's clothes even if we were the same size."

She nodded. "Understandable. Sorry."

"It's okay."

"But do you see anything in here that I'm missing? That's why I brought you upstairs. I thought maybe your eyes would notice something that mine don't."

Scott walked around the room, stepping over piles of clothes and shoes. He pointed to the chest of drawers. "You searched here?"

"Oh yeah. That's his, and most of what was in there is on the floor now."

"Hm." He went into the bathroom and looked around, but he felt a little uncomfortable doing so. Just for show, he pulled out the drawers in the cabinet, stooped down, and looked underneath them.

"What are you doing?" she asked.

"Oh, I saw a spy movie once where they taped something under a drawer like this. Just thought I'd look." He stood and came out of the bathroom. "Did John have a collection of anything? Books or CDs or something he wouldn't think you'd have any interest in?"

"Hm. We have some old vinyl records and CDs downstairs. They were always considered ours, not just his. Some are definitely mine. There are books, I guess. They're mostly kept in the next bedroom. I didn't think about that."

They went to look at the books, but nothing stood out to Scott. "Most of them are mine," she admitted.

"Did John have any hobbies? Was he a sportsman? Does he own golf clubs or anything like that? Something he knows you wouldn't have a reason to touch?"

"He liked bowling. He has a bowling ball."

"Did you look at it?"

"No. It's downstairs in the laundry room. He kept it there so he wouldn't have to lug it up and down the stairs."

"Let's go take a look."

They went down two levels to where the family room, laundry room, and exit to the garage were located. This layout was the same as Scott's house. Thomas was in the family room, headphones on his head, his eyes on the television, and his hands on a video game controller.

The dryer was on, humming along. "Here's the bowling bag." She pointed to a shelf against the opposite wall by the furnace and water heater. All kinds of items were stored on the shelves, from tools and cleaning supplies to rubber boots and umbrellas. Scott picked up the bowling bag and opened it. He really didn't know anything about bowling balls, but this one was a gorgeous shiny 900 Global with streaks of red in the black. He held it in both hands as if testing its weight, and then stuck his fingers in the holes.

He felt something inside the thumb hole. "Hm. What's this?" He used his index finger and thumb to pull the object out. "There you are," he said.

It was a flash drive wrapped inside a sandwich baggie.

"Oh my God," Rachel said. "I never would have thought of looking there."

"It was just a hunch."

"Let's go stick it in the computer."

He put the bowling ball back in the bag and then followed her back upstairs to the bedroom. The laptop, which was already on, was sitting on her vanity in the area that was obviously her side of the room. She sat, plugged in the drive, and waited for the notification to pop up. She then opened the drive and revealed its contents.

Two folders: "Pics" and "Stuff."

"Just like what was on Marie's," Scott said. "You'll probably find copies of the pictures from their trip to the Caymans. They're not pleasant to look at."

"I can take it," she said. "I knew he'd gone there—on 'business,' he said. I didn't know it was with her."

She went instead to the "Stuff" folder and opened it. Just as what was in Marie's drive, there were statements and documents. John Bergman, too, had an account at Seashell Bank in George Town, Cayman Islands, as well as a secret account at First Lincoln Bank.

"I take it that's not your bank," Scott said.

"Nope. We bank with the Chase branch in Town Center."

Like Marie's, according to the Seashell statement, John had $10,000 in the account. Another document revealed his username and password, so they went to the Seashell site and checked the balance there. His account currently contained only $1,000.

"Hey," she said. "What happened to the other nine grand?"

"I don't know. Maybe he spent it."

"You said Marie had five hundred thousand?"

"Five hundred and ten thousand."

She looked at him. "What does this mean?"

Scott rubbed his chin. "I think maybe . . . maybe Marie was holding their money for both of them. They were going to split it but, see, the deposit of five hundred thousand dollars wasn't made until the day they were killed. They were probably waiting for it to show up in the account."

"That bastard," Rachel said. She gently pushed away from the vanity and stood. "All this money they got . . . "

"What?"

Her eyes met his. "It could be ours."

Rachel was standing so close to him that he could reach out and touch her. Not good for social distancing, but excellent for the adrenaline and dopamine and oxytocin surging through his body.

They both had the same idea. The attraction was palpable.

Scott and Rachel removed their masks, put their arms around each other, and kissed with a passion that surprised them both.

26

Dawn can be a good thing, and it can be a bad thing.

If you've had a productive night's sleep, the sunshine streaming in from the bedroom window can be a pleasant reminder that you're alive, you feel good, and all is right with the world. Never mind that a minute later you'll realize that the third thing isn't exactly true. At first, though, you feel all snuggly and warm between the sheets as you stretch and yawn and daydream about the breakfast you're going to make and savor.

On the other hand, if it's been a bad night, the daylight might not be so welcome. Perhaps you had a case of insomnia, the old "mind racing" syndrome, or you're upset or anxious about something. Nine times out of ten, you eventually fall asleep out of pure exhaustion around four or five o'clock . . . and boy, do you *not* want to wake up at sunrise.

Unfortunately, even if you did sleep well, the dawn can remind you of various problems in your life. Maybe you're a worrier. I'm one of those. If it's in your nature to worry, it's damned difficult to stop. That said, there is that old saying: Worrying is interest paid for money never owed. I try to remember that, and so should you.

In this case, though, the morning has brought a new day and a new beginning for our friend Scott Hatcher.

Monday, May 18, 2020
8:05 a.m.

Birds chirped in his ear.

He opened his eyes to see bright light over the wall in front of his nose. He was lying on his side, maybe four feet away from the surface. His head rested on a pillow.

Where the hell am I?

Scott gasped and jerked a little, and then he realized he was in bed. But not his. There was just enough room on his side between the bed and the wall for a person to move through. This was not his bedroom.

What?

Then it all came crashing back to him. It took a second, and then he relaxed.

This is . . . by golly, this is comfortable.

The sunlight gushed through the window above him. Rachel had carelessly forgotten to close the blinds. Had anyone seen inside? Nah, probably not. They were on the top floor, facing the backyard of the Bergman house.

Birds were singing outside the window. That was quite a change from the cacophony of buzz saws and hammering from the Blunt house.

This was downright . . . lovely!

Scott had slept better than he had in weeks. The evening prior had been sinfully wonderful, and so had the first few hours of the night.

Did what I recall happening really occur?

He turned his body to the presence he felt beside him. Rachel Bergman was on her side, facing away from him, breathing softly and steadily. Still asleep.

Oh . . . my . . . God . . .

What had he done? What had *they* done?

A sudden surge of guilt, anxiety, and fear flooded his chest. He felt his eyes well with tears. Scott held his right hand to his mouth and bit into his index finger to keep from making a sound.

Hang on, buddy! It's all right! What happened was . . . Okay, it was wrong, it was terribly wrong, but wasn't it . . . fantastic? Didn't you feel great? Didn't you sleep like a baby? What the hell is bad about that?

The two of them had barely talked about what they were doing while it was happening. Rachel insisted that it was meant to be. They were the wronged parties. Why shouldn't they find solace in each other? To hell with what others might think. To hell with the "moral ambiguity."

Scott told himself that Rachel was right. What was that old proverb? "Worrying is paying a bill before you've even received it," or something like that.

Rachel stirred and stretched. There was a quiet, peaceful sigh uttered from her throat, and then she rotated to look at him.

When Scott saw her face, those eyes, that smile . . . all his concerns vanished. The pressure in his chest disappeared with a breath of air.

"Good morning," she whispered.

"Hey there."

"Was I snoring?"

"No." He smiled back. "I think the birds woke me."

"Oh, those crazy birds. There's a nest in the eave right outside that window." She made the cutest yawn. Scott thought he could fall in love with that yawn. She continued, "There's a new family that moves in every year. The mother lays her eggs and they hatch, and then she and the father help feed the noisy little things. Then, when they're grown, they all fly away and go somewhere else. They must leave good reviews on the Airbnb for Birds website, because it never fails. That spot rents out every spring."

He laughed. "It's actually quite pleasant. A lot better than the noisy neighbor behind my house who insists on building a second house in his backyard at an ungodly hour of the morning."

They both took turns going to the bathroom, and then were back in bed, clinging to each other. Neither of them was dressed . . . in anything. When they had first divested of their clothes, Scott had complimented her on how good she looked, and she had said, "You're not so bad yourself." He quoted the old Groucho Marx line, "If I told you that you have a beautiful body, would you hold it against me?" She had laughed, and they fell into bed. The gymnastics had been fiercely awkward at first. It had been months since Scott and Marie had enjoyed any sexuality together, and there had been only sporadic moments of intimacy over the last several years. He imagined the same was true for Rachel. They were both out of practice. Nevertheless, the mission was accomplished, although there was room for improvement. The second attempt, however, was, as Scott put it, "a promising premise to an outstanding romantic comedy." With the third time, he said they'd broken all box office records.

He kissed her, and their hands began to move over each other's skin once again. In between the breathless gnawing and nibbling of their lips and tongues, Rachel asked, "Do we know what time it is?"

"Not a clue." The only thing on his radar was that his body was telling him he was ready for Round Four.

There was a knock at the bedroom door.

Scott and Rachel froze.

"Mom?"

"Yes, Thomas?" she called.

Scott was horrified when the boy opened the door and came in the room and stood a few feet away from the bed. Luckily, a sheet covered all the naughty bits. Scott thought he probably resembled a deer in headlights.

"I'm going to make omelets. Do you and Mr. Hatcher want one too?" Thomas asked.

It was as if nothing out of the ordinary were taking place. The boy was absolutely unfazed by the sight.

Rachel looked at Scott. "Thomas makes incredible omelets. You want one?"

"Uh . . . I . . . sure . . . uh . . . "

Rachel chuckled and turned back to her son. "Yes, please, Thomas. Thank you."

"Okay. They'll be ready in twenty minutes." Thomas turned and left the room, closing the door behind him.

Scott dropped onto his back and pulled the pillow over his face. "Oh my Lord . . . "

Rachel laughed. She removed the pillow and kissed him on the cheek.

He asked her, "Is this weird?"

"Not for me. Is it for you?"

"I'd be lying if I said it wasn't, but that doesn't mean I don't . . . it doesn't mean I don't *like* it. I'm more concerned about Thomas. What does he think?"

Rachel sat up. "He and his stepfather were like oil and water. Thomas takes after me, thank goodness. To tell you the truth, he's probably incredibly happy about this." She raised her eyebrows at him. "Twenty minutes. I think that means we have to get up, handsome."

"Oh *okay*, if you say so."

Rachel gave Scott a terrycloth bathrobe to wear over his T-shirt and underwear. "Don't worry, it's not John's. It's one I have especially for guests. Not that we ever have any guests." She put on sweatpants and a tank top, and then donned a silk robe over that. They went downstairs and joined Thomas in the kitchen, where he was busy preparing omelets with sautéed mushrooms and onions. He was also frying some strips of bacon. Cups of coffee were already on the table.

"I hope you eat bacon, Mr. Hatcher," the boy said. "It may not be kosher, but it's good."

"Oh, I eat bacon, Thomas."

Rachel said, "I don't, but I can't keep it away from Thomas. You two enjoy yourselves."

"I have to say, I'm impressed," Scott said. "He's a better cook than I am."

"Thomas is the little man of the house." She rubbed her fingers through her son's hair, and then she and Scott took seats at the table.

The food was delicious and filling. While he was eating, Scott had an odd sensation that he was out of his body and subjectively gazing at the scene as a fourth entity. There he was, sitting at a table with another woman and her son.

Brian would have been just a little older than Thomas.

The conceit was convincing enough, though. Scott felt as if he was gazing at his *family*. That he belonged there.

When they were done, Thomas took away the plates and loaded the dishwasher. Again, Scott watched with incredulity. "Wow, he really does everything around here, doesn't he? I've never seen a teenager be so helpful. But then, I don't have one, myself."

"He *is* a big help around the house," Rachel answered.

Thomas turned to them. "For my next trick, I will disappear. *The Witcher 3* is calling me from the PlayStation downstairs."

"*The Witcher 3*?" Scott asked.

"A video game," Rachel said.

Thomas left them at the table. Rachel started to giggle.

"What's so funny?"

"Us. We are. The look on your face."

The doorbell rang. Rachel's laugh ended abruptly, and she frowned. "Who rings the door this early on a Sunday?"

"It's Monday," Scott reminded her.

"Oh yeah. It sure feels like Sunday, doesn't it?"

"Yeah."

She got up and left the kitchen as Scott sipped his coffee and waited. Then he heard Rachel and another voice he recognized.

Oh shit.

Detective Dante was at the front door.

27

There's a subgenre of crime stories that we refer to as "lovers on the run." These tales feature a spirited man and woman who have perhaps committed one or more crimes and are fleeing the law. If you're of a certain age, you might remember *Bonnie and Clyde*. An early B-movie called *Gun Crazy* is also one of these. I happen to be something of a movie buff, so I know these things. *Badlands, The Honeymoon Killers, True Romance, You Only Live Once, Something Wild, The Getaway, Wild at Heart* . . . just to name a few.

I bring this up for no real reason except that our tale seems to be turning into one of these nuggets.

Monday, May 18, 2020
9:02 a.m.

A dozen thoughts zipped through Scott's head. Should he run upstairs? Should he open the sliding glass door to Rachel's backyard and hide outside? Should he crawl under the table? Is Rachel about to get arrested? Is *he* about to get arrested?

Before he could act at all, he heard the voices growing in volume. Rachel and Dante were coming through the foyer, on their way to the kitchen.

" . . . not really a good time," Rachel was saying.

"It's just after nine, and this is important." When they appeared and Dante saw Scott sitting at the kitchen table with a forced grin on his face, she stopped in her tracks. "What. The. *Fuck*?"

Silence.

"What's going on here?" she asked.

"Scott and I are just being neighborly," Rachel answered with a shrug.

"In bathrobes?"

Scott stood. "Good morning, detective. Is it a problem? Rachel and I have suddenly found that we have a lot in common."

Dante blinked. "Is that in addition to both of you losing your spouses while they were having an affair?"

"Would you like some coffee, Detective Dante?" Rachel asked.

"No, thank you. Mr. Hatcher, Ms. Bergman, this does not look good. You're both under investigation."

"And we're both innocent," Scott rebounded.

Dante shook her head. "I have to say, this was not on my Bingo card this morning. Fine. I'll talk to you both. I had planned to visit you, Mr. Hatcher, at *your* house after I spoke with Ms. Bergman. Would both of you mind putting on your masks, and may I sit down?"

"Certainly," Rachel said, grabbing one from the counter and placing it over her mouth and nose.

"Mine's upstairs," Scott said.

"*Upstairs?*" Dante scolded.

Looking sheepish, he said, "I'll be right back."

As he scattered out of the kitchen and up the stairs, Rachel asked again if she could get the lieutenant anything. Dante refused, sat on the far side of the table, and produced her notebook. There were some handwritten lines on the first page. Scott returned with the mask on, and he and Rachel sat side by side across from the detective.

"We may be making some arrests today," Dante announced.

"Really?" Scott said, drawing in a breath. "That's great news!"

Dante held up a hand. "For the arson. We believe the two events are separate and unrelated. The suspects who burned down the house may very well not have known that Mr. Bergman and Ms. Hatcher were upstairs in the bedroom. We'll learn more later today."

"Can you tell us who they are?" Rachel asked.

"No. Not at this time. Sorry. Now, I want to know about any dealings you've had with a man named Fyodor Volkov."

Scott said, "Remember, you saw him leave my house the other evening and you asked who he was."

"Yes, that's why I'm asking."

"Is he one of those 'persons of interest' you hear about on TV?"

She didn't answer that. "Have either of you had any other dealings with him?"

"No."

"What exactly did he want when he was at your house, Scott?"

"He said that Marie had been helping him find a house. He mentioned the one next door to me and asked if he could see it without Marie. He wanted me to give him the code to the lockbox. I told him I didn't have it, and that only Marie could show him the house. I'm pretty sure I also told him Marie was dead and that whatever business he had with her is probably finished. I haven't gotten around to talking to Marie's realty firm to see if they would get back to him. I don't know. He struck me as . . . fishy."

Dante nodded, then turned to Rachel. "What about you?"

"He came to the house once. I didn't know who he was, but he introduced himself and told me his name. He was looking for John."

"When was this?"

Rachel creased her brow. "Uh, it was after I reported John missing, but before the fire. It must have been last Tuesday afternoon or so. I don't think it was Monday. I'm sorry, the days all run together for me. It's been that way since March."

"I understand. Did he say why he wanted to talk to your husband?"

"No. Only that he had some business with John and that he needed to speak to him immediately. I told him John wasn't here, and that was that."

"Is he a suspect?" Scott asked.

Again, Dante held up a hand. "You know I can't talk about—"

"Okay, okay."

"Scott, Rachel . . . Did either of your spouses ever mention the name 'Scoutmaster'?"

Scott found it odd that Detective Dante often alternated between being more formal and calling him by his surname, and then a few seconds later she would be more familiar and address him by his first name.

"What do you mean?" Scott asked. "A Boy Scout scoutmaster?"

"No, just a name, or nickname, rather. Someone who goes by the name Scoutmaster."

He looked at Rachel. She shook her head, and he did too. "Not me," Scott said.

"Me neither," Rachel echoed.

Dante consulted her notepad. "All right. Do either of you know Don Trainer?"

Scott leaned forward. "Don? Don Trainer, the kid who lives at the end of the block?"

"He's the one."

"Well, I know who he is. Don't really know him."

"Same here," Rachel said. "I know he sometimes bullies my son. Why?"

"Have you ever seen him hanging around the Wilkins house in the past?"

Scott answered, "Hm, no, I don't think so."

"Nope," Rachel confirmed.

"Ever seen him in Dodge Park, or any other park?"

They both shook their heads.

Dante closed her notebook. "Okay."

"That's it?" Scott asked.

"For now, yes. I'm sorry. The investigation is still ongoing, and Agent Carlson is doing some deep digging, but there's nothing to report yet. The tech team hasn't turned up anything yet on either Marie's or John's personal computers, but they've only had the machines since Friday. These things can take time. Interestingly, someone—presumably the owner—had erased all browsing history from both computers. We have computer forensics folks who can get around that, though, but it takes time."

"When will you be needing *our* personal computers?" Rachel asked.

"Have you been served with a search warrant?"

"No."

"Me neither," Scott said.

"Then you don't have to surrender your personal computers. Yet. You may not have to. It depends on how the investigation goes. But . . . " She pointed a finger at Scott and then at Rachel and moved it back and forth between them a couple of times. " . . . *this* concerns me. Tell me the truth. Did the two of you have a . . . a relationship prior to your spouses' disappearances?"

They simultaneously answered, "No."

"This just . . . happened," Scott said. "Last night."

Dante carefully gazed into each of their sets of eyes. "All right, but I'd better not find out anything differently. I'm not sure what Agent Carlson will think of this development. You may get those search warrants sooner than you think."

Scott reached over and took Rachel's hand. "I don't . . . I don't think we have anything to hide."

"That's right," she agreed.

Dante sighed. "Well. Okay. Oh, let me ask you again. Have you encountered anything suspicious regarding a hidden bank account, or unexplained deposits into your spouses' accounts, or anything out of the ordinary that might indicate a sum of money coming into their possession?"

There was a long pause. Finally, Rachel answered, "Not that I know of."

"Nope," Scott said. "Believe me, considering what's going on in the country, I'd know if I suddenly had a windfall."

Dante nodded and stood. "Thank you for your time. I'll be in touch." They both stood as well, and Rachel said she'd walk the detective out. Dante hesitated and addressed them both. "Be careful, you two. I'm giving you the benefit of the doubt only because I myself was in a similar situation a few years ago."

"Oh?" Rachel asked.

The woman held up a hand—her universal gesture to stop further inquiry. "Let's just say it involved a man, two other women, a dog, and a parakeet." With that, the woman left the house.

When Rachel returned to the kitchen, Scott asked, "'A man, two women, a dog, and a parakeet'?"

She laughed. "It's a strange world, as you know."

"That sounds like the briefs you get at a comedy club before an improv."

"Scott."

"What?"

"We just lied to a police detective."

"I know."

"Are we going to get in trouble?"

"We might."

"What will we do?"

"I don't know."

She paced to the stairs leading down to the family room. Thomas was apparently still there playing his game. Rachel came back, closer to Scott, and asked quietly, "What if we get that money out of the offshore accounts and leave?"

Scott returned to his seat. "Leave?"

"Get out of here. Leave town."

"*Together?*"

She sat down across from him. "Yes. Do you want to stay *here*? On this street? After what's happened?"

"Not really."

"Then let's go."

"We'd look guilty as hell."

"Who cares? We're not," she said.

"Don't you think we need to wait until they clear the case? Then everyone would know we're innocent. Otherwise they're going to think the worst."

"That might take a long time."

"So will the pandemic, Rachel. Do you really want to travel during *this*?" He made a swooping gesture with an arm toward the backyard.

"Scott. John owns a cabin in the Michigan woods. No one knows about it. Well, I do, because I've been there. It's a property that he's had forever . . . I don't know, passed down from a grandfather or something. It's isolated, it's got running water and indoor plumbing, and I'm pretty sure John never put it on his taxes. Like I said, no one knows about it. He used to go up there occasionally to get away from it all. Mostly I guess it was to get away from me and Thomas. Maybe he had other women join him up there. I have no idea. I'd bet money that Marie was there with him at least one weekend."

"I think you're right," he said. "There were some photos on the flash drive of Marie and John in the woods somewhere, and there was a cabin."

"That's it. It has to be."

Scott realized they hadn't removed their masks since Dante had left. He did so, and said, "This is a habit now."

"Uh-huh." She reached out and took his hand. "Look, it's just an idea. Something to think about. I know we can't just jump up and get the hell out of Dodge."

"Or Dodge Park."

She laughed at that. "Or Dodge Lane."

"We'd be dodging bullets."

Still snickering, she said, "But I won't be dodging you." She squeezed his hand. "Let's go upstairs."

"What about Thomas?"

"He's perfectly capable of amusing himself."

Scott thought about it for a few seconds, and then he allowed Rachel to lead him back to the bedroom.

28

Ah, to be a teenager again. That era of my own life was a long time ago. I'm not sure if any of you, friendly readers, are teenagers right now, but if you are, please allow me to give you some advice. For those of you who have grown out of your teenage years, and I'm sure most of you are in the adult-and-counting bracket, the same counsel applies to you too. Of course, you can take it with however many grains of salt you wish.

Temptation to do something reckless can be a powerful thing. It can grab hold of you and convince you that the act it wants you to commit will be good for you. It'll make you feel swell or powerful or whatever. Deep down, though, you may know that the undertaking that seems so attractive is wrong. Will you listen to that modicum of conscience? Unfortunately, the high that temptation has promised you to commit the deed is the number-one goal on your bucket list at that moment in time.

The odds of getting away with it are fifty-fifty. You either get caught, or you don't. Then there's that pesky demon called guilt that may poke and prod you every now and then, regardless of whether you're caught or not. We've talked about guilt already, and perhaps that fiend plays a larger part in our story than we first thought. Hell, guilt may very well be another character in our tale.

I think I'm digressing. Back to the advice I want to impart.

Hm, I'm not sure I remember what it is now. Oh well. I guess it's not important.

Monday, May 18, 2020
2:55 p.m.

Seth Schoenberg was lounging in his room as he pondered commenting on a Facebook post from a classmate named Luke who had announced that he was going to throw a party over the coming weekend. All his homies were invited. Several boys and girls had indicated they were in, but one girl had asked if everyone would be wearing masks and social distancing. Luke had replied that if she was going to insist on that "bullshit," then she was uninvited. She had responded to that with a meme of an extended middle finger. Seth "liked" her post and then went ahead to comment, "My mom is a nurse on the front lines. Wear a damn mask."

He moved on to examine more posts on his newsfeed. He heard the doorbell ring downstairs, but his father would get it. Seth came across posts from another girl he had been interested in during his sophomore year and clicked on her photo albums to have a look.

"Seth?" His father was at the bedroom door. An urgent knock followed. "Could you come downstairs? The police want to talk to you! Seth?"

An iceberg of fear floated down Seth's back.

"Uh, yeah," he called. He closed Facebook, got off his bed, and opened the door.

Mitch Schoenberg was red in the face. "What's this all about, Seth?" he whispered.

"I don't know!" The boy pushed by his father and went downstairs.

Two patrolmen were waiting for him in the foyer of the house. One was tall and blond, the other stocky with a crewcut. They wore masks, but the severity in their eyes indicated that they meant business.

"Seth Schoenberg?" the tall, blond one asked.

"Yes?"

"I'm Officer Sandrich and this is Officer Lewis. We need you and an adult guardian at the police station right now. Is this your father? He should accompany you unless you designate someone else. You can bring an attorney if you wish."

Mitch had followed his son down the stairs. "Is he under arrest?"

"No, sir, he's wanted for questioning."

"About what?"

"That's between the investigator and him, sir."

"It's okay, Dad," Seth said. "I'll go."

"I'm coming with you!"

"Sir, you'll have to follow in your own vehicle. The boy will ride with us in the patrol car."

Seth grabbed a mask from the counter near the front door and then allowed himself to be escorted outside.

The party walked into the Lincoln Grove police station lobby, where a man and woman in their forties sat waiting. The man had a mullet haircut, wore a tank top, and sported a tattoo of the American flag on a muscular left bicep. The woman was a platinum blonde who wore tight clothing meant for someone twenty years younger. Seth groaned inwardly when he recognized them as Doug and Nancy Trainer, Don's parents. They stood when they saw Seth.

"You!" Doug Trainer shouted. "You corrupted our son! How dare you! You little shit!"

"You ate *my* cookies and milk!" Nancy Trainer sobbed. "And now you've gone and told *lies* about Don! I thought you were his *friend*!"

"I . . . I . . . " Seth couldn't speak from the shock of the verbal assault.

"Don's been arrested!" Trainer spat. "You little shit!"

Officer Sandrich stood between them and Seth. "Please, folks, sit down. No need for this."

Doug Trainer got in Mitch Schoenberg's face. "What kind of kid are you raising, Schoenberg?" He pronounced it *Shoinaberg*. "If you think you can falsely accuse my son of things he didn't do, I'm going to sue you! I'm going to take you for everything you got!"

Mitch, a rather mild-mannered person, jumped back several feet to protect himself. "I don't know what you're talking about!" he stammered.

"*Sit down*, Mr. Trainer!" Sandrich commanded more forcibly. "I mean it!"

Trainer looked at the cop and back at Seth and his father. He pointed at Mitch. "You'll be hearing from my lawyer! We're waiting on him now. He'll be here *real* soon!" Then he took his wife's arm and they grudgingly sat.

All that increased Seth's anxiety. He stood with Officer Lewis for protection, and his father waited behind them. Sandrich moved to the reception window and spoke to the officer behind the glass. There were some nods and whispers, and the other man made a call. After a moment, the "Authorized Personnel" door opened, and Detective Dante appeared.

"Seth Schoenberg?" she asked, as if she were a nurse calling a patient into the doctor's office.

Sandrich gestured for Seth and his father to go with the detective. Once the door was closed behind them, the woman spoke to Mitch. "I'm Detective Dante. You must be Mr. Schoenberg?"

"Mitch Schoenberg." He raised his hand for a shake, but then remembered that no one had shaken hands since March.

"And you must be Seth," she said.

"Yes, ma'am."

"Both of you come with me."

She took them into a small interview room and asked Seth to sit on one side of a table and remove his mask. Another patrolman and a video camera on a tripod stood facing the boy. "Mr. Schoenberg, why don't you sit over there." She pointed to a chair at the side against a wall. "And I'll take a seat here." She positioned herself across the table from Seth.

"Can you tell us what this is about?" Mitch asked.

Dante ignored him. "Seth, we're going to videotape our interview. I've asked your father to join us, since you're a minor. You are not obligated to talk to us. You can ask an attorney to join us, and we'll postpone the interview for a reasonable amount of time so that he or she can get here, but I'm afraid we can't let you leave today until we conduct the interview."

"But what's it about?" Mitch asked again. "Is he under arrest?"

"Not yet, Mr. Schoenberg."

"Is he being detained?"

Dante shifted her gaze from Seth to his father. "Yes."

"Let's just do it," Seth said. "Turn on the camera. I'm ready." He swallowed and placed his clasped hands on the table. His father watched with a combination of outrage, confusion, and fear.

Dante gave the operator the signal to begin recording. "Please state your name and birth date, please." Seth answered, and she added, "That would make you sixteen?"

"Yes."

The detective swiveled and reached for something on a small table behind her. Seth saw that it was an evidence bag that contained a cigarette butt.

"Do you know what this is?" she asked.

"A cigarette?"

"Right, but have you ever seen it before?"

"Uh, I don't think so."

"It's a Marlboro. Does that ring any bells?"

Seth thought there was *something* familiar about it, but what was it? "I . . . no, I don't think so."

"Do you know anyone who smokes Marlboro cigarettes?"

"No." *Wait.* Don had told him that he'd stopped vaping and moved to real cigarettes. "Uh, maybe."

"What if I told you that we found this cigarette in the backyard of 507 Marigold Way? You know, the house that burned down?"

A tremendous wave of paralyzing guilt squeezed Seth's chest. All he could do was open his hands and shake his head slightly, as if he didn't know what she was talking about.

"Seth, we received an anonymous tip that a friend of yours is responsible for the arson that burned down the house on the night of Tuesday, May 12, 2020."

Mitch's jaw dropped.

She continued. "I'm betting that you know who this friend might be?"

Seth swallowed, looked at his dad, and back at the detective. An anonymous tip? Who would do that?

Then he remembered . . . *Thomas.*

"Yes," Seth replied.

"Can you name him?"

"Don Trainer."

"What kind of cigarette does Don Trainer smoke?"

Seth nodded. "Marlboros. He . . . he used to vape, though." His voice cracked. "Now I remember. He switched to real cigarettes."

"Are you aware of Don Trainer doing anything illegal in our parks? Dodge Park, for example?"

Seth hesitated. No one wants to be a rat.

"I don't know," he mumbled.

"Pardon?"

"I . . . don't know."

Dante cocked her head. "Are you sure? What if I told you we have evidence of him doing illegal acts? Videos shot on a phone that were sent with that anonymous tip?"

Again . . . *Thomas.*

"Uh . . . "

"Seth?"

"He might . . . he might have set some trash cans . . . on fire."

Dante nodded slightly. "Did you witness him doing this?"

Seth dropped his head. After a few seconds, he told the truth. "Yes, ma'am. A couple of times. Most of the times he did it, he was alone."

"Did you not think to call the police?"

"No, ma'am."

"Seth, were you with Don Trainer at 507 Marigold Way on the night of Tuesday, May 12, 2020?"

Seth took a deep breath. "I was," he muttered.

"I'm sorry, could you speak louder, please?"

"*Yes*. I was."

Mitch spoke up. "Seth! What is—?"

Dante snapped at him. "Mr. Schoenberg, please!" She addressed Seth again, taking the gentler approach. The Good Cop method. It seemed to be working. "Seth, do you remember what time you were in the house?"

"I think it was close to midnight. Between eleven and twelve, but closer to midnight."

"How did you come to be in the house?"

The floodgate was open now. Seth told her how he and Don had ridden their bikes to the house, parked them at the side, and gone through the gate to the backyard. He related how Don had smoked the cigarette and then picked the screen off the back window. They'd crawled into the lower-level family room.

"Did you see anything in the room?"

"Boxes of medical supplies."

"What kind of medical supplies?"

"Masks and stuff. Gloves, hand sanitizer, hospital gowns. Not all in the same boxes, they were separated. Some of it was upstairs in the kitchen and living room."

"Did you open any of the boxes?"

"No."

"Seth, do you know who started the fire in the house?" she asked.

He couldn't speak. Seth *wanted* to tell her, but he couldn't bring himself to do it.

"Seth," she said, "Don is saying you did it. Is that true?"

What?

After their promises not to talk to anyone or say anything about it. After Don pushed him into lighting the Molotov cocktail. After all the horror of it . . . Don ratted on him. And yet *Don* was the firebug who had been vandalizing village property.

"It was Don who did it, obviously," Seth said with as much conviction as he could muster. "I tried to stop him. Don doesn't like to be told no."

Dante nodded slowly. "How did he start the fire?"

"It was a Molotov cocktail. You know, you put gasoline in a soda bottle and—"

"I know what that is, thank you. The arson investigators believe that to be true. It was a Molotov cocktail that started the fire. Why do you think Don is accusing you of this crime?"

Mitch spoke up. "Isn't it obvious? He wants to throw the blame on—"

"Please, Mr. Schoenberg. I'm talking to your son." Dante regrouped and asked Seth, "Can you answer my question?"

"We . . . we had a fight. A disagreement, really. We haven't been talking to each other the past few days. Well, since the fire. I was mad at him."

Dante seemed to be satisfied with Seth's answers. "Seth, I'm afraid I have to place you under arrest for aiding and abetting the arson. It's pretty clear that Don Trainer is the one who did this, given the evidence of the videos that we have of him making practice runs with our park trash cans. You could have told the police about the crime, but you chose not to do so. That, in and of itself, is another crime, Seth. I'm sorry."

Seth wanted to cry. "I was afraid. I did call 911. I'm the one who reported the fire!"

"We know." She then turned to Mitch, whose face was white. "Mr. Schoenberg, we're going to have to keep Seth here tonight. I suggest you engage an attorney. I'll let you know the exact time, but the arraignment will be before the judge tomorrow. You can probably make bail then, and Seth can be released. I'm sure that if Seth—" Dante eyed the boy "—*cooperates*, then there's a good chance he could get off with probation and community service. But that will be up to the district attorney."

Mitch put his arm around his son and held him tightly.

29

There was a time many years ago when the landscape outside of Chicago was farmland, fields, forest wilderness, and very few roads. The "suburbs" weren't called that then, but they did exist as small villages and towns and hamlets. We're talking the first thirty years of the last century, of course. You know, there was a pandemic that occurred back then too—they called it the Spanish Flu. I've spoken of it before. It hit America something awful in 1918. People *really* had to stay inside. Doing so wasn't that big of a deal then, though. It was when the main mode of transportation was by horse and buggy. Automobiles were just starting to appear. Maybe they were more plentiful in the cities, but out in the boondocks, it took longer for cars to be a common sight.

Lincoln Grove had its humble beginnings in the late 1800s and consisted of farms. Neighbors were half a mile to a mile apart. Talk about isolation! Most folks made their own clothes and shopped at what we today would call farmers' markets. Town Center was clustered around one well-attended church. Law enforcement consisted of a county sheriff and whoever he could deputize in any given week. Schools were the stereotypical "little red schoolhouses" that were one or two rooms in size. Plumbing came to the village later than one would think. There were still plenty of outhouses in the 1920s! Electricity was generally available by then, though. Most significantly, everyone in Lincoln Grove knew each other. You could remember the names of the baker, the butcher, the grocers, the banker, and the priest. Lincoln Grove was Thornton Wilder stuff. A picture of Americana. The only scandals that occurred were when Hank or Joe or Walter got too drunk at the tavern and maybe started a fight.

Back then, people mostly stayed at home because it was the natural thing to do. Social occasions were held on weekends because the weekdays were for work. Families ate breakfast, lunch, and dinner together in their places of residence. There wasn't a lot of "hanging out," as the kids call it, except maybe at that tavern I mentioned. It was the only one in town, by the way.

Things have changed. A hundred years later, we're connected by your invisible air waves and your fiber optics and your Wi-Fi and your telephone towers. Your neighbor is in a structure ten feet from yours. Your street might have dozens of houses on it. It's true that we're better connected as a result. You might know everybody on your street. But because the methods and channels of communication have exploded, scandals have taken on a whole new significance in the social fishbowl.

Ironically, a new pandemic has come around, and yet folks are having a heck of a time staying home. A hundred years ago, they were *used* to staying put, but now the uncertainty, frustration, and angst have caused some individuals to go, well, a little crazy.

Monday, May 18, 2020
6:20 p.m.

Scott had spent the rest of the morning at Rachel's house and then went home. There wasn't a soul on the street. Once inside his own house, Scott took a shower and dressed in shorts and a Dire Straits

T-shirt. He then sat alone in his living room, contemplating what had occurred over the last fifteen hours.

He was in a bit of shock. The gravity of what he and Rachel had done could be serious. They had taken perhaps a foolhardy risk with how they would be perceived by officials of the law. It was even too late to reverse course! All it had taken was a one-time sleepover.

That made Scott smile. *That's right, officer, it was just a sleepover. No big deal.*

Did he feel bad about what had happened? Yes, but only because he still felt the loss of Marie. It was especially true when he was in his house. He had thought of his deceased wife as soon as he'd walked in the door, and she continued to occupy his thoughts now. Was he regretful about Rachel? No, not at all. Was he sorry about Marie? Yes, absolutely.

Scott spent the rest of the afternoon handling Marie's estate details. He picked up copies of his deceased wife's death certificates. He would need them when he went to close any of Marie's accounts. In fact, he needed to get moving and start canceling her credit cards, health insurance, and other subscriptions from which monthly bills and dues would come. Since it was a Monday, that's what he did until dinnertime. A can of beans and a homemade screwdriver hit the spot, and now he was ready to get on his phone and see what was up in the rest of the world.

He found that he had a ton of emails. Much of them were junk, as usual, but there were also notes from old friends, current acquaintances, and some crackpots. How the zanies got his email, he'd never know. One anonymous email that was obviously from a neighbor suggested in a polite but no-nonsense tone that he should move away from Marigold Way. In an email that had been sent earlier in the day, his attorney asked how things were going and relayed that there was no movement in the investigation that had been revealed to him.

Scott wondered if he should tell Harry Edmonds about Rachel. Surely, the lawyer would strongly advise him not to continue what he was doing. No brainer, right? He didn't call Edmonds. The truth was that he didn't want to be told to stop seeing Rachel.

The doorbell rang. Scott found it crazy that it never used to ring before all the trouble started. No one ever came to the front door. Now it's become Port Authority. He got up, went to the foyer, remembered to put on his mask, but forgot to look through the peephole.

Fyodor Volkov was outside the storm door. No mask. Light jacket. He looked as if he hadn't slept for a couple of days. Was he a drug addict? Was he sick? Scott didn't move.

Volkov spoke when he realized Scott wasn't going to say anything. "Let me in, we must talk."

"I'm not letting you in."

"I have information—" He jerked and coughed into his jacket sleeve, repeating the reflex three times.

"Are you sick?" Scott demanded.

"No!" He took a deep, wheezy breath, and then seemed to be all right. "I have information about your wife and her lover. You *want* to talk to me, Mr. Hatcher."

Scott narrowed his eyes. Should he trust this guy? The police had indicated they were looking into him. Would he really be able to find out something new from this Volkov character?

"I'll come out there," he said. "Where's your mask?"

Volkov waved his arm away from him. "No mask."

Scott cursed to himself and opened the storm door. The two men then walked down the driveway and stood beside Volkov's truck. "All right, talk," Scott said in a lowered voice. He wasn't exactly six feet from Volkov, but the space would have to do for them to speak quietly and still hear each other.

The man turned away from Scott and coughed again. The spasm lasted a few seconds, and then he breathed normally. He turned back and said, "Sorry. Have cold. Not coronavirus, don't worry. I had test."

"Negative result?"

"No result yet. But I had test."

"Jesus, man," Scott took a step back.

Volkov held up his hands and was more direct in tone and demeanor. "Stop. I will say this only once. Listen. Your wife has money that is mine and is stashed somewhere. I want it back. She has it somewhere. You have to find it and give it to me."

"How much money are we talking about?"

"A large amount."

Scott did his best to feign shock and surprise. "I don't know anything about it, and even if I did, why the hell should I believe you? Get out of here!"

"Mr. Hatcher," Volkov said through clenched teeth. "Your wife and her lover are not the only ones who could end up with bullets in their heads."

Scott was more aghast than afraid. "Are you threatening me?"

"I have tough friends, Mr. Hatcher, very tough friends. Maybe your house will burn down next."

"My God, are you the one who set the fire next door? You are, aren't you!"

"Shut up!" Volkov threw a business card on the ground. "My number is on it. Do not call the police, Mr. Hatcher. Do not tell anyone what we talked about. If I hear from the police because of you, my friends will kill you. Is that clear, Mr. Hatcher?"

"Sure. Whatever."

"I mean it. You will end up like your wife. You have twenty-four hours to find that money!"

"Thanks for the generous deadline. So, were Marie and John Bergman in cahoots with *you*? Were you involved in the theft of the PPE? Is that what this is about?"

Volkov half smiled. "You catch on quick. Do not go to the police. They interviewed me already. They have nothing on me. You go to the police, you will die. That is promise. Clock is ticking. Find that money and get it."

With that, Volkov went around to the driver's side of the truck, coughed, got in behind the wheel, and backed out of the driveway.

Scott then noticed that David Woo had been in his front yard tending to his garden two houses down, but he was now looking at him. Not only that, but Paul Justice was on the sidewalk across the street walking a dog that Scott didn't know he had. Justice was staring at him as well.

Why have I suddenly begun to see Paul Justice outside a lot? Was he spying on me too?

Had they overheard the conversation with Volkov? Probably not, Scott decided. He and the trucker had been speaking in lowered voices. It was still disconcerting. Woo's frown indicated great displeasure with Scott, and it apparently wasn't about the visit from Volkov. Woo seemed to be directing animosity at Scott just for being Scott.

30

How many of you have ever been threatened with violence? As it can be a rather common occurrence in America, no matter where you live, I imagine that a lot of you have. For those of you who have never experienced it, how would you handle it? Are you a concealed-carrier type of person who might go all Dirty Harry on someone who threatened you? Are you proficient enough in martial arts or plain old barroom brawling that you could defend yourself against an opponent? Or are you what we'd call just a "regular person" who has lived an entire life of peace and love and has never been in an altercation? If the latter is the case, what would you do?

Some folks might do the sensible thing and contact the police. Others might take the law into their own hands. Still others will run away, pretend the threat doesn't exist, and put on blinders.

I suppose the point here is that people make rash and irrational decisions in times of stress or when facing a threat. It's human nature. Maybe before we're done here, I'll tell you about the doozy of a choice *I* made that I'll regret forever.

Monday, May 18, 2020

8:15 p.m.

Scott sent Rachel an invitation to jump onto Zoom. Fifteen minutes later, she responded with an "A-OK" text message, so he got online and logged into his account. Rachel appeared a minute later, looking fresh and bright-eyed.

"I can't believe it was only this morning that I last saw you," Scott said. "And yet I feel like it's already been a week."

She gave him a big grin. "I miss you too. Want to come over?"

"Ha! Well, it's tempting, I'll tell you that much, but maybe we should slow down for appearance's sake."

She shrugged. "I'm not that concerned . . . unless you're guilty of something that you're not telling me."

"I've nothing to hide. Hey, listen, I wanted to talk to you because I just got a visit from that guy Volkov!"

"So did I!"

"Really? When was he there?"

"An hour ago? Maybe less."

"He must have come to see you before me. He left here about thirty minutes ago. What did he say to you?"

"Basically, he threatened to kill me," Rachel said. "Not in so many words, but it was definitely a threat. I'm supposed to find John's money from the PPE theft and give it to him, or he'll send his 'friends' after me."

"Yep, that's what he told me too. Well, of course, it was Marie's money he wanted."

"I was about to call you to tell you about it, and then I got your Zoom invite. I had to finish up with dinner and all. Thank goodness Thomas does the dishes!"

Scott asked, "So, how do you feel about it? What do you think we should do?"

"I don't want to give Volkov any money, that's for sure!" she said, indignant. "Who does he think he is? Even if the cash was gained illegally, you and I aren't responsible for the crime. The payment came from bad guys, right? It's not like it's money that belongs to Cassette Labs or anything. The money goes to the deceased's heirs."

"I agree. Do you think we uncovered all of John's accounts? Is five hundred thousand the full amount?"

"Unless he hid another flash drive somewhere, I think so. I agree with your original suspicion that Marie was holding on to the entire amount and that they were going to divide it."

Scott nodded. "That's what I think, too, unless . . . well, unless they were planning to run off together and share the amount as a couple."

"That's a possibility." She raised an eyebrow and gave him a look that was part flirtation, part politician. "You know, *we* could do that too. Just run away together—well, with Thomas too—and share the amount as a couple."

"We did talk about that, didn't we . . . " he acknowledged. "Rachel, we don't want to rush into anything. We have to be smart. The law is watching us. We can't underestimate Detective Dante. Or the FBI."

"No, you're right. I was just thinking out loud. Hey, speaking of Detective Dante, did you hear about the arrests?"

"No! I forgot about it. Is it on the news?"

"Not really, but Thomas found out through social media gossip. Seth Schoenberg and Don Trainer were arrested for the arson."

"What? Really?"

"Yep. To tell the truth, I'm not surprised about that awful Don Trainer, but Seth Schoenberg? He lives right next door to us. He and Thomas are buddies. It makes me sad. Seth has always seemed like a good kid."

"Yeah, I've thought so too. He mows my lawn. Surely it's a mistake?"

She shook her head. "Nope, they're in jail, and they'll have to spend the night. Tomorrow's an arraignment, so maybe they'll get out on bail. Arson is a serious charge. I feel sorry for Mitch and Harriet. Do you know them?"

"Only by sight and a wave. I know Seth better, I guess. I don't know the Trainers at all, and frankly don't want to. So why did Don and Seth start the fire? Was it an accident, or did they do it deliberately?"

"I don't know," she answered, "but it sounds like it was intentional. An act of vandalism. The Trainer boy is also charged with the trash-can fires in the parks."

"Oh my."

"I guess Valentina Wilkins will get a big insurance check and not have to worry about selling the house anymore."

Scott said, "You know, I really didn't know the Wilkinses. I mean, they were next-door neighbors and all, and we were friendly. They were a lot older than Marie and me—they were in their sixties or seventies. Doug Wilkins was a nice man, sort of a grandfatherly Jimmy Stewart type, if you know what I mean. I was really shocked when he killed himself."

"I know. Well, I knew Valentina. We'd have coffee together every now and then. Their kids were grown and away. The Wilkinses had grandkids."

"Do you know anything about what happened? Why he did it?"

"I didn't talk to Valentina after it happened. She left in a hurry, didn't she? I think she stayed long enough to take care of Doug's estate and all, and then arranged to move out. They have a daughter in Tucson, so Valentina went to be near her and her family. I guess she was too distressed and mortified by what her husband did that she couldn't face talking to me or any other friends or neighbors."

"That's what I thought. Doug Wilkins was a contractor, wasn't he?"

"He was retired, and his company was taken over by another one. It was responsible for that disaster in Waddell last year."

Waddell was a town to the west of Lincoln Grove. Scott frowned. "I don't know what you mean."

"Oh, surely you know. The high-rise apartment building in Waddell? The one that caught fire due to faulty wiring? Seventeen people died."

"Oh yeah! Now I remember hearing something about it. You said it was a year ago?"

"About that, yes."

"Damn, that was Doug Wilkins's building?"

"Well, no. His old firm, which was under new management, did the construction. There were lawsuits. They cut corners with the materials."

"So, Doug really didn't have anything to do with it, did he?"

"I'm not sure that's the case. It was in the news everywhere, but his name was kept out of the papers. The firm and their managers got in the most trouble, but Doug was still a silent partner in the company. At least that's what Valentina told me after it all went down. Let's see, what did she say? Her husband didn't tell her everything, so she had to piece clues together. She said that she thought Doug was being blackmailed. Somebody had copies of emails from Doug to the new management telling them how to cut corners. Something like that. He had to pay someone a lot of money or those emails were going to be given to the police. That someone wanted him to take the fall. Doug would have then been part of the lawsuits and maybe could have faced criminal action. Valentina was afraid he'd be indicted. She was embarrassed and humiliated by it all. I think their marriage suffered because of what happened, although they had been together many years. Doug was usually such a kidder, a folksy kind of guy, and then after the tragedy he became morose and depressed and started drinking a lot. I guess that's why he hanged himself in the closet."

Scott was flabbergasted by this news. "How did I not know this? We lived right next door! I must have been way lost in my own problems and didn't pay attention to what was going on. Geez, poor guy."

"Hey, I just thought of something," Rachel said.

"What?"

"Valentina told me that Doug had somehow gotten mixed up with organized crime. She claimed that the mobsters were the ones who pressured him to recommend the cheap materials, because there was a rivalry between the mobsters' construction company and Doug's old firm. Maybe Doug accepted a bribe to recommend the cheap stuff. I'm not sure. For some reason, though, none of this came out in the lawsuits. Maybe the cops couldn't prove it or didn't know. I never found out more because Valentina left. She couldn't sell the house for months, as you know."

"Could you have gone to the police with this information?"

Rachel laughed. "Right. I just told you everything I know. No proof. What do they call it—hearsay? I don't think they would have taken me very seriously. But don't you think it's interesting? The police are saying that the robbery of all that PPE from Cassette Labs in Fornham might be mob related. What if it's the same gang of criminals? Do we have that much of an organized crime issue in the Chicago suburbs?"

"Apparently so."

"Scott."

"What?"

Rachel pointed a finger at him. "Who came to see us today?"

He sat back in his chair. "Mr. Volkov."

"And he was involved with John and Marie. It's why he wants the money."

Scott snapped his fingers. "The money came through Volkov, probably paid to him by his bosses, and he paid Marie and John their fee for stealing the merchandise. Volkov and his people were going to sell the PPE elsewhere and make even more money . . . but because of the fire, they're unable to. The stuff was destroyed. That's why he wants his money back!"

"Bingo!"

They were both proud of themselves. "We've got it all figured out!" Scott proclaimed. "Damn, maybe we should call Detective Dante! We'd get a medal!"

"Surely they're figuring this all out themselves. They've got to be as smart as us."

"Ha ha, who knows? Maybe we should open our own private investigation outfit. I could dress in a trench coat and call you 'Velma.'"

After they laughed about that, Rachel asked, "Scott, do you think we need to be worried about Volkov? Is he really going to come after us?"

"I don't know. Maybe. Should we tell the police?"

"You forget—then they'd find out about the money."

"Oh, right. Yeah, we can't go to the police."

"Scott, I have a gun."

"*What?*"

"Yep. It's a Beretta BU9 Nano handgun. Both John and I went to the range every now and then to practice. It's one thing we had in common. I know that sounds weird coming from a liberal hippie chick like me, but I've had a gun ever since a near-assault happened to me back in the nineties. Believe me, I'm not in the NRA, and I'm not one of those gun kooks. I believe in responsible gun ownership. I keep it locked in a safe here at the house. It's where John kept his Smith & Wesson, too, the one he used on . . . well, you know."

"Wow. I've never . . . I've never even thought of owning a gun."

"In this day and age . . . and especially with Covid raging around us . . . you never know what kind of self-defense you're going to need."

Scott considered Rachel in a new light. "You continue to surprise me," he said. "I thought you were a Woodstock flower child, peace and love and all that."

"I am! I just want to protect my peace and love!"

"Do the police know about your gun?"

"Of course! It's one of the first things I told them. They even examined it. It hasn't been fired in months. Remember, it was John's gun they found in the Wilkins house, and the bullets came from it. His was a Smith & Wesson. The last time I took my Beretta to the range was way before the pandemic. Sometime before Christmas. The point is, I have a weapon. Maybe you should come stay with me at *my* house. That way you won't be all alone in yours, unprotected and unarmed."

That gave Scott pause.

"You make a good case," he said. "Maybe for the next couple of days I'll do that. Volkov gave us twenty-four hours. That's tomorrow night."

"Come on over, you're very welcome."

"Can I let you know in the morning?"

She gave him that flirtatious smile again. "Okay, but don't wait too long. I'll hold your reservation just so long before I start considering other takers!"

31

In Alcoholics Anonymous, the ninth step of recovery is to apologize. To make amends for any hurt or damage you may have caused other people.

That's a lot harder than it sounds. An admission of something you did wrong can often be a big fat surprise to the loved one to whom you're confessing. In that case, the apology could be more hurtful than you intended. The adage "what they don't know won't hurt them" can be apt. A deathbed confession may very well bring a sense of relief from guilt for the one who's coming clean—but it may also deliver a bucket of pain to the confessor.

Here, though, the act of apologizing will go a long way toward one young man's rehabilitation for a misstep. Unfortunately, the number of missteps in a person's life can be profound. I say, look at life as if it were a dance.

You just have to learn the steps.

Tuesday, May 19, 2020
12:05 p.m.

The arraignment had gone as well as it could have.

Mitch Schoenberg had hired an attorney, a woman named Deborah Klingman, to represent Seth. The charge was arson, a Class I felony. Prior to the court appearance, Mr. Schoenberg and Ms. Klingman argued about whether Seth should plead guilty or not guilty. Mitch insisted that his son was not guilty, that Don Trainer had set the fire, and that Seth was bullied into taking part in the crime. Ms. Klingman explained that aiding and abetting the commission of the crime was just as grave, and she felt they would get better traction with the judge if Seth pled guilty. Seth remained silent during their heated exchange. He knew the truth of the matter, and he was loath to reveal it.

Klingman then met with the prosecutor. She argued that Seth had been led astray by the other boy and that Seth had no prior criminal record. "In these uncertain times, with children home from school, the stress and isolation can trigger acts of rebellion that were never meant to cause harm," she had said. They struck a deal, provided that Seth testified against Don Trainer.

In the end, when the judge asked him how he pled, Seth stood and said softly, "Guilty, your honor. I'm so sorry."

As for a sentence, Klingman recommended community service, while the prosecutor echoed the same plus a fine that made Mitch's eyes bulge. Maximum penalty could be four to fifteen years in jail! The judge said he would take everything into consideration. After a bail payment of $5,000, the judge released Seth to the custody of his father—with strict instructions that the boy was to remain housebound and not leave the house without parental accompaniment until sentencing, which would take place in a little over two weeks.

Harriet Schoenberg was sorry she couldn't be at the arraignment. She was needed at the hospital, as there had been a sudden surge in Covid cases in the area. Mitch had brought her up to date over the phone while they were still at the courthouse.

Seth and his father were home by lunchtime.

Mitch prepared a couple of sandwiches, and they ate together at the kitchen table in silence. Seth knew his father was upset and disappointed in him. He felt terrible, although the guilty plea went a long way toward easing his guilt. He didn't look forward to testifying against Don, though.

"I'm sorry, Dad," he said.

"I know."

After another painful few minutes of awkward muteness, Seth asked, "Do you know what happened to Don?"

His father nodded. "Ms. Klingman told me that he pled not guilty and that his bail was high. The trash-can fires were also part of the charges. He's in a heap of trouble, and his parents haven't bailed him out. That's all I know. When you're done, Seth, I want us to go over to the Hatcher house, and I want you to apologize to Mr. Hatcher for causing the fire and burning the body of his wife."

Seth swallowed hard. *That wasn't going to be pleasant.* "Okay."

"And then I want you to do the same thing next door. Apologize to Ms. Bergman. All right?"

"All right. But I didn't know they were in the house. I told you—"

"I know, I know. Don did it, Don was responsible, you had nothing to do with it. Sorry, Seth, it's like Ms. Klingman said. You were there, you helped, and you didn't try to stop him. Furthermore, you didn't tell the police that you and Don did it, and they spent time and money investigating the crime."

That shut Seth up.

When they finished lunch, Seth was ready to make his amends. He wanted to do it alone, but because of the court-ordered admonition, his father insisted that he go too. They walked across the street and passed in front of the blackened hull that was the Wilkins house. Seth gazed at it with shame. He then approached the Hatcher front door while his father remained at the bottom of the steps. Seth put on his mask and rang the doorbell.

Scott Hatcher, a mask on his face as well, answered the door after half a minute. "Seth! Hello." He looked past Seth and saw his father. "Mitch."

"Hi, Mr. Hatcher," Seth said. The boy then found that he was at a loss for words.

"Seth has something to say to you, Scott," Mitch prompted.

"Are you all right, Seth?" Scott asked.

Seth nodded. "I . . . uh . . . I want to apologize for burning down the house next door, and . . . well . . . for burning up Ms. Hatcher too. I'm sorry if this caused you pain."

Scott seemed genuinely touched by the boy's words. "Thank you, Seth. I appreciate that. I heard that it was Don Trainer who actually started the fire. Is that true?"

Seth chose not to answer the question directly. Instead, he said, "I pled guilty to doing it because I was there." He couldn't look Scott in the eyes.

"Seth, there's a saying: 'the company you keep can determine the kind of person you are.'"

Seth raised his head. "Did someone famous say that?"

"Yeah. Me."

That elicited a bit of a nod from Seth. "Okay, see you later, Mr. Hatcher. I'll have to call you about mowing next week."

"Okay, Seth."

The door closed, and Seth removed his mask. His eyes had started to well up; he wiped them on the back of his forearm.

"That wasn't so bad, was it?" his father asked.

Seth sniffed and shook his head. They crossed the street and went straight to the Bergman house. Once again, Mitch held back. Seth donned the mask and rang the doorbell.

Thomas answered it. "Seth. How are you?"

"Okay. Is your mom home?"

"Yes. Just a minute." He disappeared and could be heard calling for her. In a minute, Rachel Bergman appeared as she put on a mask.

"Hi, Ms. Bergman."

"Seth. Oh my." She saw Mitch a few yards behind him. "What can I do for you?"

"I just came over to apologize for burning down the Wilkins house and . . . you know . . . Mr. Bergman. I'm truly sorry for any pain that I caused you and Thomas."

She seemed surprised. "I'm not going to lie to you, Seth, it has been difficult. But thank you. It was brave of you to come over and tell me this."

Thomas appeared at her side. "What is it?"

"Seth just apologized for the fire, Thomas."

"Oh. Okay." Thomas stared, emotionless. He then looked up at his mother and asked, "It's still okay for me to play video games with Seth, right?"

Rachel sighed. "I don't see why not. That's probably a good thing. It will keep him out of trouble."

"I'll . . . I'll talk to you later, Thomas," Seth said, and then he turned and joined his father. The door closed behind them, and they walked to their own house next door. When they got inside, they found Harriet Schoenberg sitting alone at the kitchen table.

"Harriet!" Mitch gasped. "I didn't expect you home. Did you just get here? We didn't see you pull your car into the garage."

She nodded. "I was about to text you."

Seth noted that she looked pale and appeared more worried than ever before.

"What's wrong, honey?" his father asked.

"I was sent home."

"Why?"

A tear trickled down her face. "I tested positive for Covid."

"Oh my God," Mitch said. "Harriet." He sat next her and wrapped an arm around her.

"We have to quarantine for fourteen days. All three of us."

Seth was unable to stay in the kitchen with them. He turned, rushed up the stairs, and stormed into his bedroom. He shut the door and fell onto his bed, facedown, and sobbed uncontrollably.

32

Love, infatuation, lust, and plain old romance—call it what you will. I'm sure you've all experienced it at one time. Can you recall the first time you felt that heavy, painful-yet-pleasurable lump in your chest that indicated you were in love? Do you remember the name of the person for whom you first felt that way? I bet most of you do. "My first serious boyfriend or girlfriend was so-and-so . . . " You've had that conversation with a friend or maybe your current significant other when you were learning about each other's histories.

There's a school of thought that whenever you experience a breakup, or a loss of a loved one, you should jump back in the saddle as soon as possible. The old "rebound." That probably works all right after a breakup—at least in the short term—but maybe not so much if your loved one has perished. Then again, it depends on what kind of relationship you had with the departed. Maybe jumping into the deep end of the dating pool is just what the doctor ordered. Maybe not.

The thing is, everyone is different, and every affair of the heart is unlike another. Sometimes the emotions—and that lump in the chest—feel the same, but the *details* are dissimilar.

I suppose that's why both Scott and Rachel have turned their backs on their deceased spouses and set their sights on each other.

That's the only way I can explain what's going on . . . Otherwise, I've got nothing.

Tuesday, May 19, 2020
5:30 p.m.

Scott had a suitcase ready and packed with essential toiletries, meds, and clothes to last four days. He felt as if he were going on a vacation. The idea of "going away" on a holiday was such a bizarre notion that it felt more like a fantasy. Never mind that he was just traveling the whopping distance of two to three hundred feet across the street and a couple of houses over.

A few factors had prompted Scott to make up his mind about moving out and staying at Rachel's house.

His sleep the night before had been sporadic. The Zoom talk with Rachel had keyed him up. He couldn't help but be concerned about Fyodor Volkov and his threat. At first he had laughed it off, but Rachel's stories about organized crime in their area gave him pause. Volkov did seem to be a dangerous person.

Then, the expected and right-on-cue noise from the Blunt backyard woke him from an elusive slumber. Power saws, hammering, and now a new component—a boombox blasting heavy metal music, although Scott felt it was debatable whether it was truly music or not. It was the kind in which the vocalist screams in a growly demonic voice, surely to invoke imagery of hell.

It was the last straw. He got out of bed, grabbed his phone, looked up the Village of Lincoln Grove, found the number, and dialed it. Like most businesses these days, a bot answered and provided a menu only after listening to the village's lengthy policy regarding Covid. Unfortunately, there was no option to choose "Report a resident for torturing his neighbors." He ultimately hit "0" for the operator. When he was finally connected, he said, "I'd like to make a complaint about the resident who lives behind me."

"What is the complaint about, sir?" a nasally female voice responded.

"He's building some kind of *town* in his backyard. He's up at the crack of dawn using power tools and hammers, and now he's blasting heavy metal music that's so loud, I'm sure they can hear it on Michigan Avenue in Chicago."

"Please state your name and address, sir."

Scott hesitated. "Do I have to?"

"Yes, sir."

"Will he be told it's me who complained?"

"No, sir."

"Are you sure?"

"Yes, sir."

He relayed his information and provided the name and address of the offending neighbor.

"I'm not sure the guy has a permit to build these structures," Scott said. "Aren't permits needed? I walked by the front of his house the other day, and I didn't see a permit in the window."

"We'll look into it, sir. Is there anything else I can help you with?"

"That's it, thanks."

The call had left him grumpy.

Then there was the visit from Seth Schoenberg. Hearing the kid's plaintive and obviously painful apology had torn at Scott's heart-strings. While he hadn't necessarily absolved the teenager of the crime, Scott had felt empathy for Seth's plight. He knew that Seth wasn't a bad boy. The juvenile delinquent who lived at the corner of the street was the real culprit. Seth had been in the wrong place at the wrong time.

The boy's remorse was palpable, and it reminded Scott of his own when he'd withheld the truth from Marie about Diana Keyes. The evidence of his fling was clear, and yet Scott had denied it to his wife. Now that Marie was gone, he had been deprived of the opportunity to come clean about it. He'd never be able to tell Marie that *he* was sorry and offer an honest apology.

This thought process began to pull Scott back into the depressed and shell-shocked state he'd been in a week earlier when Marie went missing and when he found out that she was dead. He had hit the vodka, blamed himself, and hated Marie and John Bergman for what they'd done. It was only the interaction with Rachel that had snapped him out of it. Granted, he hadn't been grieving for long. Perhaps the pain was still inside, but the excitement and novelty of a new relationship had temporarily buried it.

Like a junkie seeking out the drug that alleviated the ache, Scott's thoughts involuntarily returned to Rachel. Even though he knew little about her, and her behavior was just as circumspect as his own regarding her spouse's death, he felt a positive connection there. She was drop-dead attractive and seemed to have the same values as he did. Her son was certainly strange, but Thomas exhibited the impression of being a good kid. Their few intimate moments had been surprisingly fulfilling.

After an hour of obsessing about her, Scott made the decision. He would get out of his house for a few days and move in with Rachel. He texted her and told her he'd be over by around five thirty. She replied with a heart emoji.

Now it was time, and he was ready to go. He shut down his laptop, slipped it into its carrying case, grabbed his suitcase, and went out the front door. Scott locked it from the outside and went down the stone steps to the little walkway that curved through the grass to the driveway. He figured his and Marie's cars were safe in the garage.

Was he being a total idiot? *Yeah, probably. And I don't care.*

"Where are you going, Scott Hatcher?"

The woman's voice came from the west. He turned to see Lois Kimmelman, of course, in her front yard. She had obviously noted that he was carrying a suitcase and was heading across the street.

"Oh, hi, Lois!" he called cheerfully. "No casseroles today?"

"I won't be bringing you any more casseroles, Scott."

"Oh? That's too bad. I'll miss them terribly. But don't worry, it's okay. I can live without them. I'm sure Al will eat them."

"Did you kill Marie, Scott?" she shouted, loud enough for others on the street to hear. David and May Woo were washing their family car together in the driveway of their house. Oh, and there were Paul and Melissa Justice gardening in front of their house, Number 502 across the street. And how about that? The Smalleys, who lived directly across the street in 504, were bringing in groceries from the back of their SUV.

They were all watching him. Every neighbor in sight. *Staring* at him.

Scott ignored Lois's question and continued to walk with his head held high. The more they speculated about him, the more confident he felt about flaunting his indiscretion.

Yep, everyone, that's right! You guessed it! My wife has been dead only a week, and already I'm moving in with the widow of the man whom my wife was sleeping with!

When he was finally at Rachel's door, he didn't bother with a mask. She opened it and beckoned him inside. She was also without a mask, and she was dressed in shorts and a T-shirt that accentuated her earthy skin tone and flawless figure. The smile she gave him did wonders to lift his spirits.

"Come in, sir," she said. "Express Check-In has got you all set up. Shall I ring for the bellboy to bring your luggage to your room?"

He laughed as he entered. She shut the door behind them, and they embraced after he set down his things.

"It was a gauntlet coming over here," he said. "The neighbors were giving me the evil eye."

"To hell with them. Come into the kitchen, there's something I have to tell you."

He followed her in, and she pointed to one of the chairs at the table. He sat as she went to the fridge, pulled out two bottles of beer, and handed him one even though he hadn't asked for it.

"What's going on?"

"I got a call from Mitch Schoenberg this afternoon," she said, sitting next to him. "He felt it was his duty to tell me that Harriet tested positive for Covid yesterday. They're going to be in quarantine for two weeks. She's not sick yet, but . . . you know."

"Gee, I'm sorry to hear that."

"Scott, both Thomas and I have been in close proximity to them. And you've been in close proximity to me and Thomas."

Scott's jaw dropped. "Oh."

"Yeah. We've been exposed."

33

Sometimes we just don't know if we're doing the right thing.

How many of you really weigh all your options, consider all the possibilities, and attempt to predict counteractions from outside forces before making an important decision that could have lasting consequences? Many philosophers have compared life to a chess game. Before you make a move, you need to imagine all the conceivable responses from your opponent. If you slide your knight to that square, does this leave any of your other valuable pieces vulnerable? How will your adversary react? Will there be a bold stroke with a rook, a bishop, or even a queen? That can be dramatic, but a simple pawn moving only one square can also have devastating effects on a game.

Decisions.

Too often, humans go with their gut. Maybe you have incredibly shrewd instincts. Animals in the wild depend on their instincts to survive. We, too, are animals, and allegedly we're the superior species on the planet, right? Tell that to a hungry tiger in the jungle during a showdown between you and him.

I'll grant you that a few of us are developed enough to be worthy of being called "superior" to the animal kingdom, but most haven't.

Otherwise we'd always do the right thing.

Wednesday, May 20, 2020
10:00 a.m.

Scott had been anxious the previous evening as bedtime approached. Rachel seemed to be taking it all in stride. She had admitted being nervous about Volkov, but she didn't show it. They had spent the time playing Monopoly with Thomas, and then he and Rachel retired to her bedroom. They had made love enthusiastically, and afterward Rachel easily drifted off to sleep. Scott, though, had lain awake with his eyes open, staring at the ceiling. His unwanted talent of mind racing had presented a command performance. Was he doing the right thing? Should he really be at his own house, dealing with his demons and Volkov's threat on his own? Would it have been better to go to the police? Did he really want to keep Marie's money? What if he confessed everything to Detective Dante? What would happen then? Was Fyodor Volkov going to show up and murder them? Would he bring his "friends"? Would he be cowering in the corner while violence unfolded? Would Rachel pull out her handgun and shoot them all dead and be a hero?

Nothing happened, though. All was quiet. Eventually, Scott had joined Rachel in dreamland, and they had awoken to the birds chirping outside the window around eight. Thomas made them breakfast again, and all seemed right with the world in the light of the day.

At ten o'clock, the doorbell rang. Thomas was up in his room with headphones on, playing a game. Scott and Rachel were still in their robes, pretending it was a Sunday. To be safe, though, they both went to the door to see who was there.

"Detective Dante!" Scott announced.

Dante wore a mask and asked to come in. Scott and Rachel put on their masks and led the lieutenant to the kitchen. After the usual offer and refusal of coffee, Dante spoke.

"Scott, Rachel, I've come to let you know that we're closing the suspicious deaths case regarding Marie and John. The FBI has declared that there simply isn't enough evidence to suggest that anything other than a double suicide occurred in that bedroom. I'm sorry to tell you this."

Scott and Rachel looked at each other. Then Scott said, "Personally, detective, I would have found it more disturbing to learn that they'd been murdered by a third party. What I can't figure out is why they committed suicide. They didn't leave notes."

Dante looked away into the backyard through the sliding glass door. She appeared to be considering how she wanted to reply to that. Finally, she turned back to them. "The FBI is still examining John's and Marie's computers, but so far they appear to be clean. I can't say when they'll be returned. Our investigation isn't over, but we keep hitting brick walls. The FBI believes that there are a couple of possibilities. One is that John and Marie were filled with remorse at what they'd done and decided to do the deed. I find that unlikely. The second theory is that whoever was behind the robbery, or whoever they were going to sell the stolen PPE to, either reneged on the deal or double-crossed them, or whatever. No evidence was found that they received any money for pulling off the crime. One would think that they would reap the reward by selling the PPE to their buyer. Maybe they learned they were stuck with the stolen property and it was too difficult for John Bergman to put it back in the warehouse. Again, there are problems with that theory too."

Rachel said, "Even if either of those scenarios are true, it doesn't explain why they didn't leave notes."

Dante replied, "Not all suicide cases involve notes. That said, I'm going to tell you what I personally think."

"Okay," Scott said.

"I don't agree with the FBI's conclusions. I'm of the opinion that Marie and John *were* murdered by a third party. I believe the scene was staged. John's gun was used to shoot them both, and then it was placed in John's hand. If the arson hadn't occurred, I am confident that the evidence would have been much easier to read. Staged crime scenes are almost always unraveled. Unfortunately, the fire obliterated any evidence that could support my conclusion."

"But who would kill them?" Rachel asked. "And why?"

Dante gestured with her open hands. "Who knows? Maybe they were cheating their buyer. Maybe they had done something to anger whoever was behind the scheme. The evidence might have given us more clues." She then leaned forward and looked at them both. "*Maybe* they were killed by a jealous spouse. Or spouses." Dante crossed her arms. "You two shacking up like this is perhaps the most irresponsible and incriminating decision that people in your position could have made."

There was silence at the table for several seconds.

"It's not true," Scott finally said.

"He's right," Rachel confirmed. "We didn't do anything."

"Rachel and I simply found in each other a measure of solace. I know it looks bad. But you know what, detective? I don't care."

"Nor do I," Rachel echoed.

Scott continued, "What matters is how we feel about everything. Sure, I'm horrified and terribly sorry about what happened to Marie. It's awful. But it appears she brought it on herself. As I laid it out for you in our countless interviews, I suspected Marie of having affairs. Did I try to stop her? Did I try to divorce her? No. I've come to realize I wasn't jealous. I wasn't . . . I didn't care. Maybe I should have done something about it. In hindsight, a divorce would have been more prudent, but, hell, it was easier for us both to just live with the status quo."

"Her salary was nice too," Dante said. "She was the breadwinner for several years."

That was a knife in the heart. Scott's head dropped, but he lifted it and said, "You may be right. What can I say? It doesn't mean I killed her. I didn't. I've never fired a gun in my life."

Dante looked at Rachel. "But you have."

"Sure," Rachel said with defiance. "You know about the near-assault that happened to me when I was twenty-one. A man broke into my apartment and attacked me, and he had a gun. I fought him, and my screams got my neighbors' attention. They called the police, and luckily there was a squad car a block away. They got there just in time. After that, I swore I'd protect myself from then on. Come on, detective, you can't blame me for owning a gun and knowing how to use it."

"Maybe it was you who shot them with your husband's gun."

"I *didn't do it.*" Rachel threw up her hands in frustration. "I'm just as mystified by what happened as you are."

"I have a question," Scott said. Dante looked at him. "Have you done any more investigating into that Volkov guy? Rachel and I are a little concerned about him."

"Why, have you heard from him?"

They looked at each other. "Uh, no . . . but after what you said before about him . . . that he might be a suspect . . . "

"I never said that," Dante answered. "We were looking into him. As a matter of fact, he's gone missing. His wife has no idea where he is as of two days ago. His truck is gone."

"Really?" Scott blurted.

Dante cocked her head. "You sure you haven't heard from him?"

"No!" Scott looked at Rachel. "You haven't, have you, honey?"

Rachel shook her head. "Nope."

"You must let me know if you do," Dante said. "It appears that he does have some ties with organized crime in the area. There's a new mob boss in the county. Scoutmaster. We think Mr. Volkov might be involved with him. You should consider Scoutmaster dangerous. He could very well supply the missing links to the case, which is why we're trying to find Volkov now."

"Didn't you already talk to him?" Scott asked.

Her brow wrinkled. "How do you know that?"

Scott clenched inwardly. Dante didn't know that Volkov had visited him a third time and revealed that he had spoken to the police.

"You implied it," he answered. "I'm just inferring that from when you asked us about him before. You did, didn't you?"

"You know I can't reveal . . . oh hell. Yes, we talked to him. I must say, he aroused my suspicions. We didn't have anything on him then, though. Since the interview, I've learned a lot more about him. That's all I'm going to say. The FBI is handling the robbery. They're still trying to piece together how it was pulled off and who was involved." She pushed back her chair and stood. "That's all I have today. You two really should reconsider what you're doing here. I'm going to be very disappointed in you both if I learn something that contradicts the FBI's conclusion about Marie and John."

"Oh, detective," Rachel said. "I should probably let you know. I'm sorry I didn't think of this earlier. Uh, Scott and I, and my son, Thomas, we're under quarantine. The Schoenbergs, next door—Harriet Schoenberg tested positive for Covid."

Dante's eyes widened. "What? Oh my God. Why didn't they call me?"

"Should they have?" Scott asked.

"Of course! We were all with them at the police station and the courthouse. That means we're all exposed too. Goddamn it. Goddamn it!" She gathered her notebook and headed for the front door. "Goodbye, I'll be in touch. Goddamn it, now the whole fucking department has to quarantine." Rachel opened the door for her, and she left, still cursing.

When they were alone again, Scott said, "Wow."

"You can say that again."

"Wow." She slapped his arm. "Sorry. So, Volkov is missing? Do we still have to worry about him?"

Rachel reached into a large pocket on the inside of her silk robe and pulled out the Beretta handgun. "I'm ready for him if he shows up."

"Jesus, Rachel! How did I not know that it was on you the whole time?"

"I'm sneaky."

"I guess so!"

Rachel caressed the side of his face. "Darling, the moon is in Taurus. Your safety depends on the need for a stable existence. You must learn to accept change and strengthen your self-respect. You will find peace in the world once you accept yourself for who you are."

Scott was mesmerized. "If you say so . . . " he whispered.

Thomas appeared in the kitchen. "I heard you talking to that police lady."

"Yes, she was here," Rachel said.

"Does she really think you killed my stepfather?" he asked his mother.

"I don't know what she thinks. I'm sorry you heard that."

Thomas shook his head. "I know you didn't do it." He looked at Scott. "Do you want to play a game of chess, Mr. Hatcher? Do you play chess?"

"Sure. I'll play you, but I'm confident you'll beat my ass." To Rachel, he whispered, "I wonder if we should stay here. If we weren't quarantining, we could go to a hotel. Volkov wouldn't be able to find us."

"The risk for Covid is greater at a hotel, Scott," she answered. "No, thanks. I'll take my chances with my Beretta." She reached out and squeezed his upper arm. "Scott, there's the cabin in Michigan. Deep in the woods. Isolated. No one knows about it except maybe the people who run the convenience store that's six miles away. They have PO boxes there, too, and we could get our mail forwarded. The deed is in John's father's name." She turned to a cabinet drawer, opened it, and rummaged for an envelope. She opened it and showed him a piece of paper with the address of the PO box written on it. Rachel scribbled the information on a notepad, tore off the sheet, and handed it to him. "Here. You hold on to that. Scott, we could live there quietly and off the radar. Volkov and his mobster friends would never find us. I hope you'll think about it."

Scott nodded. "I will." He then turned to Thomas. "Okay, let's break out the chess pieces, buddy. Do your worst."

34

When night falls, does our ability to think clearly diminish? Perhaps not for those of you who work night shifts somewhere, certainly, but what about other folks who keep "normal" hours? We've already talked about anxiety and how it can be exacerbated when you're alone with your thoughts in bed. Those so-called night terrors can mess with a person's head once the sun goes down.

It seems that from an early age, we are afraid of the dark. Why is that? What was instilled in our young minds that convinced us that there's a threat under the bed or in the closet? How many times has a parent had to go into a child's bedroom and try to convince him or her that there are no monsters lurking about?

Maybe the makers of night lights are the culprits! That's it! Ha! It's all a big scheme to scare kids and sell more night lights!

Well, I have news for you.

Our capacity to think rationally does weaken at night.

And there *are* monsters in the dark.

Wednesday, May 20, 2020
12:00 p.m.–11:50 p.m.

The rest of the day had passed quietly. Thomas beat Scott's ass at chess, as predicted. Scott and Rachel discussed how seriously they might have been exposed to the Schoenbergs and decided that it likely wasn't bad. They were living recklessly, and they accepted it as part of the mad circumstances in which they had found themselves. Still, they wore masks when they went for a walk through the park together. They didn't care if neighbors saw them and gossiped. Scott remembered the street where Fyodor Volkov lived, and the couple strolled past the intersection to see if the truck might be there. It wasn't. In the afternoon, Scott volunteered to go grocery shopping for the household. He had scooted back to his own home, grabbed the envelope he had received from the coroner, retrieved his Altima from the garage, and headed for the store he had been shopping at for years. On the way, though, was the First Lincoln Bank, where he stopped, put on a mask, and went inside. They had only recently reopened with limited hours and in-person business. He met with an account manager and presented Marie's death certificate, their marriage license, a copy of Marie's will that named Scott as beneficiary, and other forms of ID that he knew would be required. He also presented the number of Marie's secret checking account. The manager didn't blink, confirming that the man didn't know that the account was meant to be concealed from Marie's husband. It took nearly an hour, but he managed to get his name added to Marie's secret account and obtain a temporary ATM card for it. The permanent card would be mailed to his home in a couple of weeks.

Before ending the transaction, Scott thought about what Rachel had told him about the cabin in Michigan. He dug out of his pocket the piece of paper with the PO box address.

"I'm going to be moving out of our house," he told the account manager. "You know, I just don't think I can live there after what happened to my wife."

"I understand, sir."

"Let's change the address of the account to this PO box. Send the permanent ATM card there, okay?"

With that accomplished, Scott got up to leave the bank. He went to his car outside and glanced over to the drive-through lanes. A Lincoln Grove police car was at one of the pneumatic tube machines. Detective Dante was at the wheel, performing a transaction with a teller behind the bank window. Her eyes met his. Scott had removed his mask since he was outdoors. He smiled at her and waved. She glared at him with a frown, as if she were thinking, *What the hell is he doing at the bank?*

Scott turned away quickly and got into his car.

Shit, shit, shit, he thought. *Is she suspicious? Will she make inquiries inside about what I had just done? Or is she just bothered that I'm supposed to be quarantining and I went inside the bank? What do I do?*

He flipped an imaginary coin and decided it was the latter scenario, so he did nothing. The clock was ticking. Scott had to get everything done today. Still . . . the encounter made him nervous.

Just go, he commanded himself. Scott moved on to the grocery store. Again wearing the required mask, Scott picked up items on Rachel's list plus some things he thought of as he browsed. The atmosphere in the grocery store had been creepy since the pandemic began. Customers peered at each other over their masks with suspicion. *Don't get near me. Don't even look at me.* When he was finished, he drove to Rachel's house to unload the groceries.

Back inside, Scott told Rachel what he had done at the bank. "Now I can transfer a little amount of money at a time from that offshore account in the Caymans and it'll automatically land in the First Lincoln account. I can use my ATM card and access the cash from anywhere. It won't attract attention if the transfers into the account are small." He took a breath and then added, "Detective Dante saw me at the bank. She gave me a scary look."

Rachel shook her head and shrugged. "Scott, the whole town knows about John and Marie's deaths. All eyes are on us." She spoke with sensible composure. "Of course it will look suspicious going to the bank. I'm going now too. Same bank. On the same day. But it's our only option. We are out of time."

He nodded, then kissed her on the cheek. Scott then returned the Altima to his own garage while Rachel took Thomas with her to the bank. She was armed with a copy of her husband's death certificate and all the proper paperwork. She made sure to speak to a different account manager than the one who helped Scott so as not to arouse further suspicion. She made the same arrangements, including changing the address to the PO box. Rachel told the bank employee, "This pandemic has got everyone looking at their finances more carefully. There's not much in my late husband's account, but I can use what's there. It's just me and my son now." Thomas appeared appropriately meek sitting by her side. Rachel thanked the man and then left with her son.

Back at her home, they found Scott on his laptop. He had gained access to Marie's offshore account at Seashell Bank. "Watch this," he said. "Let's hope this works." Using the mouse, he indicated that he wanted to transfer $5,000 to "Route 66," which had previously been set up in the drop-down menu as an account. He clicked the various buttons and made the transfer. The total in the Seashell pot was now $5,000 less. Scott then set up online access to Marie's account at First Lincoln Bank and checked the balance.

The $5,000 had been deposited.

"Magic," he said.

"Wow." Rachel stood behind Scott and rubbed his shoulders and neck. "I feel deliciously scandalous."

Later, before dinner, Scott and Rachel watched the local news on TV while Thomas played his video games. The anchor surprised them by announcing that the Lincoln Grove Police Department had been hit hard with the virus. Officer Sandrich appeared on the broadcast to speak via Zoom. He didn't look well.

"Yes, I have to confirm that everyone in the department has tested positive," he said. "Lieutenant Pat Dante went to the emergency room late this afternoon. She had no symptoms earlier today, but it suddenly hit her like a ton of bricks. She was having trouble breathing, so she went to the ER. I've got mild symptoms at the moment, but I'm self-isolating. We've put all the neighboring police departments on alert, and any 911 calls will be directed to the first available and nearest PD. Just please be aware there could be some delays in getting help, so I'm imploring Lincoln Grove residents to stay put, stay safe, and be careful."

Scott and Rachel absorbed this with their jaws dropped.

"Jesus," Scott muttered. He looked at Rachel and asked, "You're feeling all right? Dante was in the kitchen with us."

"I'm feeling fine. You?"

He nodded.

Rachel raised an eyebrow. She didn't have to say a thing. He knew what she was thinking.

It wasn't going to be difficult to slip away.

After dinner, Scott experienced another odd out-of-body sensation as he sat on the couch with his new love. There he was, pretending that he had a new family and that the events of the past week and a half had never occurred. For some reason, this thought process brought on a mild panic attack. Scott excused himself and went into the powder room on the middle level. He splashed water in his face and looked in the mirror. His eyes revealed confusion and uncertainty, and for a moment he wondered who the person staring back at him was. After a few deep breaths, though, he felt better and more like himself. He returned to Rachel on the couch. She asked if he was all right, and he replied that he was.

Now, as the time was nearing midnight, Scott found that he couldn't sleep again. Rachel was in slumberland beside him in her bed. He tossed and turned a bit, and then he felt another panic attack coming on. He was too worked up to keep still. Scott quietly slipped out of bed and treaded softly out of the room. In the hallway, he could see there was no light shining beneath Thomas's bedroom door. Scott went downstairs into the quiet, dark house.

Because the structure was the same model as his own home, Scott's senses played tricks on him. Standing at the bottom of the stairs on the middle level was hallucinatory. It was as if he were in his own house, and yet it looked different. His imagination told him he was walking through an alternate universe of his existence.

Maybe I need a drink.

He went to the kitchen without turning on the light. Outside, security lighting shone through the sliding glass door, and it was enough to illuminate the space well enough. He looked in the pantry where Rachel kept the booze. He grabbed the vodka and got a glass from the cabinet near the sink. He started to pour some of the liquid, but then he stopped.

Maybe I just need some fresh air.

He could go for a walk. Marigold Way was normally safe at night, at least until all the craziness started. There was little crime in Lincoln Grove; it wasn't like Chicago or other metropolitan areas. This was the suburbs. No one would be around. He'd have the street and the stars and the new moon all to himself. It was pleasantly cool too.

Unless Volkov was around.

Screw him, Scott thought. *I'm going out.*

Scott made his way back to Rachel's bedroom, grabbed the clothes and shoes he'd pulled off before going to bed, and then left again as noiselessly as possible. He dressed on the middle level and then went out the front door.

The neighborhood was bathed in a ghostly, silver glow from the barely adequate streetlamps on the lane—one at the corner of Marigold and Temple, and the other near the curve on the east end of the street. The houses on the block displayed very few lights in windows. It was darker than Scott had expected. Nevertheless, the air was fresh and cool, and it felt good to be outside.

He crossed the street and headed toward his house. It wouldn't hurt to check it out and make sure it was secure. Scott passed the Woos' home and then the ugly black mark of the burned-out Wilkins house. However, the sight of a shape at the end of the street stopped him dead in his tracks.

Just up a few houses west near the corner of Marigold and Temple sat the black Volkov Trucking vehicle. It was parked in front of the Justice house.

"Holy crap," he said to himself.

Should he call 911? Detective Dante had said they were looking for Volkov.

That would have been a good idea, but Scott had left his cell phone in Rachel's bedroom, plugged into a charger. Besides, the Lincoln Grove PD was out for the count. The 911 call would go to some other village, and there was no telling how long it would take for the cops to show up.

What now? Perhaps he should turn around and get back to Rachel's house, but he was closer to his own place now. The keys were in his pants pocket. He could accomplish two tasks: check his house to make sure it was all right, and call the cops anyway from his landline. At least there would be a record of his call.

As he walked closer to his front yard, Scott scanned the street for any other figures who might be out for a late-night excursion. Fyodor Volkov, for example. No one was about, though. Where was Volkov, and why was the truck sitting there? Scott hurried along the paved path to the steps and went up to the front door. He removed the key ring from his pocket and . . . he heard someone cough nearby. Scott whirled around to see Volkov standing behind him in the yard.

Volkov raised his right arm to reveal the pistol. "Don't make a sound. Unlock your door."

"Whoa, hey, don't—"

"*Shut up!*" Volkov spat in a whisper. "I will shoot you and run. No one will catch me. You will be dead. Open your door and let's go inside. Now."

Scott did as he was told. He inserted the key in the lock and went in. Volkov was too close behind him to be able to slam the door in the man's face. Incongruously, Scott reached for a mask on the side table in the foyer, but there wasn't one. It was over at Rachel's.

Volkov shut the door and marched Scott into the kitchen. "Sit down," he ordered, and then he closed the blinds on the sliding glass door. "Where is the light?"

"Over there," Scott pointed as he sat in one of the chairs at the table. Volkov turned it on and the brightness was blinding. Scott squinted and held a hand in front of his face. "What do you want?"

"You know what I want!" The man nearly choked on his words, and then he coughed violently without holding his arm or hand over his mouth and nose.

It was only then that Scott could see how terrible Volkov looked. His face was deathly pale, his eyes were bloodshot, and his lips were chapped.

"You've got Covid," Scott said.

Volkov struggled to breathe, but he kept the gun on Scott. Finally, he got control of his lungs and inhaled deeply. "Maybe so," he wheezed. "Where's my money?"

"Where's your mask?"

That was the wrong thing to ask, apparently. Volkov swung his hand across Scott's face, striking him with the butt of the gun. Scott screamed and fell off the chair onto the floor. He was blinded by the bolt of pain on his right cheekbone and nose. Scott gagged and coughed and spit. Blood sprayed over the tiled floor. He lay there, writhing in agony, unable to think clearly or defend himself. Then he was aware of his arms being pulled behind him. Volkov was binding his wrists together with sharp, tight plastic. A zip tie?

Scott groaned and attempted to speak. "I don't . . . know any-thing . . . about your money . . . "

Again, it was the incorrect thing to say. Volkov kicked Scott in the side and then slammed the heel of his shoe on the back of his vic-tim's head. Scott screamed again and tried to curl into a fetal position, but his bound hands prevented him from doing so.

Volkov squatted by Scott's face and showered him with his foul-smelling breath. "Even if I don't get my money, I'm going to make sure someone suffers, and that will be you. Your new girlfriend will be next."

35

As I said before, a decision we make after everybody else has gone to bed might not be too prudent. Especially if you're sixteen years old. There's a reason why you're not legally an adult until you're eighteen. Even then, I'm not sure how mature you are. Some people never grow up. Suffice it to say that while some sixteen-year-olds might be reasonably smart and conscientious, it doesn't mean they know everything. They may think they do, but it's just not the case.

Let's turn back the clock a few minutes and check in on Seth Schoenberg.

Wednesday, May 20, 2020

11:50 p.m.

Butch the Dachshund growled at the window. He was standing on the edge of the bed at Seth's feet, where the dog usually slept at night. Seth was awake. He had been scrolling through Facebook on his phone.

"What is it, boy?"

Butch looked at him as if to say, "A *person*! Are you deaf?" He barked.

"Shh, don't wake up Mom and Dad," Seth whispered. He got up from his prone position and moved to the window that faced the front of the house.

Sure enough, a man was out there in the dark. He stood on the sidewalk and appeared to be focused on the house next door—the Bergman place. Although there wasn't much light, the man was illuminated a little by the streetlamp at the end of the lane by the curve. Seth recognized him as the gangster Thomas had told him about. The Volkov Trucking guy. What was he doing?

Volkov moved closer to the Bergman house. Seth had to change positions to get a better view. The man was almost out of his line of sight. Volkov appeared to be casing the home.

Butch continued to growl.

"Shh, Butch."

Seth slipped back to his bed, picked up his phone, and sent a text to Thomas. Are you awake? He then went back to the window. Volkov had turned and was walking west in front of the Schoenberg residence and started to cross the street toward the Woos' and the burned-out Wilkins place. Seth continued to watch as the man stopped in front of the Hatcher home.

Should he call the police?

Volkov ascended the steps and approached the Hatcher's front door, disappearing behind a jog in the exterior wall. Seth couldn't see the door itself from his window, only the front facade and the yard.

Then another figure came into view in front of the Bergman house. Another man. He walked slowly, stood and surveyed the street and sky. He appeared to be taking deep breaths.

It's Scott Hatcher!

He had come out of the Bergman house. What was he doing there?

Seth watched Mr. Hatcher cross the street and saunter toward his home. Did he know Volkov? Was he meeting Volkov there?

I'm awake, came the text on Seth's phone.

Seth replied. I just saw Volkov in front of your house.

Thomas: Really?

Seth: And Scott Hatcher too.

Thomas: Mr. Hatcher is staying with us.

Seth thought, *What?* He almost asked Thomas why, but he decided not to go there. Instead he texted, Hatcher walking to his house now. Volkov is there.

Thomas: Oh no.

Seth: What's going on?

Thomas: Don't call police. On the news it said they are all sick. I am waking my mom.

Seth: Should I do anything?

There was no reply.

Seth continued to peer out the window. He couldn't see anyone now. The dog had ceased growling, but he was curious as to why his master seemed agitated.

"Go back to sleep, Butch."

Seth texted again. Are you there?

Damn.

Seth felt as if he should do *something*. Wake his parents? No, that wouldn't be a good idea.

He eyed the metal baseball bat that was propped upright in the corner of his room. He knew that a bat could be a deadly weapon. Clobber someone on the head with a metal bat, and they are guaranteed a concussion at the least. It could also bash a person's brains out.

This was his chance. Seth thought he could finally act in a way that would redeem him in the eyes of his parents and the law. Perhaps he could solve the big mystery about the strange events that have occurred on Marigold Way. What if Scott Hatcher and that Volkov mobster were in cahoots? What if what happened to Ms. Hatcher and Mr. Bergman wasn't a double suicide? What if Mr. Hatcher and that Volkov guy had killed them?

He took another look out the window. There was no one in sight.

Seth picked up the bat. At a minimum, maybe he could learn something he could relay to the cops. When they realized what a good—and brave—citizen he was, perhaps they would drop the arson charge against him, and it wouldn't be on his record.

Let's go.

Seth dressed, put on shoes, and gave Butch a scratch on the head. "Stay here, boy." He then left his bedroom, shut the door, and quietly snuck out of his house.

36

Have you ever noticed how bad guys in movies or television simply love to brag about their diabolical schemes, especially when they've got the hero trapped? I guess that must be a prerequisite for villainy—an oversized ego. Even stupid criminals will not miss a chance to gloat to their prisoners about how clever they think they are.

Well, I'm glad this guy does it here. It saves me from having to explain his evil plot to you.

Thursday, May 21, 2020

12:10 a.m.

Scott must have passed out, because he found himself sitting in one of his kitchen chairs. He didn't remember getting off the floor. Volkov must have picked him up and placed him there. His hands were still tied behind him, so it made sitting awkward and uncomfortable. His face hurt, his head hurt, his back hurt, and his right side hurt. Scott was afraid he had a couple of broken ribs where he'd been kicked. Blood still ran from the cut across his cheek and nose. Had the bastard broken it? He couldn't breathe through his nostrils.

Through blurry vision, Scott looked around the kitchen. Volkov wasn't there. In fact, the man's handgun lay on top of one of the counters near the sink. There was a voice, though . . . Scott attempted to concentrate on it, but his head was spinning.

" . . . if you come now, we can make him talk. Right."

Volkov. He was nearby, maybe in the living room. Talking on his phone.

"Yes. I'll wait. Bye." The man then went into another violent coughing spell. After a few moments, Volkov staggered back into the kitchen. He shoved his phone into his pants pocket, went to the cabinets, and opened a few until he found the glasses. He grabbed one, moved to the sink, and filled it with water. He drank it down, coughed a little more, and then set down the glass. He approached Scott.

"How do you feel? Hurts, eh?"

"Please," Scott said. "What can I do . . . to make you believe me? Please don't hit me again. Can we just talk?"

Volkov leaned against a counter and closed his eyes. His breathing was labored and wheezy. Scott thought the guy looked as if he might faint.

He has a high fever. The man is horribly sick.

"Can you tell me . . . what my wife did for you?" Scott asked. "Please? I want to understand. Maybe if you tell me what this is all about . . . I might remember something she said, or . . . something."

Volkov opened his bloodshot eyes. He stared at Scott, sneered, and then retrieved his gun. He held it loosely in his hand, pulled out another chair, and sat in it. "We wait," he said hoarsely. "Scoutmaster is coming."

Scoutmaster? That rang a bell. *Oh, Detective Dante mentioned him. The BOSS.*

"We have done business with John Bergman for a couple of years," Volkov said. "He skimmed drugs out of the Cassette Labs warehouse, we paid him, we sold them again for distribution." He coughed again, caught his breath, and continued. "Scoutmaster has a pipeline around the country and overseas. Some call it a black market. We call it opportunity." He started to laugh at that, but his lungs and diaphragm didn't like it. He coughed again. Volkov winced in pain. He swayed in his chair as if he were seasick. The man grabbed the edge of the table with his free hand and groaned in misery. Eventually, he seemed to settle.

"Coronavirus hit," he went on. "We could make a big score. John Bergman had the PPE. The good stuff. Masks. Gowns. Gloves. Sanitizer. You name it. We paid Bergman a very handsome amount to steal enough PPE and other drugs to fill my truck. My truck is big. It holds a lot. Bergman fixed the security at the warehouse, then we took the stuff. Me, Bergman, and one helper. But the timing was off. Supply lines got cut because of coronavirus. We had to store the stuff someplace until Scoutmaster found new channels of distribution. That's where your wife came in."

Scott wiggled his hands and wrists to see if there was any play at all in his bindings. They were tight and painful. There was no way he could escape. He didn't have the know-how or fortitude. Was he going to die tonight?

"Bergman and Marie . . . your wife . . . they were . . . " Volkov grinned. "They were together. Did you know? Probably not. You are a coward and a weakling. You did not know."

Asshole.

"She offered to open the house next door. She was the realtor for it. We robbed the warehouse in the middle of night, Marie met us next door, opened the garage, we unloaded everything. But only she and Bergman had the code to the lockbox on door." He coughed again, got up, refilled his glass with water, and chugged it. "Ohhhh. I feel like shit."

"You should go to the hospital," Scott said.

"Shut up."

"What about the money you're looking for? How did you pay Marie? Where would it be? How much cash was it?" Scott genuinely wanted to know how the funds got into Marie's offshore banking account.

Volkov returned to his seat. "Did not pay in cash. Bergman had set up offshore bank accounts for him and Marie. Bergman set up accounts so he and Marie could access the money easy, transferring from an offshore account through many banks in other countries and finally to here. I do not know details. Scoutmaster gave me the money to pay them before the robbery. The night it was done, I made the transfer from *my* offshore account. Bergman said to transfer all of it to Marie's account. I did that. I think they planned to split it. Maybe run off together. I don't know."

Scott had figured it was something like that.

"Then those bratty kids burned down the house. Destroyed the merchandise. Scoutmaster wants his money back. If I don't get it back, he will . . . not be happy with me."

"But why did they kill themselves?" Scott pleaded. "Tell me! You must know something about that! Or were they murdered?"

Volkov grinned and shook his head. "I do not know why. That part is crazy. Maybe they were nuts. That's another thing Scoutmaster is unhappy about. He thinks I did it because I was mad at them for some reason. Now, what about the money?"

"If Marie had a secret bank account," Scott said, "why would I know anything about it? If she and John were going to run off together, do you really think she'd tell me where she had hidden five hundred grand?"

Volkov's eyes flared. He coughed a little, stood, and then said, "I do not remember telling you how much I paid her."

Oh shit. I blew it.

"You *do* know something."

"That was just a guess," Scott moaned.

"Liar." He slapped Scott across the face with his open left hand. When Scott was able to open his eyes again and look at his captor, Volkov was pointing the gun at him. "Where is it? Scoutmaster will be here soon. We will make you tell. If you don't tell, then you will die. How will you die, Mr. Hatcher? Quickly? Slowly, with pain? Would you rather me shoot you?" He grinned. "Or shall I *cough* on you?"

37

I'm just going to shut up now. You don't want to hear from me at this point.

Thursday, May 21, 2020
12:20 a.m.

Scott noticed movement behind Volkov at the corner of his line of sight. He had the wherewithal not to move his eyes in that direction for fear of alerting his captor that they had company.

Seth Schoenberg was peering around the side of the archway that connected the kitchen with the dining/living room. Scott figured that he and Volkov had left the front door unlocked when they'd entered the house.

Call the cops! Scott screamed silently. Even though the Lincoln Grove police were out for the count, a neighboring precinct would send someone.

Seth slinked into the kitchen. He held a baseball bat, and his expression exhibited determination mixed with a palpable degree of fear. The boy could see that Scott was in trouble.

Volkov straightened and stepped back just as he began another coughing fit. This one was bad. Scott thought the man's eyeballs would pop out of their sockets. Volkov bent over as he coughed, grossly spewing phlegm on the tile floor.

Seth moved closer. He raised the bat.

Volkov tried to gasp for air and ended up coughing harder. He staggered—just as Seth swung the bat at the man's head. Because Volkov was already falling over, the bat only glanced its target. Volkov hit the floor hard and rolled. Reflexively, he swung his gun arm forward and squeezed the trigger.

BANG!

The round whizzed past Seth's ear and shattered the cabinet door containing the glasses. Glass shards and wood splinters showered a few feet over the kitchen. Seth yelped, jerked to the side, and then raised the bat again. Volkov continued to cough and lost control of his aim. The bat came down on the man's gun arm. Volkov screeched and dropped the pistol. It slid on the floor toward Seth, who quickly kicked it sideways toward the sliding glass door. Volkov curled into himself, grasping his broken arm.

"Hit him again!" Scott shouted.

Seth hesitated, but then he lifted the bat and brought it down on Volkov's shoulder. The man cried out again, and then he twisted further into a ball and whimpered.

"Help me!" Scott pleaded.

Seth tucked the bat under an arm and supported Scott as he attempted to stand. Seth examined the zip ties.

"Can you get them off?" Scott asked.

Seth pulled at the bindings, but they were too tight. "I need scissors or something."

"Did you call the police?"

"Not yet. Should I?"

"Uh, *yeah*!"

"*Stop right there!*"

Both Scott and Seth looked toward the archway that led from

the kitchen into the foyer. *Another* man with a gun stood there, the barrel pointing at them.

Scott thought he looked familiar.

"Drop the bat, kid," the man said. Seth did so. The thing clanged on the tile floor. "Both of you—stand over there and face the wall."

Oh my God! Scott realized where he'd seen the man before.

He was Mr. Blunt, his neighbor behind his house.

Seth and Scott, whose hands were still bound, did as they were told.

Blunt moved toward Volkov and squatted beside him, the gun still trained on Scott and Seth. "You all right, partner?" Volkov raised his head and immediately coughed again, spewing droplets into Blunt's face. "Ugh!" Revolted, the man leaped backward, nearly falling on his butt. He stumbled but managed to stand. "What's wrong with you? Are you *sick*? Oh man, why did you *do* that? You coughed all over me!" He desperately wiped his face with the bottom of the Slipknot band T-shirt he wore.

Volkov got on his knees and struggled to inhale. "I'm . . . sorry . . . I tried . . . "

"You *idiot*!" Blunt yelled. "You fucked up everything with our deal! You stole the stuff before I told you to, and then what did you do? What did you do?"

"I . . . I paid my team with the money." Volkov coughed again.

"You paid them before I told you to, didn't you! And then what happened?"

Volkov gasped for air. "The merchandise got burned up!"

"Right! And you were supposed to get the money back by now, you dumb *shit*!" Blunt impulsively pointed his pistol at Volkov and shot him in the back of the head.

BANG!

The man collapsed onto the floor in a pooling sea of blood.

"There," Blunt said. "Now there's one more ICU bed that's up for grabs." He then directed his attention to Scott and Seth. "So, I've got the noise complainer and the arsonist in one room together. What, are you two a team? Did you *know* about the stuff stored next door?"

"Can . . . can we turn around . . . and talk?" Scott asked.

"Slowly. Stay where you are, though."

They rotated and kept their backs to the wall. Both were terribly frightened, but Scott managed to ask, "So . . . you're Scoutmaster?"

Blunt squinted. "How do you know that name?"

"The police asked me if I'd heard it before. And your buddy on the floor said you were coming."

"Huh. I thought the cops might be getting close. God, I hate that nickname. I should have plugged the smart-ass who started calling me that. All because I was once the den leader of my kid's Cub Scouts. The damned thing stuck."

"I . . . I thought . . . you were the boss of a gang. Organized crime."

Blunt grimaced again. "That's what the cops think. It's just a group of five guys. Four now. Jesus. When my construction company tanked two years ago, I started working with ex-cons I know who are black market dealers. Now, let's get down to business. I want my money back. Either you hand it over to me, Hatcher, or I shoot the kid." He pointed the gun at Seth.

"No, wait!" Seth cried.

"Don't!" Scott yelped.

"Then talk."

"Wait, wait. Look, I told Mr. Volkov the same thing. I don't know where the money is. Marie and I . . . we weren't on good terms. She wouldn't have told me. She took that secret to her grave!" Scott was surprised by how easy it was to lie now. "But I want to know . . . did you kill her? Did you shoot Marie and John Bergman?"

Blunt rolled his eyes. "Yeah, sure, I shot your wife and Bergman. Shot 'em right in the head. Blam, blam. Of course I did." He paused and then growled, "Are you nuts? Why would I shoot the golden geese? I wanted them alive! They had my money! Now *you* have it. I want it back. And I mean it!" He thrust the pistol again toward Seth. "I'm going to count to three. You'd better talk. One . . . !"

Seth whimpered.

I have to tell him, Scott thought. *I can't let him shoot Seth.*

"TWO . . . !"

"All right, you win, I—"

BANG!

Blunt's head exploded like a watermelon being struck with a hammer. Blood and fragments of skull sprayed the kitchen.

Scott and Seth screamed simultaneously and then stood there with their mouths open.

Blunt wavered on his feet for a few seconds, his arms now limp. The gun fell to the tile. His knees buckled, and his body plummeted like a stack of cards.

Scott and Seth turned their heads to see Rachel Bergman, her Beretta in hand, standing in a Weaver stance in the archway to the foyer. Thomas was behind her, pointing a phone at the scene. Was he capturing it all on video?

"Tell me you got it, Thomas," Rachel said.

"I got it," Thomas replied. "Just give me a sec." He moved into the kitchen, carefully stepping over the blood, the bat, and the bodies. He went near the sink, set his phone on the countertop, and began to manipulate an app.

Rachel approached Scott and ran a hand over the wound on his face. "You poor thing. I'm sorry I didn't get here sooner."

"I'm just glad you got here at all!"

She looked at the zip ties. "Hold on, let me grab a knife." She did the same awkward step-dance over the mess on the floor, went around to the drawers, pulled one out, and found a steak knife. She brought it back to Scott and quickly cut through the ties.

"Oh Lord," he said with relief. "I can't tell you how good that feels." His wrists sported red lesions where the bindings had dug into his skin. "What's Thomas doing?"

"You'll see." She addressed Seth. "Are you all right?"

"I think so."

"You did a brave thing."

"I don't know . . . "

"Let's go into the foyer so we don't have to look at all . . . this."

Scott pointed to the two pistols on the floor. "Do we leave those there?"

"Yes. Seth, leave the bat too. It supports our story." Rachel led them out of the kitchen, and then said to Scott, "Listen. I have the car outside. Your suitcase and computer's already inside. Your phone and charger too. Thomas and I had bags already packed in anticipation of this moment. They're loaded and ready to go. Grab anything else you think you might need from your house. Let's get out of here, Scott. We'll go to the cabin in Michigan. We can quarantine there."

Scott had no reason to argue. "I think I have . . . everything . . . for now. When winter hits, I'll need warmer clothes."

"I think we'll be able to buy them."

Thomas called out from the kitchen. "Okay, it's done." He went through the living room to meet them in the foyer. "Take a look."

He played the edited video he'd shot. The video featured Blunt pointing a gun at Scott and Seth, and Blunt saying, "Yeah, sure, I shot your wife and Bergman. Shot 'em right in the head. Blam, blam. Of course I did." The video ended there. Thomas had deleted the rest.

Thomas said, "I'm going to email his *confession* to Detective Dante right now. If she doesn't come home from the hospital, then someone from the police department will get it."

Scott said, "I have to go upstairs." He left them, rushed to the top-floor bathroom, and splashed water on his face. The rip across his nose was still bleeding, but it wasn't terrible. He touched the area and it stung like the dickens. The intense pain had subsided a little, though. "Maybe it's not broken after all," he said. He grabbed some antibiotic ointment, applied it, and stuck on a bandage. He shoved the tube of ointment and extras bandages in his pocket, and then he returned to the group on the middle level. He asked Rachel, "So we just leave? That's the plan? Leave my car, Marie's car, our houses, and that bloodbath in the kitchen?"

Rachel shrugged. "We'll send an email to Detective Dante and tell her what happened. She'll get it with the video. Let the police find the bodies and they'll do what they do. We defended ourselves against intruders, Scott. We were traumatized, so we left town for a while. Maybe we'll be back. Maybe not. If they have to talk to us, we'll do it by Zoom, damn it."

He gestured to the foyer. "I still have a mortgage. So do you."

"If we don't come back, the bank forecloses, takes all the contents and the houses, and they're gone. Out of our hair. I don't want to live here anymore, Scott. Do you?"

Scott felt defeated and elated at the same time. It was a strange sensation. "I'm not sure it's that easy, but . . . yeah, I don't want to live here anymore either. I think I made that decision when I was at the bank getting my name on the account."

"Good."

"What about me?" Seth asked.

Rachel turned to him. "You'll have to give a statement. Just tell the truth. You didn't do anything wrong."

"I was under house arrest. I snuck out and came over here."

"And it's a good thing you did," Scott said. "I think you saved my life." He addressed Rachel and Thomas. "I mean, you *all* saved my life, but if Seth hadn't shown up when he did, I might have undergone more torture."

Rachel said, "Seth, we need you to do something else for us." She dug into her pants pocket and pulled out a wad of bills. "Here's three hundred dollars. It's for you. Would you please gather Scott's and my mail every day, stick it in an envelope, and then once a week mail it to this address?" She gave him a slip of paper with the PO box location in Michigan. "I trust you'll keep that piece of paper secret. We'll continue to send you three hundred bucks a month if you do this for us until a time when we think it's safe to officially forward our mail." She looked at Scott for his approval, and he nodded.

Seth took the money and the paper. "I can do that. Thank you."

"Thank *you*."

Thomas then said, "Let's go."

Scott reached into the kitchen and turned out the light, and then they were out the door.

38

Folks, we're nearing the ending of our tale.

Well . . . maybe.

Let's just say that this is how I, as your storyteller, choose to finish it. A raconteur is, in many ways, "god," in that he or she selects what parts of a story to relate. I explained this way back at the beginning. I did hint at some Missing Pieces, though, which we'll get to. I've decided to show them to you.

I assure you that true accounts of crimes never really have complete and satisfying endings. There are always questions that go unanswered, evidence that isn't found, or facts that are never presented at trials. There are plenty of innocent folks in jail for crimes they didn't commit, and even more hardcore criminals who are acquitted due to some technicality or incompetence of the prosecution or police. Many offenders are never even discovered and arrested.

With that in mind, for now, let's wind up our sordid saga.

Thursday, May 21, 2020

1:15 a.m.

Scott looked at Rachel's car, a 2014 white Kia Rio, which was parked in the driveway.

"Hey," he said. "Why don't we take my Altima? It's newer and it's . . . bigger. I also got brand-new tires last fall. I've hardly driven since March. What do you think?"

Rachel and Thomas exchanged glances and the boy shrugged. She spoke. "My car is fine. It's not going to break down. It's already packed and it's here. There's also the chance your neighbors might have heard the gunshots and called the cops. How many shots were there? Three? Four?"

"I lost count. But I doubt the police are going to show up if someone called them."

Seth laughed a little. When they looked at him, he said, "I can just imagine a sign on the door at the police station and on their website that says, 'Please don't commit any crimes in Lincoln Grove, people. The police are unavailable.'"

That made Scott and Rachel laugh, too, which released some of the tension they were all feeling. The adrenaline rush had left them a little loopy.

Rachel placed a hand on Scott's arm. "We need to leave. Are you coming?"

I can't let her go without me, he thought. *For better or worse, she is my destiny.*

"Fine," Scott said, "we'll use your car." He turned to Seth. "Thank you again for your help." He held out his hand to Seth, who almost shook it, but hesitated.

"We're quarantined. I can't shake your hand. Social distancing!"

"I think it's a little late for that. You know, I haven't shaken *any-one*'s hand since March. Put her there, Seth."

Scott and Seth shook hands. Then Seth and Thomas did so, and Rachel gave the boy a hug.

"Be careful," she said. "Take care of yourself. I hope you don't get sick. Don't worry about the police. We'll just make sure they know that all you did was hit Volkov with the bat because you thought Mr. Hatcher was in danger."

They said goodbye, and Seth turned and walked toward his home.

Rachel got behind the wheel of her Kia, while Scott slipped into the passenger seat. Thomas climbed into the back. She started the car, backed out, and headed west to Temple. It would take them ten minutes to get to the interstate, which would then steer them around the southern end of Chicago and the Great Lake, and up north into Michigan.

The trio was silent for some time. The roads were empty. Even the interstate had little traffic on it.

Scott eventually broke the hush. "We still don't know what really happened to Marie and John. Did they commit suicide, and if so, why?"

Rachel sighed. "I don't think we'll ever know, Scott. The police closed that part of the case. It's one of those mysteries of life and death. In the meantime, you have your flash drive, I have mine, and we've got enough money to last us quite a while. We'll have some explaining to do to the police for what happened tonight, for sure, but we did nothing wrong."

"We're running away," Scott said.

After a moment, Rachel responded, "I look at it more as running *toward*."

They were silent for a while longer until Scott spoke again. "Do you ever wish you could move back the clock and start over?"

Rachel thought about it as she watched the road. "No, because we'd discover missing pieces of our lives that we probably don't want to face or think about."

After a pause, Scott added, "I don't know. I think there's something to be said for examining past events by going backwards in time to the start. You can learn something." He turned his head. "What do you think, Thomas?"

The boy in the back seat simply answered, "Whatever you say, Dad."

Scott blinked. He turned to Rachel, who gave him a knowing grin. Scott smiled in return, and then glanced back at Thomas, who was staring out his side window.

Scott sighed, faced forward, and shut his eyes.

The occupants of the Kia were quiet as they traveled around Lake Michigan and headed for an unknown future, not knowing if they were carrying the coronavirus or not. They did take comfort, however, in the knowledge that they were escaping the claustrophobia of their little, locked-down street as the car sped forward on the lonely, lost highway.

39

Right.

So, do our characters go off and live in the Michigan woods happily ever after?

Hell, *I* don't know. I'm not privy to what happens to them after they leave Marigold Way. However, as I promised, I can reveal scenes that occurred off camera, so to speak. Stuff from the cutting-room floor that may or may not shed some light on what you've just witnessed.

For example, during the telling of the tale, I chose not to relate much from the point of view of Rachel Bergman. What if I were to "turn back the clock," as Scott said, and cast a spotlight on her and her son? How about we "go backwards in time to the start," as Scott mused?

We'll begin with a brief snippet that took place immediately after Seth texted Thomas about seeing Mr. Hatcher and Mr. Volkov on the street in front of his house.

Folks, here are the Missing Pieces.

Wednesday, May 20, 2020

11:55 p.m.

Thomas texted to Seth: Don't call police. On the news it said they are all sick. I am waking my mom.

Thomas then quickly put on his pants and a shirt, and slipped his feet into shoes. The boy then left his bedroom, walked swiftly down the hall to his mother's room, and knocked.

"Mom? Are you awake? Mom?"

He went ahead and opened the door. Rachel bolted up from her pillow, startled. "What? What . . . Thomas? What's wrong?" She looked over at the side of the bed where Scott was supposed to be. "Where's Sc—where's Mr. Hatcher?"

"Seth just told me he saw Mr. Volkov outside our house. Now he's at Mr. Hatcher's house. Mr. Hatcher left just now and is going over to his house."

"Oh dear." She immediately swung her legs out from under the sheets and made for the pile of clothes on the floor. As she dressed, she said, "Thomas, I want you to get the suitcases we packed and put them in the trunk of the car. Then get Mr. Hatcher's computer, his phone and charger, and put those in the car too. I'll get my computer and the cooler of groceries we set aside. It's time to get the hell out of Dodge. You, me . . . and Mr. Hatcher. Go. I'll meet you downstairs. Hurry!"

As soon as Thomas left the room, Rachel moved to the nightstand beside her bed and opened the drawer. She removed her Beretta and set it down. Next, she grabbed the box of ammunition and the gun case from the drawer and stuck both in a carry-on bag that contained her meds and toiletries. Scott's overnight bag was in the bathroom, so she quickly gathered his things from the counter and threw them inside.

Rachel caught sight of herself in the mirror. No makeup, her hair was a mess, and there were dark circles under her eyes. The stress of the past week and a half had indeed taken its toll.

"Are you ready to do this?" she asked herself aloud.

Of course I am. My life as "Mrs. Bergman" is over. It's time to reinvent the wheel.

"Let's do it, then."

Rachel juggled both bags and her laptop and carried them downstairs, where she met her son in the hallway. "Get in the car," she ordered. "We're going to pick up your new dad."

40

Granted, that didn't tell you much.

Okay, let's go back a little farther to the end of the Zoom call in which Scott considers moving in with Rachel for a few days.

Monday, May 18, 2020
9:20 p.m.

"Come on over, you're very welcome."

"Can I let you know in the morning?" Scott asked her.

She attempted to give him the flirty smile he seemed to like. "Okay, but don't wait too long. I'll hold your reservation just so long before I start considering other takers!"

That made him laugh. He waved at her through the computer screen, and then he was gone. Rachel closed the Zoom meeting and sat back in her chair.

She was thrilled.

The conversation with Scott had eased her anxiety about the earlier visit from Fyodor Volkov. That awful man had threatened her, insisting that she give him John's money from the Cassette Labs robbery.

There was no way in hell she was going to do that. Besides, Scott had it all. John had allowed Marie Hatcher to hold on to his portion.

Talking to Scott had made it all better. It had been a wonderful Sunday with him in the house and in her bed. He was a kind, passionate lover, and they seemed to be compatible. Could a new relationship really work out so soon after John's betrayal and death?

She snickered to herself when she thought about Detective Dante's visit that morning. The expression on the lieutenant's face had been priceless. Yes, the cuckolded spouses of the deceased adulterers were shacking up. Rachel had done her best to act nonchalant, as if it were the most natural thing in the world to do. It was hilarious.

Rachel got up from her vanity and stuck her head out the door. "Thomas?"

"Downstairs, Mom!"

She descended to the middle level, where her son was snacking on cookies and milk at the kitchen table. "I feel like a schoolgirl with a crush," she said.

Thomas wiped his mouth with a napkin and looked at her. "I'm happy for you, Mom. You talked to him on Zoom?"

"I did. I think he's going to move in with us starting tomorrow. For a little while, anyway."

He nodded without showing much emotion. "That's nice. I will like him as a new stepfather."

"Whoa, don't get ahead of yourself, kid," she said with a laugh. "We're not getting married. Yet."

"I know you're thinking about it, though. Right?"

She moved to him and ran her fingers through his hair. "You've always been such a smart boy. My little genius."

He took another bite of cookie.

"Listen," she said. "I need you to help me get the house ready. We've got to clean the kitchen, run the vacuum, and clean my bedroom and bathroom. It wouldn't hurt to clean your bathroom and bedroom too. I want the place to be sparkling when Scott comes back over."

"Sure, Mom."

"There's something else on my mind, Thomas."

"What?"

She sat at the table and looked at him. "We need to be ready to get out of here at the drop of a hat. Don't you agree? Let's pack bags as if we're going on a long vacation. Pack your suitcase with clothes for summer and winter. Use one of your stepfather's if you need more than one. I'll do the same. Let's have them ready in case we need to disappear. Are you with me?"

"Sure, Mom. I'm with you."

41

Now let's go back to the prior weekend when Scott first agreed to enter Rachel Bergman's house and have iced coffee with her at the kitchen table. It was the true beginning of their relationship. Earlier that day, they had both given separate interviews with FBI Special Agent Carlson. What happened right after Scott left Rachel's house to go back to his own?

Saturday, May 16, 2020
2:45 p.m.

Rachel peered out the front room window and watched Scott walk across the street and head for his own home.

What a handsome man, she thought. *Kind, considerate. He's going through a lot. Just as I am.*

She went to the kitchen and put away the cups as she thought about seeing Scott at the police station that morning after her interview with the FBI agent. Detective Dante had escorted her to the lobby, where Thomas was in conversation with Scott Hatcher, the other poor soul who had also lost a spouse to an adulterous affair, suicide, and arson. Once again, despite him being masked, Rachel had been struck by Scott's dark good looks.

"All done," she had said to her son. "Let's get out of here." She had then greeted Scott with a "Hello" and an eye roll that indicated, *Whew, it's a relief to get that over with!* On the way out to the car with Thomas, Rachel had wondered if Scott had picked up that she was flirting with him.

The interview with Agent Carlson had gone as well as could be expected. Carlson had the same queries about her relationship with John. Where she was on the night of his disappearance and on the night of the arson. He had asked about John's business and what she knew about it. The subject of John's gun. Her own weapon. The safe at home where they kept the firearms. Rachel had also detailed how she had been familiar with guns since the attempted assault she'd experienced when she was in her twenties. Guns were one of the things she and John had in common. They had met at a gun range.

She had responded to Carlson's questions with honesty and straightforward sincerity. She knew that there was no evidence that could possibly suggest she had anything to do with what had happened to John.

Carlson had asked if she had ever noticed her husband storing medical supplies at the house or in his car. She replied truthfully that she had not. The agent then inquired about "windfalls of money." Had she seen unusual activity in the family's bank accounts?

"He bought a BMW last year," she had answered. "The one that was in the garage of the Wilkins house when it burned down. Oh, and he spent time away from home. On 'trips.' He'd say it was for business, but I know now that he was having an affair . . . with *her*. Hotels in Chicago. Probably fancy dinners. He took a trip to the Cayman Islands in January. Again, he said it was for Cassette Labs."

Carlson had then revealed something interesting. "Ms. Bergman, a month ago, a shipment of PPE and drugs recently touted as treatments for COVID-19—hydroxychloroquine—was confiscated by authorities in New York. It was being distributed by an organized crime outfit. The source of the goods was Cassette Labs. Do you know if your husband has been on the phone at home with any suspicious characters, or was *he* behaving suspiciously when talking on the phone?"

"No," she had answered. "The only thing I ever heard about involving organized crime was what happened to the owner of the house that burned down. Doug Wilkins. He committed suicide in the house. I understand from his widow, Valentina, that he might have had something to do with that apartment building in Waddell that also burned down last year. She had no proof, but she thought Doug had been involved with some mobsters. I really don't know."

Carlson had paused to study some notes. He mumbled something to himself and nodded. "I've been made aware of Mrs. Wilkins's suspicions. There was no evidence to support her claims."

"Then the answer to your question, Agent Carlson, is no, I don't know anything about organized crime in Lincoln Grove."

Thomas appeared in the archway between the living room and the foyer, bringing Rachel out of her recollections of the morning and back to the present in her kitchen.

"How did your visit with Mr. Hatcher go?" he asked.

"Mr. Hatcher is very nice. Do you like him?"

"I do."

"We're going to have a Zoom chat later this evening. Maybe we'll get to know each other better."

She moved away from the window and went into the kitchen. Thomas followed her.

"Well," he said, "I'll make sure I stay in my room and give you privacy."

"That's grown up of you."

"May I make a suggestion?" She nodded. "Perhaps you should hint to Mr. Hatcher that his wife might have hidden something in the house that's a clue to where the money is. Like a *flash drive*."

Rachel opened her arms to her son, and he approached. She folded him into her and held him tightly. "I love you so much!"

"I love you, too, Mom."

"I'm so sorry you and your stepfather had all that trouble. You never could call him Dad, could you?"

"No. He called me the R-word."

"That was horrible of him." Rachel let Thomas go and held him by the upper arms. "You're incredibly smart. Smarter than me. Smarter than your *stepfather*, that's for sure! And you're only fourteen."

"Am I smarter than Sarah?"

"Of course you are. Sarah is not a part of our family anymore. She doesn't count."

Thomas nodded. "I'm going upstairs now, Mom."

"Okay, honey. I'm going to start going through those drawers now."

"Let me know if you find anything."

"I will."

42

The clock moves back a day. Do you remember when Scott was at home, and Thomas surprised him by ringing his doorbell and coming in to say that Scott would make a good stepdad? They barely knew each other. Rachel then showed up, looking for her son. Scott awkwardly invited her in. They had coffee. They chatted. It was friendly. They spoke about the case. It was the first time they had more than a "Hi, how are you?" conversation. Afterward, Scott had wondered what the hell just happened. Did Rachel feel the same way?

Friday, May 15, 2020
11:45 a.m.

Rachel and Thomas removed their masks and walked away from the Hatcher home. Thomas took her hand. Normally a fourteen-year-old boy wouldn't be caught dead holding his mother's hand in public, but Thomas had no problem with it. Neither did Rachel.

The woman next door to the Hatchers—*what was her name? Lois something.* She was doing something in the yard, but Rachel wasn't sure what it was. Snooping, perhaps? The woman gave her the stink eye something fierce. Rachel ignored her, and they walked along the sidewalk in front of the burned-out Wilkins house, then crossed the street to their own place.

Once inside, Thomas said, "I like Mr. Hatcher."

"Well, I like him too. He seems nice."

"Maybe you can get to know him better."

They went into the kitchen. Thomas sat at the table, and Rachel went to the fridge. "How about some lunch?"

"Okay."

She began to make sandwiches. "You think I should get to know Mr. Hatcher better, huh?"

"Yes. You're not unhappy about Stepdad."

She looked at him sharply. "Thomas, we both know your step-father was a difficult person. It's clear you didn't get along with him. I know that."

"You didn't either."

Rachel finished making the sandwiches and set a plate in front of her son. She poured glasses of orange juice for them both and she joined him at the table. "Your stepfather and I clicked for a while when we first got married, but things went sour. It happens."

"It happened with my real father too."

"I know."

"And Sarah's father."

"You don't have to remind me."

"Too bad Sarah's father died." She shot him a look that said, *Don't go there.* Thomas continued to talk. "My stepdad was a crook. Crooks are not usually very good people."

Rachel smiled at that. "Oh, Thomas." She shook her head and then reached out and ruffled his hair.

He displayed no pleasure in that, but simply took a bite of his sandwich and asked, "Will people think it's wrong if you get friendly with Mr. Hatcher?"

"Well, probably. I'm supposed to be in mourning."

"You're not, though."

"I am, Thomas. I feel bad your stepfather is dead. But I'll admit that it opens up some possibilities for us."

Thomas nodded. "I know what that means. There's some money stashed away somewhere." He looked at her with humorless eyes. "Are we going to get it? Maybe Mr. Hatcher can help us."

Rachel gazed out the sliding glass door to the backyard. A squirrel was rustling in the grass, looking for something to eat.

Scavengers . . . every one of them . . .

"Mom?"

She snapped out of her brief reverie and said, "Let's just see if Scott Hatcher gets in touch again."

43

The sands of time seep upward back into the hourglass. Now we're traveling back to the morning after the fire. The Lincoln Grove Police have already visited Scott Hatcher to break the news that Marie's and John's bodies were discovered in the charred remains of the Wilkins house. From there, the police moved across the street to the Bergman home to do the same for Rachel.

Wednesday, May 13, 2020
9:50 a.m.

Her hysteria was real. She screamed and cried and tore at her hair.

"My husband was with . . . *Ms. Hatcher*? How can that be?" She lowered her head onto her arms, which rested on the kitchen table, and wailed. Thomas sat beside her, mortified, staring at Detective Dante and Officer Sandrich as if they were the culprits. If he'd been equipped with laser beams in his irises, he probably would have used them.

Dante and Sandrich exchanged glances. While they had to deal with grieving family members on a near-daily basis, this case was especially difficult. And then there was that creepy kid . . . They let the woman express her anguish until it subsided to a more manageable sobbing.

"Ms. Bergman, may we ask you a few questions?" Dante gently prodded. "It's important."

Rachel lifted her head, wiped her cheeks, and nodded. "Just a sec." She turned her head, removed her mask, and grabbed a tissue from the box on the table. She blew her nose and wiped her face again, then replaced the mask. "Sorry."

"It's quite all right, Ms. Bergman. We understand."

"Do you?"

Dante took a breath. "Did you have any suspicions about your husband and Ms. Hatcher?"

Rachel sniffed and nodded. "Some. I wasn't sure. I suspected he was . . . cheating. I knew he talked occasionally to her. I suppose it's a . . . shock to find out for sure. A wife always knows." She narrowed her eyes. "Did Mr. Hatcher know?"

The detective mumbled, "Uh . . . "

"Did you ask him? You came here from his house, right?"

"We did. He didn't seem to know about it. Ms. Bergman, do you know Mr. Hatcher?"

"Only by sight. We wave. We say hello. That's it."

Dante nodded, then made a note. "When you talked to my colleagues on Monday, you told them that your husband owns a gun. You also confirmed it with me yesterday. Can you tell me again what kind of gun it is?"

Another sniff. "A Smith & Wesson M&P9 Shield. Nine-millimeter."

"You indicated that the gun was missing from your safe."

"Yes. And I showed Officer Sandrich my Beretta that I keep in the same safe."

"Right. Ms. Bergman, we recovered a Smith & Wesson M&P9 Shield at the scene. It was in your husband's hand."

Rachel gasped. "What are you saying?"

"On preliminary examination, it appears that he shot Ms. Hatcher in the head and then turned the gun on himself."

"He . . . shot *himself*?"

"We're still investigating, but that's what it looks like."

"*Why?*"

"Have you found any kind of note?"

"No! I would have told you. Wait a minute, wait a minute. Are you saying my husband and that woman set the house on fire and then shot themselves?"

"Maybe, maybe not," Sandrich said.

Dante cast him a look and continued. "Crime scenes can be staged. Did a third party shoot them and start the fire? It's possible. We have to wait for the autopsy reports. Hopefully, the coroner can determine the time of death for both victims. Unfortunately, everything is burned. Vital evidence is probably destroyed."

Rachel inhaled sharply. "You mean they might have been . . . murdered?"

"Could be," Sandrich said.

Dante glared at him and turned back to Rachel. "It's not what it appears to be, but we have to consider everything. Now. There's another thing."

"Oh, what else could there be?" she snapped sarcastically.

"The house was full of the stolen merchandise that was taken from Cassette Labs the other night."

"No."

"Yes. PPE and cartons of drugs. At least we think it's the missing stuff. It, too, was destroyed in the fire. What that tells us, though, is that your husband may have been involved in the robbery."

"Oh my God." She moaned loudly and lowered her head into her arms again. Thomas continued to laser-beam the police officers with his eyes.

Dante moved away a little. "I think perhaps that's all for now. We'll talk again later after we know more. I'm leaving these pamphlets with you. It's information about grief counseling in case that's something you want to look into. I know this is hard. We're going to get to the bottom of this, I promise you." She dropped the literature on the table. "We'll need you to come in and identify the gun and other items tomorrow."

"What . . . what about his phone?" Rachel asked. "Did you find his phone?"

"It was there. Smashed. Destroyed. That's one of the items we want you to identify. We're not sure if it was somehow damaged in the fire or if he deliberately broke it before the fire. There are a lot of unanswered questions right now."

"Jesus."

"Will you be up to coming in tomorrow? If not, we can—"

"I'll come in! Just let me know what time."

"Thank you. Again, my deepest condolences."

Yeah, right.

She saw the officers out, removed her mask, and went back to the kitchen to sit with Thomas. He held out a hand and she took it.

"You're my rock," she said to him.

"Are you all right?" he asked.

"Yes. Of course." She sniffed and blew her nose on another tissue. "We knew your stepfather was a bad man."

"We should reach out to Scott Hatcher."

Rachel looked at her son. After a moment, she replied, "The stars tell me that it's our destiny that we do."

44

Now we're moving back in time another day, prior to the fire at the Wilkins house. You'll recall that Scott received a phone call from Detective Dante on that Tuesday evening around dinnertime to inform him that the phone company pinged his wife's phone, and they determined that it had last been somewhere around the Hatcher home, or certainly nearby. Scott went outside and searched for it, but he couldn't find anything. Then, around seven thirty, Fyodor Volkov showed up at his door for the first time and asked about Marie and when she would be home. Scott was put off by the guy and sent him on his way.

Well, just prior to Volkov's visit to Scott, he had stopped by the Bergman house first.

Tuesday, May 12, 2020
7:10 p.m.

Rachel hung up the phone after speaking to Detective Dante. The lieutenant had called during dinner as she and Thomas shared a frozen pizza they'd baked in the oven. While money was tight, she found it significant that the only money they were spending was for bills and food. She wasn't shopping for clothes or shoes for herself or for her son. John had regularly deposited his paychecks into their joint checking account, from which she handled the mortgage and the other monthly expenditures. The stimulus check from the government had helped, too, so with inexpensive meals like frozen pizza, they were doing all right.

The call from Dante didn't reveal anything that was a surprise to her. The phone company had pinged John's cell. Dante said that it indicated that his device was somewhere across the street near the Hatcher and Wilkins houses—maybe in between. The ping wasn't always exactly accurate. Furthermore, the ping pinpointed only where the phone was last turned on. If John had shut it off and taken it elsewhere, then the ping wouldn't be accurate at all.

The big question, Dante wondered, was why John's phone would be across the street near the Hatcher and Wilkins homes. Rachel didn't answer that. While she knew that Marie Hatcher was also missing, she didn't ask the detective if Ms. Hatcher's phone was in the same place, and Dante didn't offer that information. The query about whether John had known Marie Hatcher had come up in their earlier in-person interview. While Rachel had previously admitted to Dante that she suspected her husband of infidelity, she'd kept it to herself that John was having an affair with Marie. She'd known for some time. He may very well have been a serial philanderer. The thing with Marie Hatcher was not all that recent.

Why didn't she tell Detective Dante what she knew? Rachel was unable to justify her silence. Perhaps she just didn't want to air the dirty laundry of her marriage until there was a resolution of the missing person case.

Did Scott Hatcher know about the affair? She doubted it. Rachel didn't know him well, but she pegged him to be rather naive. A nice guy—and good looking, too!—but a little clueless as to what was going on around him.

Rachel had always been a private person. She wasn't on social media. She had few female friends. Ever since her marriage with John had begun to unravel, she had tightened the circle around herself and Thomas. It was them against the world. She had been conditioned to think this way after the collapse of her first, and then second, marriage.

At any rate, the investigation was still going on.

When would they find John and Marie?

The doorbell rang. Thomas had gone upstairs to get on his computer, probably with headphones covering his ears. Rachel got up from the kitchen table, moved to the foyer, and looked through the peephole in the front door. A man she didn't know stood on the porch. He wasn't wearing a mask. Rachel put hers on and opened the door.

"Can I help you?" she asked.

"Oh, I am sorry to bother you, madam . . . look, I stand here six feet away." The man spoke with a pronounced Eastern European or Russian accent. The man continued. "My name is Fyodor Volkov. Maybe you have seen my truck in your neighborhood or around the vicinity of Dodge Park?" He gestured to the black truck parked in the driveway. "Volkov Trucking" was painted on the side, along with a phone number.

"What do you want?"

"Is John Bergman at home?"

"No, he's not. Why do you want to know?"

"Oh, I have business with John. We work together sometimes. I have a trucking and delivery business. Volkov Trucking. He mentioned me maybe?"

"Never."

"I see. I deliver medical supplies and things for him. I am trying to reach him. He does not answer his phone."

Rachel didn't like the sound or the look of the guy. "I don't know when he'll be home. Sorry." She started to close the door.

"Wait! Please!"

She hesitated. "Yes?"

The man's demeanor changed abruptly. He no longer smiled or exhibited a submissive attitude. Now the man's face was a hard frown, and his voice almost growled. "Tell him I came by. Fyodor Volkov. Tell him I am not happy. He must call me."

Rachel felt a presence at her side. Thomas had come down the stairs and joined her at the door.

"I'll tell him," Rachel said. "Goodbye." She shut the door before the man could get in another word.

Thomas went to the living room and discreetly peered out the window. He watched Volkov get into his truck, back out, and drive away.

"That's him, Mom," he said.

45

Earlier that same day, Rachel met Detective Dante for the first time, as did Scott Hatcher, when the lieutenant and Officer Sandrich paid a house call to both residences to discuss the separate missing persons cases. The police showed up at the Bergman house first. Since Dante asks Rachel many of the same questions that she put to Scott, we'll skip over a lot of that and just cut to the tail end of this Missing Piece.

Tuesday, May 12, 2020
9:05 a.m.

Detective Dante wrote in a notebook as Rachel answered the questions the best she could. The other officer, Sandrich, stood nearby. Both police officers wore masks, as did Rachel and Thomas. The boy sat quietly at the table and listened attentively. Dante had not minded that he was present for the interview.

Rachel had never met Detective Dante before. She was happy, though, that Sandrich had brought someone with more seniority over to follow up on the missing person report she'd made the day before.

Nevertheless, it had been a difficult night. Rachel hadn't slept well, and the uncertainty of the situation had brought on a great deal of anxiety.

Dante had asked about John's daily routines, whether he was taking medications, and if Rachel thought he might be a danger to himself or others. There were questions about the last time she'd seen John, which was Sunday morning, and what his mood and demeanor was then. Dante got more personal than Sandrich had done the previous evening. She queried Rachel about her marriage to John and how it was going.

Rachel answered everything transparently. She told the detective that the marriage was on the rocks and that she suspected her husband of unfaithfulness. "I should have left him a long time ago, but I didn't. It's my third marriage, and I wanted to work extra hard to keep it together. Unfortunately, there is a strain between my son, Thomas, and John. They don't get along. My second husband is Thomas's father."

"Has there been any domestic abuse going on?" Dante asked.

Rachel hesitated, then looked at Thomas. The boy's eyes bore into Dante's as his mother answered, "No. You might say there's a battle of wills going on between Thomas and his stepfather. It's been that way for a while."

"Are you able to keep the peace?" Dante asked.

"More or less. I usually take Thomas's side, and John doesn't like that." Rachel shook her head. "It is what it is. John's never hit anyone, if that's what you're asking."

Dante wrote in her book.

This led Rachel to revisit what Officer Sandrich had previously told her.

"I understand Ms. Hatcher, across the street, is also missing. Has she turned up?"

"No," Dante said. "Did your husband know her? Is there any connection between them that you know of?"

"We know the Hatchers only well enough to wave hello. We've barely spoken to each other over the years," Rachel answered.

Dante nodded, indicating that was the response she had expected. She moved on. "You told Officer Sandrich yesterday that your husband owns a Smith & Wesson?"

"That's right. I showed him the safe. The gun is missing."

"And you own a Beretta BU9 Nano?"

"Officer Sandrich saw it in the safe."

"That's right," Sandrich confirmed. "It had not been fired recently."

"I haven't been to the range since before the pandemic started," Rachel explained.

Dante then outlined what the next steps would be in investigating the missing person case—asking the phone company to ping John's cell, which Dante would arrange that afternoon, and entering information into LEADS. There wasn't a need to go into John's personal belongings—yet.

"However, we are concerned that your husband has gone missing so soon after the robbery at his place of business. This gives us pause. The crime at Cassette Labs was well planned and clean. That's not our jurisdiction, and we're letting the Fornham Police handle that. It's possible you'll hear from someone there if Mr. Bergman doesn't show up soon. Can you tell me where he was this past Friday night?"

"I have no idea. I was asleep by ten o'clock and wasn't up until nine the next morning. We . . . don't always sleep in the same room. Lately, he's been sleeping in one of the other bedrooms. I have no idea if he was home or not that night."

"I see." She wrote that down.

Dante wrapped up the interview and stood. "Try not to worry, Ms. Bergman. We'll find your husband."

"Will you?" Thomas asked.

"Yes, Thomas, we will. We'll do everything we can."

Rachel thanked the officers and showed them the door. She and Thomas then removed their masks and looked at each other, and Rachel took him in her arms.

46

It's Monday afternoon, the same day it was when we first began the story. You'll recall that Seth Schoenberg and Don Trainer were in Dodge Park. Thomas appeared just as Don was about to light one of his Molotov cocktails and throw it into a metal trash can. Thomas took some nasty abuse from Don, and then he received a phone call from his mother, telling him to come home. As soon as Thomas left, Don lit the explosive and the two older boys fled the scene.

Monday, May 11, 2020
1:50 p.m.

Thomas entered the house, removed his mask, and found his mother in the kitchen wiping down the counters with vinegar-based cleaner. "There you are," she said. "I sure wish your father had brought home some Clorox wipes. We have a supply of masks, hand sanitizer, and vinyl medical gloves, but no wipes. It's crazy that none of the manufacturers can get these things in the stores. First there was that mad run on toilet paper, which was really stupid, and then everyone realized they needed gloves and masks and *wipes*. Your father could have given us wipes!"

"He's not my father. He's my stepfather," Thomas said.

Rachel stopped what she was doing and looked at her son. "I know that. I'm just a little stressed out right now, as you can imagine."

"It will be all right, Mom. Everything will turn out okay."

"Are you sure? People make mistakes."

Thomas sat at the table and scrolled through his phone.

"Where were you just now?" Rachel asked.

"At the park."

"Did you see anyone?"

"I saw Don Trainer and Seth."

Rachel continued to wipe the counter after spritzing it with her homemade solution. "I don't like Don Trainer. Does he bully you?"

"Yes."

"You need to stay away from him."

"He lit a Molotov cocktail, and it exploded in the trash can."

She stopped working. "What?"

"I told you Don is the one who is doing that."

"You saw him do it?"

"Yes. I even got it on video." He held up his phone and showed her the footage.

"Did he see you shoot this?"

"No. They thought I'd left. I was behind a tree. See, they're kind of far away. But you can tell it's him."

She sat down and watched the video on her son's phone. "They could get in a lot of trouble for this."

"Seth is okay, though," Thomas insisted. "He's my friend."

"I know he is. You've known Seth a long time."

"We talk a lot on FaceTime. We play games together."

"I know."

"Don is a pyromaniac. He's been setting things on fire for years. I know."

Rachel chuckled. "I'm surprised you know that word."

"What word?"

"'Pyromaniac.'"

"Mom, I'm fourteen."

"I know. I'm not sure *I* would think of that word. I'd just say, 'He sets things on fire,' or 'He's a firebug.' You're such a smart boy. I wonder if we should tell the police about Don?"

Thomas took the phone from her. "No. Not yet."

"Maybe Don will get really creative and set fire to that eyesore house for sale across the street," Rachel said. "Burn it down and everything inside it."

"I agree, Mom. That would be a good thing. It would bring some excitement to the neighborhood. I'll ask Seth to suggest it to Don. I bet Don will do it if someone dares him."

47

Now we move back in time to the day before our story began.

The fateful night.

The essential Missing Piece.

Sunday, May 10, 2020
11:50 p.m.

Wearing medical-grade vinyl gloves, a disposable shower cap, and one of the protective hospital gowns that Cassette Labs sold wholesale, Rachel opened the gun safe on the floor of the clothes closet with the combination she knew by heart. Inside was her Beretta, which she hadn't touched for months, and John's short-barreled Smith & Wesson M&P9 Shield. It, too, had not been fired in some time. She removed the Smith & Wesson and a box of the 9mm rounds, as well as the seven-round magazine that was already full. She expertly inserted the magazine and examined the weapon to make sure it was ready for use. Rachel then closed and locked the safe.

Thomas stood nearby, watching her. He, too, wore vinyl gloves, a shower cap, and a smaller-sized gown.

Rachel straightened from her crouch and gently nestled the handgun in a canvas shopping bag that she wore around her neck. A hammer and a flashlight were already inside the bag.

"Are we ready?" Thomas asked.

"Yes." Rachel took a deep breath and then followed her son out of the bedroom, down the stairs, through the foyer, and to the front door of the house. Thomas opened it and held it for his mother as she stepped outside into the night air.

Together they stood on the porch and surveyed the street. There was a light on in a window here and there, but most of the houses on Marigold Way were dark. Nearly everyone had gone to bed.

Rachel studied the Wilkins house across the street.

There.

A dim light flashed in one of the top bedroom windows.

"Stepdad and Ms. Hatcher are in that room," Thomas whispered. "Let's go."

They quietly moved to the end of the driveway and then to the middle of the street. Thomas had suggested that they walk in the center of the road to avoid being caught by any ring cameras that might be in use on some of their neighbors' porches.

No one saw them. No one heard them. If there hadn't been a pandemic scouring the landscape, it wouldn't have been so easy. Now, though, everyone was indoors. Staying home. Social distancing.

They reached the Wilkins house front door. The lockbox was in place. Rachel and Thomas knew that Ms. Hatcher possessed the garage door opener, and that's how the couple would enter the house instead of using the front door. Rachel reached into the bag and handed Thomas the flashlight. He cast it on the lockbox, and Rachel punched in the code. Thomas had hacked into John's cell phone months ago, and Rachel had gained access to John's text messages. That's how she had learned the lockbox code. Marie Hatcher had texted it to John. Thomas had also planted malware on the phone that was essentially spy software meant for parents to monitor messages on their child's device. Anytime Marie and John texted each other, Rachel could read the conversation. The adulterous couple thought they were being careful by deleting the texts as soon as the exchange was finished. By then, though, Rachel had seen everything.

The lockbox opened and revealed the house key. Thomas took it, carefully inserted it into the door, and turned the knob. Together they entered the foyer of the house. At first it was a bit disorienting because the layout was a mirror image of their own home. As expected, there were stacks of cartons in the living room, carefully arranged away from the window. They could see more cartons through the archway to the kitchen at the end of the foyer. Thomas and Rachel shared a glance. *The stolen goods from Cassette Labs!*

They heard noise upstairs. Rustling. Voices. A man and a woman. Moaning, laughing, grunting . . .

Rachel winced. She knew those sounds. Thomas stared at the darkness at the top of the stairs. They could see dim illumination in the hallway, coming from a small lamp in the occupied bedroom.

Thomas made for the carpeted stairs. He had always possessed the ability to move with stealth and silence. He turned back to see his mother frozen at the front door. He gestured with his head.

Rachel's eyes were wide with fright. *I can't*, she mouthed.

Thomas nodded. He slowly moved back to her and slipped the bag from her shoulder. He put it around his own neck. He held a finger to his lips and then gestured for his mother to wait there. She clutched his arm to prevent him from going ahead with the plan. He looked back at her.

His eyes were cold, dark, and brutal.

Rachel released him.

Thomas took the steps one at a time. The man and woman upstairs were likely too engaged with each other to hear him anyway. Rachel watched her son fade into the shadows as he reached the top of the stairs. He turned and disappeared down the hall and toward the light.

Except for the vocal passion of the two adults upstairs, there was no extraneous noise.

Headlights suddenly panned across the living room front windows, followed by the rumble of an engine. Rachel tensed. It was a car driving from east to west, on its way to the intersection of Temple and Marigold. Then it was gone. It had likely come from the end of the street near the curve. Someone was out late. Odd.

The house grew silent again except for the ugly gutturals of lust.

Rachel waited. She felt the sweat drip from her underarms down her sides. Her mouth was cotton dry.

What's taking so long?

The seconds ticked by.

She waited.

Although she knew it was coming, the discharge made her jump. BANG!

This was followed by a woman's half-scream of confusion and surprise. BANG!

Then all was dead quiet, except . . . Did she just hear John *groan*? Then . . . nothing.

Still, Rachel waited. At least a full minute passed. Maybe more. Then—BANG!

She heard a bit more rustling above.

Did the neighbors hear the gunshots? Is someone calling the police?

Thomas had assured her that three isolated "bangs" around midnight on quiet little Marigold Way in safe, suburban Lincoln Grove would not attract attention. Even if heard, the barks of the handgun wouldn't be recognized for what they were.

She heard something break upstairs. A pounding. Then another shattering, followed by two more hammer strikes.

Their cell phones.

Another two minutes passed.

What's taking him so long?

Finally, Rachel saw Thomas appear at the top of the stairs. He calmly and coolly descended and handed her the shopping bag. He nodded at her. His eyes were dark slits of cold granite.

Rachel opened the front door and they stepped onto the porch. She replaced the key in the lockbox and shut it.

They were home within minutes.

Once they were safely inside their house, Rachel and Thomas removed the vinyl gloves, shower caps, and gowns. She stuffed them in with the kitchen garbage that was full of stinky food scraps. Rachel removed the trash bag, tied the ends and took it, along with two other bags of trash they'd been collecting, into the garage to place in the Waste Management garbage bin. She would set her alarm, get up early, and roll it and the recyclables bin to the curb, since pickup day was Monday. By noon, the only evidence of the murders would be compacted in the garbage truck and on its way to the landfill.

"No problems?" she asked Thomas.

"None."

"What happened?"

"I shot stepdad first in the side of the head. It was not perfect. He was still alive, but he was helpless. I did her next before she could yell. It hit her just above her nose. Not the best spot, but it will be fine. It took a little time to arrange the bodies. Stepdad made some noise. I put the gun in his hand, pointed it to his head, and fired the gun a third time into his temple. Then I smashed both of their cell phones."

"What were they . . . oh, never mind."

"They were on an inflatable mattress with a blanket over them. He didn't see me at all. She might have seen my silhouette, but that's it. The police will believe it's a double suicide. The two shots in him might confuse them, but it will look like he botched the first shot, and then managed to fire the gun again."

Rachel sat down in the kitchen. Thomas stood in front of her. She was impressed—and a little disturbed—by how calm he was.

"We should both take showers," he said.

She nodded. "On television, they always figure out if a crime scene is staged."

"Mom, it's going to be days, maybe even weeks, before someone discovers them. Tomorrow, you report him missing. You just have to be convincing. Like me."

She held out her hands and shook her head. "I don't know anything about it, officer. I was at home with my fourteen-year-old son."

"Mother, you will win an Oscar for your performance."

48

And now we come to the final Missing Piece. The following conversation took place that morning before the murders.

Sunday, May 10, 2020
10:30 a.m.

Rachel sat at the kitchen table eating a plate of scrambled eggs and a toasted English muffin. It was a late start to the day for her. The trouble with John had been increasing, and he had threatened to hit her the previous evening. Her hot coffee did wonders to heighten her mood, though. It perked her up.

She studied the text messages between her husband and the woman on her phone, thanks to the spy software Thomas had secretly installed on John's device. The couple discussed how Volkov's payment had been made and would land in Marie's Seashell account on Monday. Once that was done, John told her, they could proceed with the next step of their plan to abandon their lives in Lincoln Grove and move to the cabin in Michigan. He was still dealing with the police investigation of the Cassette Labs robbery. Marie asked if he was under suspicion, and he replied that he was, but that there was no way they could pin anything on him. Once he was cleared, they would act.

Rachel was tempted to forward these texts to the police. However, she and her son had other plans.

The text messages ended with John and Marie agreeing to meet "at the house" that night to celebrate their good fortune. Marie said that she should be able to slip out around eleven o'clock and meet him there. She would open the garage door and they could go in "the same way as before." John said he'd bring a bottle of wine. Marie said it would brighten her otherwise depressing Mother's Day.

Hmpf, Rachel thought.

The texts were deleted a minute later and were no longer available.

Thomas came down the stairs. "Stepdad is gone?" he asked.

"He left the house an hour ago. I don't believe we'll see him again today," she replied.

He held up a flash drive. "His offshore account has only a thousand dollars in it."

Rachel indicated her phone. "I just saw some texts between him and his *girlfriend*. The money they're being paid for the robbery has been transferred and will supposedly land in her account tomorrow. I guess they're going to split it up later. You'd better put that flash drive back in the bowling ball."

"I will."

As her son went to find her husband's bowling bag and replace the incriminating evidence, she thought about the pair of pistols upstairs in the safe. While she was proficient with her Beretta, John's Smith & Wesson was just as user-friendly. He had let her shoot it a few times at the range. Thomas was also extremely skilled with both weapons.

The money that John and Marie were going to receive could be a boon of a nest egg. She and Thomas could live very comfortably in the Michigan woods on that money. The problem was that it was going to be in Marie Hatcher's account. Should she wait until the woman transferred John's portion to him? What if she didn't do that? What if their scheme was for John and Marie to run off together *first* and then share the money out of her account?

When Thomas returned, Rachel asked him, "What do you know about her husband? Mr. Hatcher."

Thomas's face remained expressionless. He blinked a couple of times. "Seth mows his lawn in the summer. He says Mr. Hatcher is a nice man. Mr. Hatcher is a famous writer, sort of. He used to be."

"I know. He hasn't been too successful lately, has he?"

"I don't think so. His wife is the main breadwinner, from what I gather."

"But he's about to be rich and doesn't even know it."

Thomas continued to look at his mother as if he were waiting for her to come to the conclusion he expected.

"Do you think Scott Hatcher might make a good father?" Rachel asked him.

"I don't know. I don't care. As long as you're happy, Mother. He would be a major improvement over Stepdad."

"Will you help me?"

"Of course, Mom."

"Maybe the three of us can live in the Michigan woods. For a while, anyway. Mr. Hatcher is very good-looking."

"Whatever you say, Mom."

She shrugged. "After we get the money, we can get rid of him. Somehow."

"It's worked before. No one blinked about Sarah's dad. We can do it again. I just wish we could have done something about *my* dad."

Rachel shook her head. "He wasn't worth the trouble. He'll always be a loser." Still sitting, she held out her arms. He moved toward her and she enveloped him in a hug. "I'm so glad I have you."

"Do you miss Sarah?" Thomas asked.

"No. She . . . refuses to accept the special relationship that you and I have."

"Neither did my father or my stepfather."

"No, they didn't."

"Maybe Mr. Hatcher will."

"Maybe. But I'm afraid it's just you and me, Thomas. The moon is in Capricorn tonight. We underestimate what we want from ourselves and for ourselves. We're not to seek approval from the outside. We have to trust our inner values. Thank heavens, you'll always be with me."

"You know I will. But we need to act before Fyodor Volkov moves the PPE and drugs from the house."

"Tonight, Thomas."

Thomas nuzzled his face into her chest. "Sounds like a plan."

Rachel ran her fingers through her son's hair. "My brave, smart boy."

49

The tale of the Mad, Mad Murders of Marigold Way must now come to a close.

I realize there are some unanswered questions. Perhaps you feel there are unresolved threads. I have news for you, folks. There always are.

That's just a part of life.

And death.

Unresolved threads.

Will the Lincoln Grove Police Department staff recover from the virus that's raging throughout the country and around the world? That I can't tell you. Detective Dante will likely come through all right. She is a smart supervisor, and I have confidence that she will do everything she can to continue protecting the residents of the village.

What's going to happen to Don Trainer? Will he convince the prosecutor and judge that he didn't personally set the fire that burned down the Wilkins house? Probably not, considering his history of malfeasance. Perhaps a little jail time will do him some good.

Will Seth Schoenberg overcome the guilt he feels for taking part in the deed? Since he's had a decent upbringing and a good sense of what's right and what's wrong, I'm fairly certain that Seth will turn out all right. The scare he received, the violence he witnessed, and his own actions in the early hours of May 21 will likely haunt him for years to come. He will surely be put through the wringer when he's interrogated about the events that took place in Scott Hatcher's kitchen. Never fear, friends—I have a good feeling about Seth. He'll survive. Oh, and while his mother may have tested positive for COVID-19, I'm betting that Harriet Schoenberg will be one of the lucky ones who has either a mild case or has no symptoms at all. She's a true hero, after all. Seth and his father will hopefully avoid getting ill as well. Fingers crossed.

As for Scott, Rachel, and Thomas . . . their destiny is more difficult to predict. Scott and Rachel obviously don't realize how easy it is for financial investigators to discover hidden bank accounts and such. But be that as it may. Given what we know now, is Scott Hatcher in for the shock of his life? Or will events turn out all right and will the members of the trio ultimately love each other and live happily ever after? In many ways, Rachel and Thomas are a lot like the coronavirus. They latch on to a subject and cause an infection. The seriousness of the illness is unpredictable. Scott may find himself asymptomatic, or with a mild case of sickness. Or it could be fatal.

We just don't know, do we? We never do.

Unresolved threads.

I can't see the future, my friends. I may be able to observe what happens on Marigold Way in Lincoln Grove, but I'm only able to hover over events and document them to myself. I can never influence anything that the living do on my street. When my wife, Valentina, picked up and fled the house where I made use of a noose in the closet, I was left alone and aimless. Yeah, that was the doozy of a bad choice I made that I'll regret forever. I should have just fessed up to my role in the Waddell apartment building fire. Not that it makes any difference now, but it was indeed Mr. Blunt and his cabal of petty crooks who got me into that mess. I lost my sense of humor . . . and I fell into an abyss. Every day I apologize to Valentina, even though she can't hear me. Now I'm doomed to stay here for eternity and watch and listen and haunt and . . . tell stories.

The great Thornton Wilder closed his classic play, *Our Town*, with final thoughts about the state of the village. Even though the characters had grown up, changed, or possibly died, the mundane routine of life moves forward. The same thing will occur in Lincoln Grove once the mad scandal of Marigold Way is a fading memory. Until those duties are no longer necessary, folks will continue to wear masks, play the social-distancing game, be wary of strangers and infection, and hopefully get vaccinated once those miracle drugs appear—less than a year after the events of our tale. Yes, the stars will persist in streaking across the sky in their never-ending and inevitable treks. The sun will surely rise and fall every twenty-four hours—like clockwork!—and there will repeatedly be rain and heat and snow and cold over twelve-month periods. Children will learn (or not), grow up (or not), find partners (or not). And they will all eventually depart this lovely, wondrous, but deeply troubled earth.

In the meantime, I advise each of you to spend a few hours every day ignoring the turmoil and engaging in an activity that gives you joy. Above all, just get some rest. Chill out, as they say.

Goodbye . . . for now.

About the Author

RAYMOND BENSON is the author of over forty books. His most recent novels of suspense are *Hotel Destiny: A Ghost Noir*, *Blues in the Dark*, *In the Hush of the Night*, and *The Secrets on Chicory Lane*. He is primarily known for the five novels in his best-selling serial *The Black Stiletto*, as well as for being the third—and first American—author of continuation James Bond novels between 1996 and 2002, penning six worldwide best-selling original 007 thrillers, among them *Zero Minus Ten*, *The Facts of Death*, and *High Time to Kill*, and three film novelizations. Benson's other novels include *Dark Side of the Morgue* (Shamus Award nominee for Best Paperback Original), *Torment: A Love Story*, *Artifact of Evil*, *Sweetie's Diamonds*, and *Evil Hours*, as well as many media tie-in works.

Benson has taught courses in film history in New York and Illinois, and he currently presents ongoing lectures about movies with Chicago film critic Dann Gire. Raymond is also a gigging musician. He is an active member of International Thriller Writers Inc., Mystery Writers of America, the International Association of Media Tie-In Writers, and ASCAP. He served on the board of directors of the Ian Fleming Foundation for sixteen years. He is based in the Chicago area.

www.raymondbenson.com | www.theblackstiletto.net